Looking for
Julie

by

Jackie Calhoun

Bella
BOOKS

2011

Bella Books, Inc.
P.O. Box 10543
Tallahassee, FL 32302

Printed in the United States of America on acid-free paper
First published 2011

Editor: Katherine V. Forrest
Cover Designer: Judy Fellows

ISBN 13: 978-1-59493-232-8

Other Bella Books by Jackie Calhoun

Abby's Passion

Education of Ellie

End of the Rope

Obsession

Off Season

Outside the Flock

Roommates

Seasons of the Heart

Tamarack Creek

Woman in the Mirror

Wrong Turns

Acknowledgments

Thanks to my faithful first reader, Joan M. Hendry.

Thanks also to Janet Elizabeth Smith for her firsthand knowledge of the American Birkebeiner, without which I would have been lost.

Special thanks to Madeline K. Snedeker for her valuable input on UW-Madison and the city of Madison.

Honorable mention goes to my editor, Katherine V. Forrest, who was my first editor twenty-some years ago.

And, as always, special appreciation to those at Bella Books, who made this book possible.

About The Author

Jackie Calhoun is the author of the following Bella Books—
End of the Rope, Wrong Turns, Roommates, The Education of Ellie, Obsession, Abby's Passion, Woman in the Mirror, Outside the Flock, Tamarack Creek, Off Season and *Seasons of the Heart* (reprint). She also wrote *Crossing the Center Line*, an Orchard House Press book, and ten novels published by Naiad Press. Calhoun lives with her partner in northeast Wisconsin.

For more information on her and her books, go to her website at www.jackiecalhoun.com.

For comments and questions, e-mail her at jackie@jackiecalhoun. com.

CHAPTER ONE

Sam leaned over and spoke into a small opening in the glass window. She had always wondered if the glass was bulletproof but had never asked. "My name is Samantha Thompson, and I want to make an appointment with Dr. Julie Decker." She had not seen Julie in months, and this person behind the glass looked unfamiliar.

The young, heavyset woman, Linda according to the tag pinned to her sweater, gave her a perplexed smile. "There is no Dr. Decker here."

"But she was here. I was one of her..." What had she been anyway? "...patients," she said.

"Let me check." Linda got up and said something to a vaguely familiar older woman seated in front of one of the computers, who looked Sam's way.

"Dr. Decker doesn't work here anymore," Linda said when she came back to the window.

"But I need to talk to her." It came out as a plea. "Do you know where she is?"

The woman stared at her for a few heartbeats, before saying, "I don't know where she is, but she's probably on the web. Almost everyone is."

"Thanks." Sam turned away.

She took the stairs to the first floor. Outside, her breath vaporized in the cold. She jumped into the backseat of the old Escort idling in one of the visitors' slots. "Let's go," she said to the driver, slamming the door and stuffing her hands back in her pockets.

"Hey, that was quick. Everything okay?" Jamie asked from behind the wheel.

Nothing was okay. Julie had been her safety net. "She's not there anymore."

"Your shrink?" From beside Jamie, Nita turned to look at her roommate. Dark eyes. Dark hair. Sculpted facial features. Sam thought she was beautiful.

She gave her a twisted smile. "Yeah, my fucking shrink. She could of told me she was leaving."

Jamie put the car in reverse and stepped on the gas. A horn blared and he stomped on the brake, his eyes wide in the rearview mirror. "Where the hell did that come from?" A black four-wheel-drive truck drove slowly past.

Jamie opened the window far enough to shove a fist out.

The truck stopped and an older, beefy guy, wearing a dirty ball cap jumped out of the driver's side. "What you say, nimrod?"

"Use your brakes, not your horn," Jamie shouted and rolled his window up tight. He began to back again, but now the guy with the ball cap was pounding on the glass.

"Hey, open up and say that again."

"Let's get out of here," Nita said in a scared voice.

Jamie shot backwards, narrowly missing the man. He put the car in drive and, tires squealing, sped past the parked truck.

"Jesus, Jamie," Nita said. "You want to get us all killed."

Sam was looking through the rear window, watching the guy climb into the truck. "Better step on it. He's coming after us."

Jamie veered out of the parking lot, turned right on a one-way street going left and weaved through swerving traffic. Horns blew. Brakes screamed. Jamie made a sharp turn onto a side street and Sam let go of the door handle she'd been clutching.

Jamie threw his violet-crowned head back in laughter just before pulling into a parking spot, seeking safety among kids and cars. "Guess we lost that dude."

"Think again," Sam said. She'd been monitoring their backside.

The truck double-parked next to them. The passenger window rolled down smoothly and a voice snarled, "Watch for me in your rearview mirror, you fucking freak." The vehicle sprang forward and turned at the next corner.

Sam's heart raced. Jamie was always mouthing off to the wrong people. He'd suffered more than one black eye that way. "Let's get out of here." She watched the cross street, expecting the truck to double back around the block.

"That was real smart," Nita said, shooting a dark look at Jamie as he drove away.

"Where do you want to go now?"

Sam wanted to go back to the apartment she shared with Nita so that she could Google Julie on her Mac.

"Take me home." Nita looked and sounded mad. "I think you should re-dye your hair brown or something. If you're going to do stupid stuff like yelling at people who can knock the shit out of you, you better look less conspicuous."

"Hey, I'll still be driving the same fucking car." The car with all the bumper stickers that said *Peace* and *If You Can Read This You're Too Close* and *Get A Life And Leave Mine Alone*. Stuff like that.

"I won't be in it."

"Aw, come on, Nita."

"Hey, everyone carries guns these days. I don't want to get shot because you hollered at the wrong person." She was yelling.

Sam said suddenly, "Better take me home too."

Nita quieted. She did that. She'd be hollering one minute and silent the next, like she couldn't be bothered. Sam nervously turned the tiny fake diamond in her nose, her eyes on the traffic, alert for the black truck.

Safely back at her apartment she typed Julie Decker in the Google slot and got some other Julie Decker who owned a business. Snowflakes swirled outside her bedroom window. Cold air seeped through.

Sam had studied Julie's diplomas on the walls of her office. She'd earned her bachelor's, her master's and her PhD in Psychology from UW-Madison. Julie had thought Sam had no longer needed her counseling. At the time, Sam had thought so too.

She threw herself on the double bed and stared at the cracked ceiling. Nests of cobwebs swayed slightly in the corners. She told herself she was okay. She had a three-point grade average and a job and an apartment. Didn't that signal progress?

She'd gone to high school with Nita, but they hadn't been friends then. When Nita asked her at the end of their sophomore year if she wanted to share an apartment with her, she'd been thrilled. Now they lived in three rooms plus a dinky bathroom cut out of a large house off campus. Tiny trees and bushes grew in the gutters. The paint was scaling off the exterior. The storm windows were no longer attached to the rotten frames and banged in the wind. The hallways and stairs between apartments were filthy.

Although Nita made Sam's skin go hot and cold, she was terrified of offending her by making a move. Besides, Nita was obsessed with grades. Every free minute, she was studying or writing a paper or working at her job.

Sam waited tables at the same place where Nita was a hostess. She didn't like the job much. Customers frequently changed their orders or complained that everything was too spicy or not cooked enough or too cold. The cook yelled at her when she returned an order.

Two days later Jamie called.

"Hey, what's up?"

"I've been texting you and getting no answer. Are you through with exams?"

"Yeah. My parents are coming to get Nita and me tomorrow."

"I'll take you home. That guy found me, the one in the truck."

A shiver galloped over her skin. "How?"

"I was getting out of my car, and he nearly took my fucking door off. He blew his horn and I damn near wet my pants. God, doesn't he have to go to work or something? I can't wait to get out of here. What time is Nita's last exam?"

"Ten."

"Well, tell her to be ready."

She called out to Nita who was in her room, studying with the door open.

"Tell him no more road rage," Nita called back.

She passed that on.

"Never again," he promised. "I'll see you at noon."

Appleton was home and Sam had been there two weeks. Christmas and the New Year were memories. She had always loved Christmas. It was like a ceasefire had been called and an ambience of goodwill and calm descended on the household. She no longer snapped at her parents or sister and brother nor they at her. But now the calm had passed. Annoyance had rippled through her at her mother's suggestion this morning—"Do you think you could do some wash? There are piles of dirty clothes in the basement."

Mostly her piles, she realized, even as she bristled. She glared at her mother, who waved a hand in defeat.

"Forget it."

"Okay, Mom, I'll do it. Anything else you want done?"

Her mother shrugged. "You could clean up the kitchen. It looks like a disaster hit."

"Whatever."

Her mother's eyes glinted dangerously, but she only said, "See you later."

"Yeah, later."

She'd cleaned up the kitchen and was lying on her bed waiting for the washer and dryer cycles to end when Jamie called.

She tucked the phone between her shoulder and ear. "Hey, what's happening?"

"If I get more bored, I'll be dead. Want to go somewhere?"

"And do what?" She stroked Buddy, who was lying next to her. Her father always had a shit fit when he saw the mixed Lab on her comforter. He'd say, "Buddy has his own bed. Look, dogs don't have shoes to take off, nor do they shower often. Get him off your bed. Now." When everyone was gone either to school or work, though, she coaxed him onto the bed with her.

"Ski. We can go to my Aunt Edie's house in Point. Granite Peak is only a few miles up the road. She might go with us and pay for our tickets."

"She might pay for yours, not mine."

"Call Nita and see if she wants to go. She's mad at me."

"I have to ask my parents first. When do you want to leave?"

"Now, before that guy finds me."

Cold bumps chased each other across her skin. "What makes you think he knows where you are?"

"I saw him when we left Madison. He was lurking around the corner."

"Have you seen him since?" Jamie was always in crisis mode. He made things up just for the excitement.

"Not yet, but I expect to any minute."

"I'll call Mom." Sam and her family had gone to the Upper Peninsula for four days of skiing after Christmas. She'd worn her new winter jacket and mittens. The trip was a present to all of them. They'd had a fun time together. Now, though, she wasn't sure whether her mother would be glad to see her go or disappointed. Sam was arguing with her about every little thing. She was so crabby that she didn't even like herself. "This is Eleanor Thompson. May I help you?"

"It's me, Mom. Jamie asked me to go to Point with him. His aunt lives there, and we can stay with her and ski at Granite Peak." It was a peak, albeit a small one when compared to the mountains out west where they had sometimes skied as a family, but there were some good, if short, runs. "That okay?"

"When will you be back?"

"I don't know. We didn't talk about that. I'll call you when I get there."

"Okay," her mom said. "When are you leaving?"

"Today." She wanted to get off the phone and call Nita.

"Have fun, sweetie. I love you."

She mumbled, "Me too," and called Nita. "Hey, you want to go skiing?"

"Can't afford it." Nita's dad contracted out to several condo complexes in town, doing repairs and upkeep. Nita lived with her family in a small house in a modest neighborhood.

Sam's dad worked in an executive position at a paper mill. Her mom took care of claims for an insurance company. She was aware of the discrepancy between her family's income and Nita's. But just because Sam's parents had money didn't mean Sam had a ton of it. Her ski equipment had been a gift from her parents, and she'd been able to sock away her paycheck, because her mom and dad sent her a weekly allowance. They also paid her tuition and rent. Nita had a scholarship and a job and occasional infusions of money from her parents.

"We're going to stay with Jamie's aunt. She lives in Point."

"Have fun. I don't know how to ski."

"Maybe I won't go." After all, she'd just got back from a ski trip with her family. She could hang out with Nita instead.

"Hey, go. Break a leg for me. Besides, I'm going back to Madison ASAP. Work calls."

"Jamie thought he saw the guy with the truck, so he thinks he has to get out of town."

"Serious? He and his big mouth are really going to get him into trouble."

Sam liked Jamie. Yes, he often spoke without thinking, but he was fun and funny and loyal and gay. Although he lived in the Fox Cities along the Fox River that included Appleton, he had gone to a different high school. She had met him on campus at a LGBT meeting. "Well, he's fucking scared now."

"He should be. I'll see you when you get back to Madison."

"I wish you'd go with us." She sounded wistful, even to herself.

Nita laughed. "I wouldn't be any good anyway, and I hate not being good at something."

When Jamie pulled into the driveway, Sam staggered out the door with her skis and boots and poles and a backpack with clothes and other necessities. He jumped out of his parents' van and grabbed the handle of the ski bag. "He'll never find me in this," he said, shoving her equipment next to his in the back of the van.

"I was wondering how we'd squeeze our stuff in your car." She climbed in the front seat. "Nita isn't coming."

"Because she's mad at me."

"Nope. No *dinero*."

"*No hablo español.*"

They crossed the bridge and headed west on Highway 10. "What's your aunt like?"

"Aunt Edie? She's great. You'll like her." He flashed a grin, and she thought how handsome he was, even with the violet hair. His fake diamond earring glittered in the light.

"Is she married?"

"She's a lesbian. I thought you knew that." He shot her another white-toothed smile. "She writes romances, but they're about men and women. Women eat them up. You see them on store shelves in groceries and drugstores. She goes by Lauren James. Nobody would guess she's gay from reading her books."

A wave of excitement swept through her, and she laughed. She'd never met a genuine author, much less a lesbian one. "I want to read one of her books, but aren't there any lesbian romances?"

"I asked her that once and she said it's a small market and she started out with this publisher and felt a certain loyalty. Maybe that's why she doesn't talk about her books much. She's a terrific skier."

Sam had sometimes wondered if Julie was a lesbian. She

had seemed to understand Sam too well. Sam had been forced into therapy when she'd made a suicide attempt. She'd had two choices—go to counseling or leave the university. She'd never regretted the choice. Julie had given her a sense of self worth. She could think of a dozen things she now wanted to run by Julie.

Jamie drove through a maze of streets with Christmas decorations on snowy lawns—blow-up snowmen and Santas and an occasional manger scene. He turned into a cul-de-sac and parked in the driveway of a brick ranch house. There were no Christmas decorations in Edie's yard, but a tree with lights stood inside the bay window.

"This is it. Grab your backpack and come on."

The woman who opened the door and ushered them inside with a smile was tall and big boned. Sam glanced at the Christmas tree and saw a comfortable looking sofa and chairs clustered around a fireplace.

"Auntie, this is my friend Sam Thompson."

Edie took Sam's hand and squeezed it. Sam was tall, but not as tall as Edie, who was only a little shorter than Jamie's skinny six feet. Her deep-set eyes resembled Jamie's and her dark blond hair was the color of his before he got the purple dye job. There was a remarkable resemblance between them.

"Hi. Thanks for letting me stay with you." Her phone was vibrating in her pocket. It was Nita, she knew. She'd been texting her during the drive. She fingered the phone and transferred it to her jeans when Edie hung their coats in the closet.

"Jamie talks about you often," Edie said.

Sam gave Jamie a crooked grin and said, "Uh-oh."

Edie laughed. Her voice was gravelly and her laugh deep as if it came from the gut. "Only good things were said. Are you two hungry?" She led them toward the kitchen. She was wearing jeans and a sweater over a turtleneck and her hips swung in rhythm with each step.

Jamie nodded toward his aunt and lifted his brows. He grinned and mouthed, "Nice, huh?"

Was he talking about his aunt's behind? She flushed and mouthed back, "Shut up." Her cell vibrated in her pocket again.

She took it out. It was Nita. She text messaged, "Hey, we're here. Can't talk right now. Later. Okay?" She shoved the phone in her pocket again as Edie turned toward them.

Edie ran a hand over her short hair and it snapped back in place. It was almost a crew cut but with a little curl, and Sam thought it looked great. She would never be brave enough to get a buzz. She'd probably look like a pinhead. Her hair was pulled back into a short ponytail. "Dinner's in the oven. We're waiting for Lynn." She put chips and salsa on the table. "I've got Diet Coke and Pepsi. Would you like either?"

Always hungry, Sam ate every morsel set in front of her. She never put on weight. Her dad called her the lean eating machine. "Thanks." She dipped the chips in the salsa and slugged back a Pepsi while surreptitiously studying Edie.

"You know, we could go skiing tonight. They're open." She began putting plates on the table and Jamie and Sam leaped up to help. "Sit down. You can do the dishes."

The garage door buzzed up. A car door slammed. The garage door went down, and a woman stepped into the kitchen. She brought a wave of cold air with her. She set a briefcase down and unzipped her jacket.

"Hey, Jamie," she said and Jamie hugged her. She smiled at Sam, and her olive skin crinkled around her oval brown eyes.

"Lynn, this is my friend, Sam," Jamie said.

Sam blushed as she got up. It was one of those uncontrollable things she hated about herself. Lynn was holding out a slender hand, and Sam, feeling awkward, walked over and took it. It was cold. "Thompson, Sam Thompson." She ducked her head.

"Lynn Chan." She had a mischievous grin. Her black hair was cut just below her ears. It was and thick and straight. "You two are here to ski, right? Let's eat, so you and Edie can hit the slopes."

"Hey, we can't go without you," Jamie said.

"I don't ski. Remember? Besides, I've got work to do."

Sam was standing near Jamie and Lynn. When Edie put a light hand on her shoulder, she started. Edie squeezed lightly and let go.

"Come on. Sit down. We're going to eat and get out of here." Edie dished food off the stove and put it on the table.

"Ah, Chinese pork," Lynn said.

"It's a bastard concoction from a recipe that Lynn's mother gave us," Edie said, and Sam wondered whether to call them by their first names.

Lynn said, "What is up with you, Jamie? We haven't seen you for months and suddenly here you are."

"This guy is following me." Jamie told his aunt and Lynn about the encounter at the mental health clinic.

"It's that violet hair." Lynn leaned back in her chair.

"Men hate it as much as they used to hate long hair on guys," Edie said. "Now that the football players have long hair, it's okay. But this violet color is hard on the eyes, Jamie. What do your parents say?"

"I didn't tell them about the guy with the truck."

"I mean the hair."

"My dad hates it. Mom says I'll get over it. It's better than a tattoo, she says." He put a hand behind his head and preened. "I think it's cool."

"Hate to tell you but it looks like a Halloween wig. Promise me you won't put those dresser drawer knobs in your ear lobes." Edie got up to clear the table, and Sam got up to help her.

"I swear I won't," Jamie said, holding his right hand up.

"I'll take care of the dishes," Lynn said. "You all go get ready and get out of here."

Sam blurted, "But we're supposed to do them."

"Nonsense. You can do the breakfast dishes."

"Wait. I have to ask Lynn something. She teaches psychology. Maybe she knows your shrink, Sam," Jamie said. "Doctor Julie Decker. Right?" He looked at Sam for confirmation.

Sam turned bright red.

Lynn, who had been halfway out of her chair when Jamie started talking about Julie, sat down.

"I'm sorry, but why are you asking?"

"She disappeared off the radar screen."

Sam burned with embarrassment. Both Lynn and Edie were looking at her. She stared at the floor and hissed at Jamie who was standing nearby with a dish in his hand, "Shut up."

"Hey, I'm just trying to help."

"I'm okay. Okay?"

"I'll keep my ears open. I'm going to a psychology conference in a couple weeks," Lynn said.

Edie put a hand on Sam's shoulder again. "You heard the girl. Shut up, Jamie."

"How do you find someone if you don't ask?"

The runs were lit, the chairlifts running. They put their boots on in the warming lodge and went out into the cold night. Their breath floated before them and their boots crunched on the snow. After snapping into her bindings, Sam pushed off with her poles, skate skiing to the lift. Edie was in front of her, Jamie behind.

A three-person chair carried them up the hill. Jamie sat in the middle. When he began to rock, Edie snapped, "Cut that out. It's a long way down and people do fall off." Elongated shadows of the skiers on the lift stretched across the snow.

"You're no fun, Auntie."

"Remember that," Edie said mildly.

To warm up they skied down the medium runs. Sam pushed off first. Skis parallel, knees slightly bent, she wove her way downward in a series of short, controlled turns. Edie caught up with her halfway and Jamie passed them both at the bottom.

After a few runs, Jamie said, "I'm ready for a black diamond. Who's coming?"

All three lined up at the top of a steep hill, which disappeared beneath a mound of snow. Edie and Jamie shoved off first. Jamie was a good skier, but Edie was better. She glided over the snow with seemingly effortless control. Sam pushed off and nearly lost her balance flying over the mound. Her skis left the surface and she landed with poles out, snow plowing for control. Regaining her balance, she turned into the hill, heart pounding.

At the bottom Edie said, "Well done, Sam," and Sam felt inordinately pleased.

They headed for Point just before nine. Sam fell asleep as

soon as they hit the road. She drifted off with a smile, looking forward to tomorrow, wishing Edie would go with them.

Jamie shook her awake when they pulled in the driveway. It took her a moment to ground herself. Oh, yeah, she thought, Edie and Lynn. She stumbled after Edie and Jamie into the warm house. One light had been left on.

"Come on, Sam. I'll show you your room. You look like you've had it."

As she lay between fresh sheets, she found herself wide-awake. Edie's and Lynn's voices seeped through an adjoining wall. She strained to hear but was unable to make out the words. However, the tenor was the same as her mom and dad talking in their bedroom at night. Perhaps someday she'd have someone to talk to like that, but so far her love life hadn't begun.

Jamie woke her in the morning. "It's snowing like crazy, girl. Get up."

She lifted her head, looking at him through bleary eyes, and fell back again. "What time is it?"

"Nine. The ski hill's open. Let's grab some food and go."

She crossed the hall to the bathroom and peered in the mirror. Her cowlick poked up like a bunch of feathers. One side of her hair was flattened. She shrugged at her reflection. She'd be wearing a hat, so hair didn't matter much. Besides, she'd put it in a ponytail. She dressed and went looking for Jamie.

There were boxes of cereal on the table with bowls and bread and butter and a note that read—*Toast, cereal, milk in fridge. Have fun. I'm in my office if you need me.*

Sam's phone buzzed in her pocket. She looked at it and saw her mom's work number. She hadn't called as promised. "Hey, Mom. I'm sorry. I forgot."

"You didn't answer when I called last night."

"I was skiing, Mom. It's snowing here. We're going to eat and go out."

"Okay. Thanks for doing the wash and cleaning up the kitchen."

"No problem."

"Love you. Take care."

She mumbled, "You too."

Careful not to disturb Edie, they quietly wolfed down a few bowls of cereal and pieces of toast, cleaned up the dishes and left. The snow was falling so thickly that the windshield wipers failed to keep up. The roads were slippery. Whenever Jamie stepped on the gas or brakes, the rear end of the van tried to pass the front, and Sam's adrenaline kicked in.

Jamie laughed nervously as they slid sideways into a snowbank. "God, I hate it when the car is in charge."

"Slow down," she said, leaning forward, trying to see through the heavy flakes.

"We're hardly moving, for chrissake."

They got to the ski resort without any accidents. Sam could barely see the nearest lift, much less the top of any hill. They carried their skis to the racks outside the warming house and went inside to put on their boots. She was excited now that they were here. There was nothing better than fresh snow.

It slowed them down, the heavy snow, and wore them out. Visibility was about two to four feet on the runs. Suddenly there'd be a person in front of her and she'd swerve. They skied the black diamonds where there were fewer skiers. At five the ski hill shut down for an hour, and everyone had to pay again to ski in the evenings.

"Let's go back to Edie's," Jamie said, stomping clumps of snow off his boots before entering the steaming warming shelter. She did the same.

Edie stood at the stove. "Chili and warm bread. You must be starving."

"It's scary out there." Jamie kissed his aunt's cheek.

"That hair gives you a ghoulish look, nephew. Does it glow in the dark?"

"Yeah, it does. Can I help?" Sam said, glancing around the warm kitchen, but everything appeared to be done. The table was set, the bread cut, bowls ready to fill.

"Lynn won't be here tonight," Edie said. "She has a meeting."

"You didn't stay home because of us, did you?" Jamie asked.

When Sam sat down, her stomach growled.

"You were a good excuse. I didn't want to go. I get tired of meetings. I get tired of trying to prevail."

What did that mean? Sam wondered.

Jamie asked.

"It doesn't matter." She turned and her mood turned with her. She smiled and her handsome face lit up.

That was the only way to describe her, Sam thought. She was tall and handsome and lithe with an athlete's grace. She filled three bowls and sat at the table with them. "So, how was the skiing today?"

"Spectacular," Jamie said. "Do you want to go tonight?"

"I don't think so. I worried about you. The roads are ice rinks."

Sam rejoiced inwardly. Her limbs were heavy and her eyelids drooped. She could fall asleep right there.

"It's a good thing Nita didn't come. Nita is Sam's girlfriend."

"She's your friend, too," Sam shot back.

"Not that way she isn't."

"Hey, knock it off, Jamie." Edie lightly punched his shoulder. "You always were an annoying kid."

Jamie laughed and dug into his chili. "I didn't mean anything. If I liked girls, I'd go after Nita Perez too. I'd bury my face in her long neck, kiss her dark eyes, run my fingers through her thick hair."

"I never went after her," Sam whispered, her face red with embarrassment just like it had been when he'd started talking about Julie.

Edie said, "You know, if you were a kid, I'd send you to your room, Jamie. I don't allow rude people in my house. It makes everyone uncomfortable. Ignore him, Sam. He's turning into a loudmouthed, ignorant man. His mother would be ashamed."

"I'm not a man," he said.

Edie looked at Sam and they laughed. It felt wonderful, their laughter. She fell in love with Edie then—not in a physical way, though. She didn't want to go to bed with her. She'd never had all-the-way sex with anyone. She'd be terrified that she'd do the wrong thing with someone like Edie. She used to imagine going to bed with Julie and would squirm with embarrassment. But Edie had Lynn. She'd never want Sam. Besides, Edie was probably as old as her mother, maybe older.

Edie asked Sam questions and Sam answered. They ignored Jamie, but he managed to worm his way into the conversation after a few moments and Sam forgave him. It was his indiscretions that made her laugh.

When Sam's parents took her back to Madison, Jamie left his car at home and rode with them. He told Sam he was less of a target without the vehicle. Besides, it sat most of the time anyway. Whenever he drove it, he lost his parking space and would have to drive around endlessly looking for another. He'd rather walk, he said.

They dropped him off at his dorm. He'd wanted to room with Sam and Nita, but Nita wouldn't agree to it. In the end, Nita had found the two-bedroom apartment, and there wouldn't have been room for him anyway.

Sam and her dad helped Jamie carry his stuff into the dorm. His roommate wasn't there, and they dumped his duffel bag, the food his mother had given him, and left. Jamie walked back out with them and thanked Sam's parents for the ride. He told her he would call.

Her dad broke into laughter as they drove away. "God, I'll dye your hair back to normal myself if you ever do that."

She was offended and stared out the window at the older homes they were passing. They were rentals, much like the place she and Nita lived in. As she neared their apartment, her heartbeat picked up. She'd missed Nita.

Sam unlocked the door and she and her parents carried in her stuff. They set the baskets of clean clothes down in her bedroom and the cooler of food in the tiny kitchen, where her mother transferred the perishables to the small refrigerator and the other stuff to the cupboards. Sam dropped her backpack on her bed. Nita wasn't home.

The sink was overflowing with dirty dishes. Books were

strewn across the floor along with a few clothes and shoes. It looked normal to Sam. She chanced a look at her mother, who was staring at the mess. She could see her itching to clean up and forcing herself to turn away, apparently determined not to interfere, not to say anything.

She said instead, "Do you want to go somewhere to eat before we leave, Sam?"

"I've got all those leftovers you gave me. I can eat those."

Her parents hugged and kissed her and said their goodbyes. She watched them go through the smudged window that faced the street, feeling a relieved sadness.

Restless, she wandered around the tiny rooms, picking up the stuff on the floors and chairs, and putting it in Nita's room. In the kitchen she washed the dishes and wiped off the counters and table. Only then did she sit down and open Hemingway's *For Whom the Bell Tolls*, required reading in her Lit class.

She awoke with a start when she heard Nita's key in the lock. Nita switched on a light and let out a little shriek.

"What are you doing sitting there in the dark? You scared the piss out of me." Nita stood backed against the door, clutching her chest as if for protection.

"I fell asleep over Hemingway."

Nita started for her room. "What happened here? Where are all my clothes?"

"In your room." Sam walked after her.

Nita glared at her. "Why?"

She didn't want a fight and that's where they were heading. "I picked things up and washed the dishes after my mom and dad left. I needed something to do."

"Am I supposed to say thank you?"

"Why don't you say hello, Nita?"

Nita was pulling her shirt off. "Excuse me." She shut the door in Sam's face.

Sam threw herself in the chair. Years of dust puffed out from the cushion. She called Jamie. "Hey, want to go out?"

"I thought you'd be hanging with Nita tonight."

"Nope." She shut the phone and picked up the book. Her chest hurt as it always did when Nita was mad at her.

Nita came out of her room. "I got my period today. I'm a bitch. Thanks for cleaning up. Bruce asked about you." Bruce was the manager at the restaurant where they both worked.

Her anger vanished, just like that. "I'll go see him tomorrow. Want to go out with me and Jamie tonight?"

Nita looked at her, her dark eyes serious. "Want some advice, Sam? You'll never meet someone if you're always with him."

"What if I don't want to meet someone?" She had met Nita. She was the one Sam wanted.

Nita shrugged. "I'm going to bed early. You missed a good party last night."

Disappointed, Sam said, "There'll be others." She followed Nita into the kitchen.

"Look at all this food. It's like manna from heaven." Nita stood in front of the open fridge. "Can I have some? Please, please, please."

"It's manna from my mama. You can have some if you promise not to eat any of it without me."

There were two chairs at the small, battered table. Sam put a few pieces of fried chicken into a tiny microwave. When she turned it on, the room lights dimmed. She leaned against the counter and admired Nita, who was waiting expectantly for the food.

When Jamie knocked on the door, Nita said, "Damn. He'll want some."

"How do you know who it is?" Sam asked, going to the door.

"Who else do you hang around with, except me, and I don't have anyone coming over."

It was true, she thought dispiritedly. She needed more friends. She unlocked the door.

"Food, my favorite thing," Jamie said, following Sam into the kitchen.

"Didn't your mother send any back with you?" Nita asked.

"Yeah." He sat in the other rickety chair. "I love chicken legs, though."

Sam put another piece in to nuke. "What's happening tonight?"

"Not a fucking thing. Campus is dead. State Street is dying. Sure you want to go out?"

"No." Now that Nita was civil she wanted to stay in.

"Can I sleep on your couch? There's a girl in our room. She and Nate were doing it under my nose."

Nita said, "Ever think about making a threesome? Nate is gorgeous."

"And get killed? He's straighter than an erection."

Sam laughed. The microwave bleeped. She put the chicken parts on the table and told Jamie to make room for her on the rickety chair.

Late in the night when Sam woke up and stumbled to the bathroom, the light was on over the sofa where Jamie lay stretched out, his lower legs and bare feet hanging over the arm. When she went over to switch off the light, he grabbed her. She screamed, and he doubled up with laughter.

"Hey, that's definitely not funny and don't wake up Nita. She'll kick you out."

"Where did you find this lumpy couch? On the curb?"

"It was left here. I won't stop you if you want to go back to your own place."

"And watch Nate and Betsy screw? No thanks. Have you made it with Nita yet?"

"Shut up," she said.

"Make a move, girl. Get in her panties. Faint heart gets you nowhere."

Sam shivered at the thought of Nita's rejection, but he was right. She'd never know if she didn't try. "Can I move in with you if she throws me out?"

"Me and Nate? You'd have to sleep with him."

"I'm going back to bed."

"Why don't you climb in with Nita, and I'll get into your bed."

"Ah, that's what you want. My bed. Well, you can't have it."

The next morning Jamie looked like he'd been on a binge the night before. His eyes were bloodshot, his hair flattened on one side like a crushed violet. He and Sam were drinking coffee, waiting for Nita to finish in the bathroom.

"What's on your agenda?" Jamie asked.

"I have to go to the restaurant and talk to Bruce about working hours. God, I hate waiting tables. All I get are complaints, and students don't leave tips."

"I'll go with you. Maybe I can land a job. I'd like to be a waiter."

She looked at his hair. "I don't know. Bruce is a pretty straight guy. Maybe he'll give you my job, though. You'd be better at it."

"You gotta stop thinking that way, like you can't do anything." He started counting on his fingers. "You can't get Nita in bed. You aren't good at your job. Nobody likes you."

Sam stared into his brown eyes floating in a red sea. "I never said nobody likes me. I just feel like an outsider, and I'm not sure Nita is queer. She had a boyfriend in high school."

"Yeah, that stud of a quarterback. I had the worst crush on him."

"And I had a crush on her." She'd hardly believed her luck when Nita had wanted to rent an apartment with her.

Nita came out of the bathroom ready to go, makeup and all. "No wonder it took so long," Sam said.

"Honey, you look terrific. I love how your hair shines. What *is* the secret?"

"Shut up, Jamie." But Nita was smiling. She must have known she looked wonderful. "Pantene," she said. "You don't want yours to shine. Trust me on this. I'll give you a bottle if you dye it back the way it was. Wasn't it a nice brown?"

"Dishwater blond," he said.

"Hey, blondes have more fun, don't they? Certainly more than violets."

"Why don't we just go with her to work," Jamie said.

"I'm going right now." Nita was putting on her heavy jacket and gloves.

"You look so cool," Sam said a bit wistfully.

Nita smiled sweetly. "Thank you. By the way, I'm bringing a friend home after work." She left a blast of cold air behind her as she went out the door.

Jamie walked with Sam to the restaurant. They made dirty snowballs and shot them at trees and each other. Chili Verde was packed, the floor slippery slurry. Nita was showing a group of students to a booth. Bruce, the manager, was guarding the cash register. He spied Sam and his pale face lit up. "Hey, Sam, ready to go to work? We can use another waitress. We're doubling up on tables."

"Sure," Sam said, turning and grimacing at Jamie. "Later."

Jamie stepped forward. "I'm a good waiter."

Bruce looked at his hair and scowled. "No thanks, buddy. Weird hair turns people off their food."

"Ridiculous," Jamie muttered as he left.

After work, a stunned Sam walked home with Nita and her friend, Carmen. Sam felt as if there were a fist in her chest where her heart was supposed to be as she listened to Nita and Carmen prattle on as if she weren't there. She stuffed her hands in her pockets and hunched into her jacket.

When they reached the apartment, Sam unlocked the door and once inside, Nita said, "Carmen and I are going to study in my room."

She looked at them as they sort of leaned into each other. Carmen's skin was kind of sallow, her hair dense and black. Sam nodded dumbly and went to her room. She did not even have the heart to call Jamie.

CHAPTER TWO

When the digital clock on the bedside table registered eleven p.m., Edie put her book down and turned the light off. She hadn't seen Lynn since Jamie and Sam had come to ski. It had been surprising that Lynn had spent that night with her. Lynn slept better alone. Edie knew that.

She fell asleep on that thought and woke up in the dark. Six o'clock and pitch black outside her window. After showering and dressing, she walked quietly to the kitchen where she made coffee and ate a piece of toast, leaning against the counter. She refilled her cup and went to her office, which had been converted from a bedroom.

What she'd wanted to do in her youth was teach literature and write—short stories and books, like the ones she read. She'd gone to the Iowa Writers' Workshop after graduating from

UW-Madison. There she'd written a pretty good short story, submitted it to a national magazine contest and won second prize. She'd taken a job as a salesperson in a bookstore to be part of the world she loved and worked on a novel in the evening. The story's main character was a salesperson like herself, who is wooed by a young man who keeps returning to the store to buy books. It was a love story, she realized when it was finished, and she sent it to Horizon Romances, a publisher of romance novels. They mailed her a contract, suggesting she write under the name of Lauren James, and offered her an advance of five hundred dollars. She was thrilled.

For years she worked at the bookshop before finally becoming the manager. She stocked lesbian and gay books, thinking it was the least she could do since she wasn't writing them herself. Her parents were still alive. Although her mother read her books faithfully and told her how good they were, Edie was sure she hoped that some day she'd write something that could be called literature. Fleetingly, she wondered how they would react to a lesbian book, but she'd never told them she was a lesbian, so how could she explain such a book?

When she felt financially secure enough to quit the bookstore, she moved back to Point. Her dad had died at fifty-five from a massive heart attack, and her mother lived alone. Edie had carried on a long-distance relationship for thirteen years with a woman she'd met at the Iowa Writers' Workshop, but when she moved to Point instead of Ames, Iowa, both knew the relationship was over. Shortly after her return home, her mother was diagnosed with pancreatic cancer and died within a year. Edie was so bereft that it took a long time to occur to her that her mother's death freed her from her expectations, imagined or real.

She was in her late thirties when she met Lynn at a Democratic fundraiser for Dave Obey. Lynn taught psychology at UWSP. She was also an advisor for the LGBT student organization. Her passion was equal rights for the LGBT community. She believed that if everyone came out, sheer numbers would demand that gays be recognized and respected.

Edie had long since given up any pretense. She didn't care who thought she was a lesbian. She and Lynn were best friends and sometime lovers who agreed on practically everything. They were pro-choice, advocates of clean air and water, fervently anti-war and, of course, active in civil rights. What they didn't agree on was living together. Edie had adjusted to living alone, and Lynn's occasional stays left her feeling lonely and unsettled.

For a few minutes she thought about Jamie and Sam's visit, how their presence had given the house life. When Jamie had stuck his head in her office to ask if she wanted to ski with them that last morning, she'd said reluctantly, "I can't. I've got a looming deadline for my next book."

"Yeah, what's it called?"

"*Midnight Magic*," she said, wincing at the title.

"Is it hot?" He grinned and opened the door enough so that she could see Sam behind him.

"Get outa here."

"Hey, thanks for having us," he said, and Sam echoed his words.

"Any time. I'll see you soon. Stay out of trouble." She went to the door with them.

"We cleaned up," Sam said.

"Good." She smiled at Sam. She was an attractive girl—sharp blue eyes, shiny brown hair, maybe a little too slender for her height, but she would fill in. "Have fun."

Jamie had given her a hug and they were gone.

For two hours she worked. The book began when a stranger (Don) showed up at the house of the protagonist (Elizabeth) at midnight. His battery had begun to die on the nearby Interstate, but he'd managed to keep it going until he exited and made it to the frontage road. Hers was the first door he knocked on.

He was good looking in a rugged sort of way—big nose, strong chin and thick dark hair. She looked at him through the side panel and, against her better judgment, opened the door to the length of the chain.

"My engine died," he said into the space between them.

"Go next door. My neighbor runs an auto shop."

She watched him cross the yard and knock on that door, saw the light come on over the front door before going back to bed.

The next day Don returned to thank her. He hung around

for days until she finally agreed to go to lunch with him. Their slow courtship filled pages. Don found work at UPS. There was something about him that made her wary, but finally, on page ninety-five, they went camping together and spent an uncomfortable night in a tent. Now they were back at Elizabeth's home and he was asking her to marry him.

This was where she got stuck. She didn't want Elizabeth to marry Don. Elizabeth had a best friend, Mary Ann, whom Edie longed to turn into a lesbian. She'd like nothing better than to write a love scene between the two women.

She looked out onto the Green Trail behind the house and decided she needed a break. There was a text message from Lynn. "Are you busy tonight?"

She shot back, "Nope."

"I need you to take minutes for me at a meeting."

"Find someone else," she replied.

Lynn called her. "I need you."

"You set a trap."

Lynn laughed. "And you fell into it."

"No fair." She'd planned a little cross-country skiing on the Green Trail after work.

However, she ended up at the meeting, scanning the twenty or so people who were there—a handful of students, several older men and a few other women. The moderator was a young guy, maybe in his twenties or early thirties. Next to him sat a forty-something woman who was taking notes on a computer. She took the chair next to hers.

"I can e-mail you a copy of the minutes," the woman said, looking at Edie's legal pad and pencil. She had a head of frizzy grayish brown hair.

"Hey, that would be great." She wrote her name and e-mail address and handed the scrap of paper to the woman. "You are?"

"Pam Dorschner. I'm subbing for a friend." She had a quirky smile.

Edie introduced herself. "I'm doing the same. How coincidental." Edie gave her a quick look-over. Framed by the unfortunate hair was a sweet face—pale blue eyes, punctuated by brown brows. Dimples when she smiled.

The moderator had begun to talk. "I'm Todd Schneider, regional director of Equal Rights For All, ERFA, ..."

Pam passed around a stack of papers with the details of the new domestic partnership law. She took one, even though she knew that Lynn would not be interested in forming such a union. Nor would she. She had been independent too long.

When Todd adjourned the meeting, some of the attendees gathered up their belongings and left, others stood in groups talking. A few approached Todd. She turned to Pam, who was putting the laptop in a backpack.

"Are you here from Madison?"

"Yep. It's a great place for lesbians. I'd love to show you around."

Edie looked into Pam's eyes, trying to determine whether this was a real invitation or a friendly remark not to be taken seriously. She decided to take it as the latter and said, "Thanks."

Pam fished around in the computer bag and came up with her business card and handed it to Edie. "You look like you'd be fun." She zipped the bag shut.

Todd turned toward Pam. "Ready?"

"I guess." Pam pulled a heavy jacket over a sweatshirt with ERFA's letters on it. "Give me a call when you're in town, Edie." She extended a hand and so did Todd.

"You're Edie Carpenter?" he asked.

Edie nodded. "How did you know?"

"Lynn Chan told me you'd be here." He smiled. "Nice to meet you."

"Same here," Pam said, giving her a thumbs-up before walking away with Todd.

Edie watched them go, then zipped up and went out into the cold night. She folded herself into her Focus and drove home.

By the following weekend, Edie had nearly forgotten Pam. She had received the minutes on Monday via e-mail with a short note and passed them on to Lynn. Every day after getting off the computer, she had stepped into her cross-country skis and strode along the Green Trail that bordered her backyard. Night fell early, and she wore a miner's lamp over her ear band. It lit a narrow pathway. Everything looked different in the shadows cast by the feeble light. One evening four deer dashed across her path. Their muscular hindquarters brushed against her, nearly knocking her over and taking her breath away. It was as if their warm hides burned her. Her heart beat wildly.

On Friday she was removing her skis when someone stepped out of the darkness into the light shining at the back of the house, startling her. "Who?"

"Pam Dorschner. Remember me? We were at an ERFA meeting together last week. I was taking minutes for someone. So were you." Pam laughed. "I love the headlamp. I'm not a stalker. I had a business meeting here and I just thought I'd look you up. I'm a skier too, by the way." All said in a rush.

Edie remembered the woman with the frightful hair. All she wanted to do, though, was go inside and belt down a glass of wine. She was chilled. "Maybe another night. Do you have equipment?"

Pam stepped closer. "Not with me." She pushed back her hood and the frizz that passed for her hair sprang up.

"You had another meeting here?" Edie asked, not quite sure what to make of Pam's appearance.

"Yes. Work related. Boring." Her eyes were hollows in her face. "I work at MATC." Madison Area Technological College. "I'm a computer geek. What do you do?"

Edie smiled and said, "I'm a book geek," as she stepped out of her bindings and picked up the skis. "Want to come inside? It's cold standing here." Sweat was drying on her skin. She shivered. With a mittened hand, she knocked the snow off her skis and stuck them and her poles in a snowbank outside the back door.

In the mudroom, Pam asked, "What's a book geek?"

"Someone who writes books." Edie sat on a bench and changed from boots to slippers. The room branched four ways—into the basement, into the kitchen, into a small bathroom and outside.

"No kidding," Pam said, looking all excited. "What kind of

books?" She took off her snow boots and hung her jacket next to Edie's.

Edie sighed. She hated this question, because she never knew how to answer it. "Fiction," she said. The kitchen tile felt warm under her feet.

"I'm so impressed, but before I ask any more questions I have to use the john."

Edie pointed the way. She was opening a bottle of merlot when she heard the key in the front door.

Lynn padded into the kitchen. "Someone is parked in front of my side of the garage."

Edie's brows shot up. "Your side of the garage? You haven't been here since the kids were here." It wasn't meant as a rebuke. At least she didn't think she meant it that way. "I didn't know you were coming."

"Who's here?" Lynn asked.

Pam popped out of the bathroom. Edie looked at her and nearly laughed. What was it about hair that made people do strange things to it? Maybe because they knew it would grow back to its original color and shape?

Lynn looked astonished. "You, Pam? What brings you here?"

"A meeting. What else?" Pam replied.

"Anyone want a glass of wine or coffee or something?" Edie asked.

Lynn said, "Sure, I'll have a glass of wine."

"Do you live here too?" Pam asked.

"No." Lynn winked at Pam.

"Something in your eye?" Edie asked, looking from one to the other.

"No," Lynn said. "Why?"

Lynn was not in the habit of winking. Edie poured three glasses and sat at the table. She felt a little foolish and pushed the glass away.

"Hey, I better take off. I didn't tell anyone where I was going. They'll be worried." Pam drained her glass.

Edie nodded. Was it a huge leap to think the wink was meant to keep Edie in the dark about something? She could understand

Lynn having another life. What bothered her was Lynn not trusting her enough to tell her. In the next moment she realized that she no longer loved Lynn in a physical way, but she did love her as a best friend. A best friend doesn't lie to her best friend.

After the front door closed, she said, "Tell me what that was about, Lynn."

Lynn looked down. "Nothing."

Edie's chest hurt. That was the problem with knowing someone so well. You caught all the nuances. "Don't play me for a fool, Lynn."

"I strayed a little." Lynn met her eyes. A worried frown was etched between her brows.

"You sound like one of those philandering politicians. It's okay, Lynn. Just don't lie to me, please."

"Her name is Frankie. I met her at a meeting. We talked for hours." Lynn drained her glass. "I'm sorry."

"Don't be. Just give me some time to digest this. You better go."

Lynn hesitated, but Edie thought she looked relieved. "You're my best friend."

"I still am your friend, but I want to be alone now."

After Lynn left, Edie remembered how she'd been bursting to tell someone about the deer that had crossed her path, brushing against her as they went. Now there was no one to tell. She got up slowly. Her muscles ached.

She took a shower and stared at her naked body in the full-length mirror. It was a nice body, even if it showed her age in small ways—graying pubic hair, slightly drooping breasts. She pulled an oversized T-shirt over her head and turned off the lights on her way to bed. She picked up the book she was reading, *Infidel*, about an amazing woman from another world, and fell asleep in the middle of a paragraph.

She wanted to avoid Lynn till she could look her in the eye and feel okay about it. When the phone rang early Saturday morning and Lynn's name and number appeared on the display, she let the call go into her message box. She needed time and space. Not even the book and its upcoming deadline could keep her home. She decided to head to Minocqua and hit the ski trails.

She was loading up her car, sliding the ski bag crossways from front to back, when a VW Jetta drove up. Pam got out of the car. Her jacket was open and her hands were stuffed into her pockets. "I just came to say goodbye. I guess you're going somewhere too."

Edie put a small cooler in with her backpack. "Skiing," she said.

"Wish I could join you. Actually, I am going skiing with a friend as soon as I get back."

"Good," she said. "See you next time." As Pam got back in the Jetta, Edie lowered herself into the Focus and backed out of the driveway. She followed Pam's VW out of the neighborhood and turned north on Interstate 39.

She was lucky to get a small room at the Concord Inn, a Best Western across the road from Lake Minocqua, where snowmobiles were zipping across the ice. She skied at Winter Park the first day, using her skate skis on the wide trails. Up and down, up and down without stopping. She wanted to be so tired at night that she would drop into sleep. The sky was clear and whenever the sun penetrated the trees, it was blinding. Her strong legs carried her till closing time, and during those hours she thought of nothing that she could remember. She picked up a sub sandwich and took it to her room. Opening a small bottle of Sutter's cabernet, she washed down the sandwich and watched the news. Afterwards she took a shower and went to bed with her book.

The next morning she drank coffee and toasted a bagel in the motel's lounge before driving over snowy roads to the American Legion State Forest. The parking lot was empty, and she waxed her diagonal skis before heading off on the trail. She hardly noticed the cold. She'd be hot once she started to move. There would be no skate skiers on these trails. The tracked paths were narrow and steep. They twisted through the forest, sometimes widening at a sharp turn at the bottom of a hill.

She was more than halfway through the one-way trails when

she stopped at a three-sided shelter. A fire, contained by rocks, burned in front of the shed. A pile of split wood was stacked nearby. Feeders, placed near the edges of the opening, hosted small birds. Chickadees and nuthatches and goldfinches sparred over toeholds, while juncos ate on the snowy ground. Two women joined her in the clearing as she leaned on her poles, captivated by the chattering birds flitting to and from the feeders. Yesterday's skate skiing was catching up with her. Her hips ached, her thighs and calves burned.

One of the women pulled off her knit cap, and Edie recognized Pam. The red-cheeked woman accompanying her did the same.

Transfixed by the sight of the woman's hair, electric in the brittle cold, Edie stared for a moment. It was a shiny chestnut color and fell in waves almost to her shoulders. She was squinting, one gloved hand shading her eyes as she watched two chickadees fight over a perch. She seemed unaware that Edie was in the clearing too.

"Claire Bouveau, this is Edie Carpenter."

Claire turned a green-eyed gaze on Edie. "Hello, Edie. Are you the reason we couldn't pause to catch a breath of air?"

Edie touched her own face, wondering if her cheeks were as rosy. Her curiosity was piqued. "Hello," she said, smiling. She bent over and put a log on the fire, and heat flared into her face.

"I always ski fast." Pam grinned at Edie. "Are you alone? That's not a good thing."

"I ski alone all the time." She always liked the sound of her skis on the snow and the nuthatches muttering in the trees and occasionally she saw deer in the woods. Once she came upon a porcupine crossing the trail.

"I'm getting cold," Claire said. "I have to keep moving."

"Want to have dinner with us? We're going to Jacobi's. They have the finest dining around."

Edie knew that. She glanced from Claire to Pam. "What time?"

"Six thirty okay? We'll pick you up. Where are you staying?" Pam asked.

Edie told her. "I'll be in the lobby."

She let the other two get a good head start before pushing off. When she reached the parking lot, Claire and Pam were loading their skis into a Ford Escape. Pam waved. Edie scraped the snow from her skis, put them in their case with the poles and fitted it crossways in the Focus. As she drove to another trailhead, she washed a peanut butter sandwich down with half frozen water.

At the end of the day, she was tired and sorry she'd agreed to go out for dinner. But a hot shower revived her, and she dressed in jeans and a turtleneck. She'd brought no good clothes with her, intending only to eat in her room.

After blowing her short hair dry so it wouldn't freeze, she went out to the lobby. The local news was on the TV and she watched while she waited. A big snowstorm was coming their way. She thought she'd rather be snowed in at home where she could ski out the back door.

Pam appeared in the lobby, her hair comically askew. The tips were frozen and glinted under the lights. Edie got up and pulled her jacket on. Outside, Claire was sitting behind the wheel of the Escape when Edie climbed into the backseat.

"What a coincidence, huh, running into each other on the trail?" Pam said.

"You never know who you're going to see where," Edie said agreeably. She felt sleepy.

"I should have known Lynn was the one you were taking notes for at that meeting."

Edie said nothing in response. Lynn was a political animal, and one Edie would rather not talk about right now. The wound was fresh.

"Lynn is the kind of person we need right now. She gets things done."

"Yes," she said, looking out the window at the snowy night. Of course, there was no way Pam would know that they'd been much more than friends.

Pam seemed to catch the drift and changed directions. "We're going to Winter Park tomorrow. How about you?"

"A big storm is coming. I think I'll head for home in the morning."

"She can ski right out of her backyard," Pam told Claire, who had yet to say anything besides hello.

"Really." Claire's attention zoomed in on Edie in the rearview mirror. "How lucky you are. I used to live in Point."

"When was that?" Edie asked, meeting her eyes in the glass.

"When I was married. I moved to Madison after the divorce. We both left. My husband taught at UW-Stevens Point those few years."

She couldn't remember a Dr. Bouveau, but why would she?

Claire seemed positively chatty now. "Stephen taught anything French—French language, French literature. He wasn't there long enough to get tenure. He moved back to France. I liked Point."

Edie asked her what she did.

"I'm a librarian at one of the branches. I took a couple days off." She smiled at Edie in the mirror. It transformed her, making her disarmingly attractive.

"Edie writes books," Pam said. "Tell me where I can find them. I want to read one."

Edie looked out her window. "Almost anywhere. I write as Lauren James."

"Why is that?" Pam asked.

"Because everyone who writes for this publisher uses another name."

"What else do you do?" Claire asked, meeting Edie's eyes in the rearview mirror.

"I used to manage a bookstore in Madison, but that was years ago." She was not offended by the question. She was well aware that most people didn't make a living wage writing books. She'd never get rich writing for Horizon, but she made enough to get by.

Claire parked in front of Jacobi's, which was tucked off the Interstate, and they went inside. The hostess showed them to a table for four in the corner. She took drink orders and handed them menus.

When the waitress left, Edie asked, "Are you active in ERFA, too?" She was trying to figure out the connection between Pam and Claire.

Claire shrugged. "Not like Pam. I go to meetings occasionally." Claire raised a thin eyebrow and smiled. Edie was enchanted.

Edie looked around the room and saw Jennifer Gottschalk, who got up from her table and walked over.

"Hey, how did I miss you on the trails?" Jennifer smiled down at them. She was tall and well muscled. Her hair was more reddish than brown, chin length and wavy. She worked as a pharmacist in Wausau.

Edie introduced her to the others. "I was at Winter Park yesterday and the American Legion today."

"Ah, that's why. I went to Winter Park today and the American Legion yesterday. I wish I'd known." Jennifer's eyes glowed. "I would have had someone to ski the expert trails with. Where are you going tomorrow?"

"Standing Rock," Edie said. "I want to get home before the storm hits."

"Next time maybe we can go together. The Birkie is coming up. Got something I can write on?"

They exchanged e-mails, and Jennifer said, "I don't know why we didn't do this before."

When Jennifer returned to her table, Pam said, "Wow. She's an Amazon."

Edie smiled. "She's no bigger than I am. She's a great skier."

When they dropped Edie off in the hotel parking lot, she looked at the stars clustered in a clear sky, took a deep breath and her nostrils froze together. Across the road several snowmobiles zoomed to life and sped across the lake. The snow squeaked under her feet as she walked toward the hotel door.

When she was lying in bed, trying to stay awake long enough to come to a stopping point in her book, her cell buzzed. She looked at the display, sure that it was Lynn calling and saw it was Jamie instead.

"Auntie," he said across the empty air, "do you think Sam and I could transfer to UWSP and live with you?"

"Why would you want to do that?" she said, coming instantly awake.

"Things aren't going so good here. My roommate's girlfriend has moved in and Nita, Sam's roommate, brought a girl home after work."

"Oh." She flashed back to her college roommate on whom she'd had a hopeless crush. How would she have survived if her roommate had brought her boyfriend into their living space? "This is not a decision to make lightly or without your parents' consent. You're not really serious, are you?"

"I can't sleep or study when they're going at it, and Sam is desolate. The girl stays overnight."

She was so glad she wasn't young and helpless to control her environment. "Can't you go to the hall advisor?"

"And be a snitch? He's a jerk anyway."

"Where are you?"

"We're in my room. Nate and Betsy, the bitch, aren't here right now. Sam doesn't want to go back to her place."

She glanced at her watch. It was after ten.

"Do you want to talk to Sam? She admires you."

Not really. She wanted to go to sleep, and forget these problems that had been forced on her. "Well, that's nice, but…"

"Sam, Edie wants to talk to you."

"Jamie, I'm in Minocqua. There's nothing I can do…"

"Hi," Sam said. The one word sounded so forlorn that Edie wished she knew what to say to make everything better. Sam took a breath that became a sob. She'd obviously been crying.

"Have you got another place to stay, Sam?" Edie asked.

"No." Said just as forlornly.

She experienced a twinge of anger at Nita's thoughtlessness. "Sweetie, maybe Jamie could move in with you for a while?" She was thinking if Jamie were there, he could act as a buffer between Sam and Nita and her girlfriend.

"She wouldn't let Jamie share an apartment with us."

"Well, she has someone there now, so how can she say no if you have someone? It would also give Jamie a place to stay other than with his roommate and girlfriend."

"Okay," Sam said, just as sadly.

"Sam?"

"Yes."

"This too will pass. Trust me. I know it hurts." How astute, she thought dryly, but nothing more original came to her. "There should be someone you can talk to at the university. They offer counseling services."

"I want to talk to Julie."

"Julie?" She vaguely remembered Jamie talking about how Sam was looking for Julie, but she was tired. She wanted to sleep.

"My therapist, Dr. Julie Decker. She sort of disappeared."

"I remember. Have you looked for her on the web?"

"Yes. She's not there."

"Keep looking. One of these days she'll turn up, that is if she's still working." She didn't know if she would turn up, of course, but it was likely.

Sam said, "Okay," in the same sad voice.

Jamie came on the phone. "Can you come here, Aunt Edie, and help us out?"

"What do you want me to do, Jamie? You don't change schools because your roommate is sleeping with someone. Get her out of there or go stay with Sam. Sam needs someone to give her moral support. Sleep at her apartment tonight. I'll call you tomorrow night."

"Thanks, Auntie. Sam says thanks, too."

She slept in the next morning. Snow was falling heavily. She packed up, wishing she'd left the night before, and checked out.

The highway was covered with the white stuff. Traffic was moving at fifty miles per hour or less. Passing was hazardous. She got stuck behind two snowplows that crossed the southbound lanes, effectively blocking everything. Claire drifted into her thoughts as she chafed at the slow pace, but by the time she reached Point, she was thinking about the book and what changes she should make.

She stopped at Copps to buy groceries and headed for home where she fired up the snowblower and blew the driveway. The world was white and muffled, buried under at least six inches of fresh snow. She loved it. It could snow till April as far as she was concerned.

Inside, she listened to her messages—two from Lynn asking her to call and one from Jamie. He said, "We did what you told us to do, Auntie. There are four of us crowded into Sam's teeny apartment. I have to sleep on the lumpy couch. Turn on your cell. I need advice."

She took her bag to her room, turned on her cell and flopped on the bed to phone Jamie. His cell rolled to voice mail and she left a message. An hour later the vibrating phone woke her. It was loosely clasped in one outstretched hand. Samantha Thompson appeared in the display. "Hi, Sam. What's up?"

"Remember the guy with the truck? Well, he found Jamie alone and beat him up. He went to UHS, but his nose won't stop bleeding. I think it's broken, and Nita wants him out of here, and his parents are in Mexico."

"Let me talk to him, Sam." She waited until Jamie came on. "I hear you got into a fight, nephew."

"I was massacred." He sounded nasally.

"Do you have cotton up your nose?"

"That and blood. Listen, it's not good here. Nita thinks I'm trouble. She wants me out. My roommate's girlfriend has moved in."

"Well, she can't do that."

"You tell her and Nate that. I can't take another beating."

She sighed. "Look, I just got back from Minocqua. Can you wait till Friday? Give me Sam's address."

She was asleep when Lynn walked in.

"Since you wouldn't answer my phone calls, you forced me to come here." She lay on the bed next to Edie and looked at her out of dark oval eyes.

Edie's anger had cooled, and her hurt feelings had healed.

"I apologize," Lynn said as they stared at the ceiling. "I should have told you, but would you have told me? What if you had a thing for Pam? Would you admit it?"

She laughed. "Don't try to turn the tide, Lynn." For some reason she thought of Claire.

"I don't have an excuse. It just sort of happened."

Edie wanted to talk to Lynn about Jamie. Losing Lynn as a friend was not an option.

Lynn started to get up. "Do you want me to go?"

"No. Tell me about Frankie and I'll tell you about Jamie."

Lynn flopped back down. "You'd like Frankie. She's a political animal."

"What does she look like?"

"She's kind of on the heavy side, but she has a pretty face and great hair. She doesn't ski or hike like you."

Big boobs and ass, Edie interpreted, and hair you could run your fingers through. Lynn would like that. "Neither do you."

"True. We go to meetings together, and you're meetinged out."

"Yeah, I am. I thought after the election we'd get good universal health care and a green economy. What we got was a recession and more war."

"We were already in a recession. You can't quit, Edie. If we all quit, the party of NO will take over."

"I want to talk to you about Jamie and Sam." And she launched into the latest phone call.

"Poor Jamie," Lynn said, rising on an elbow to look at Edie. "See what I mean? We have to fight for equal rights and respect."

"I'm going down there Friday afternoon and see if I can straighten this out. He claims his roommate will beat him up if he tries to get the girlfriend out of their dorm room. God, I wish his parents were home."

"What will you do?"

"I thought I'd talk to the hall advisor first, if they have one. Maybe he can put him in with someone else. I don't think I can help Sam."

"Could they room together?"

"Not in Sellery. The boys and girls wings are separate. God, why do I get stuck with my nephew's messes?" There were no good solutions. She realized that. Her power was limited.

She left for Madison before three on Friday. It took a little over two hours from Point to Sam's apartment on West Washington. The streets were cleared of snow. As she stood on the decrepit porch knocking on the door, she looked around at the rundown rentals that had once been two-and three-story residences.

Jamie opened the door. His taped, bloodied nose and bruised face shocked her. His eyes were lost in the swelling, and his violet hair made his entire head look black and blue. She figured Sam had been exaggerating about the beating, as Jamie would have, but now she wished she'd come when Sam called.

Inside were Sam and another girl, whom Jamie introduced as Nita—a slender, dark haired, dark eyed beauty. Edie stood in the doorway, wondering what should be done first. "Okay, let's talk for a few minutes before I take Jamie to the health center."

"I went, twice. All they did was tape my nose and give me pain medication."

"Did you get this guy's license plate number?"

"Yeah. We told the doctor," Sam said. "He said he'd report it. Jamie doesn't want to talk to the police."

"He might come looking for me again."

It was painful to look at him. "You don't want to press charges?"

Jamie lifted his chin and said with a bravado he clearly did not feel, "The cops have his license number. It's up to them to do something."

She let it go. "Well, maybe we should start a conversation about the rooming situation."

"Sit down, Auntie." Jamie patted the empty spot on the couch next to him.

Sam looked at Nita. "Want to go first?"

Nita appeared taut with anger or something like it. She spoke in rapid-fire sentences. "I don't feel safe with Jamie here. He's right. That guy could come back any time and break in. This is a small apartment. I don't want someone sleeping on the couch. You know? I want my space."

"Your girlfriend is taking up my space," Sam shot back.

"I ought to be able to have friends here. Jamie is Sam's friend but he's here all the time, like he lives here. He's got a room of his own. He should sleep there."

"Your girlfriend is sleeping here," Sam said. She was sitting on the other side of Jamie.

"Jamie should sleep in your room then. This is living space that he's taking up."

"I can't go back to my room," Jamie said. "They're always fu...making it right under my nose." Edie had told him before she didn't want to hear the F word coming out of his mouth.

"Tell the hall advisor. Don't be such a coward," Nita snapped.

He cringed. "Nate will beat me up. He said as much."

Edie put up a hand to silence them. "I don't think Jamie should or can endure any more beatings. I'm going to the dorm now. Jamie, I want you to come with me. Maybe we can get you in another room." She felt badly for Sam, who sat with her arms hanging between her legs, but she couldn't help her.

The knock startled all of them. Nita jumped to her feet and opened the door. She pulled the girl inside and whispered something in her ear. The girl's dark eyes widened when she saw the others.

"Maybe I should go," she said quietly.

"No. This is my friend, Carmen Jimenez," Nita said, looking defiant.

"Hello," Edie said, smiling at the girl who appeared scared. She introduced herself as Jamie's aunt. "We'll go now."

"Come with us, Sam," Jamie said in his stuffed up voice.

Sam grabbed her backpack and fled.

CHAPTER THREE

Sam felt as bruised inside as Jamie was on the outside. She wasn't going to be left alone with Nita and Carmen and watch them making it, although she'd never seen them so much as kiss. She feared Nita's caustic tongue as much as Jamie was afraid of the guy with the truck. She went with Edie and Jamie.

Because of heavy traffic, it took about twenty minutes to get to Jamie's dorm and find a place to park. Sam settled down to wait. She'd brought a book with her.

"Hey, you can't stay here," Jamie said, when she opened the book.

"I want to talk to you too, Sam. Come with us," Edie said.

She followed them into the dorm. "Who is your hall advisor?" Edie asked.

"Mike Paltzer, but he's a wimp. He's not going to tackle

Nate." Jamie hunched into his jacket. He'd told Sam that the cold and talking hurt his face.

Sam tagged along behind. She thought Mike would probably say, "Okay, okay," and when Edie was gone, everything would go back to the way it had been.

Mike was in his corner room, nodding his head to something on his iPod when Edie tapped on the doorframe. Jamie was out of sight, backed up against the wall in the hallway, breathing shallowly. He looked like a Halloween mask. Sam stood behind Edie, interested in how she was going to handle this.

"Hey, Mike. I'm Edie Carpenter." Mike jumped to his feet and shook her proffered hand. "I think we have a problem here."

"What's that?" He began working a zit and Sam looked away.

"I understand Nate Bloomburg's girlfriend has moved into Room 315."

His chewed fingernails kept at the zit as he stared at Edie. "Yeah? That would be Betsy Schmidt. I think she just spends a lot of time there."

"Like overnight and all day." Edie turned around as if to confirm this with Jamie and only saw Sam, who nodded.

"Who is this?" Mike asked.

"Samantha Thompson. She's a friend of Jamie's."

"Oh, yeah. Does she want to move in too?" He snickered.

"Who is head of student housing? Stuart Evans? Is that who I should talk to?"

"Where's Jamie? Can't he speak for himself?" Mike stuck his bristly chin out. The red zit glowed.

Jamie slid around the corner, presenting his Technicolor face to Mike, who gasped. "Jesus, did Nate do that to you?"

"No, but he's probably going to do worse. Can you get that girl out of my room, please? They go at it like rabbits and don't care who sees."

Mike smirked. "Maybe I should go take a peek." One look at Edie and he backtracked. "No, no, I didn't mean that. I'll tell him."

"He won't listen," Jamie said, sounding defeated.

"He'll listen to Stuart Evans and Mr. Evans will wonder why you haven't done anything about the situation, Mike."

Sam wondered who the hell was Stuart Evans, but she thought Edie was awesome. Maybe Edie could get Nita's girlfriend out of the apartment. Maybe she could threaten Nita with the landlord, but then Nita would hate Sam and she didn't want that either.

Mike's eyes shifted away from Edie's. "I said I'd tell him."

"Let's tell him together right now."

"I don't know if he's there," Mike said sullenly.

"We can find out. You go first. We'll follow."

Jamie said sotto voce, "Oh God Oh God Oh God. He's going to kill me."

Edie must have heard him too, because she said, "No, he's not. Come on, Mike, The day is almost over."

"Was it some straight dude who hated the hair, Carpenter?" Mike led the way with dragging feet.

"Something like that," Jamie said.

The door of Jamie's room was closed. Mike knocked on it. They heard feet shuffling, and Nate yelled, "We're busy in here. Go away."

"Open the door, Nate," Edie said.

More shuffling and a girl's voice said, "Wait, Nate." Sam figured she was putting on her clothes.

Nate opened the door halfway. He had the body of a football player, which he had been in high school. No wonder Jamie was afraid to displease him. "What do you want?"

"I want my room back," Jamie said, stepping forward.

"Yeah, who took it away from you?" Nate's eyes widened. "And I didn't do that to his face."

"Your girlfriend can't live here. She has to go wherever home is at night. You can't fuck here."

Nate grimaced. "Look at him. He even looks like a fairy with that purple hair. All he needs is tights and a wand."

Edie moved to the fore. "I think we've got a grievance we can take to the Student Housing Administration. We're wasting our time here." She turned and started walking away. "Have you got any rooms where Jamie could bunk in the meantime, Mike?"

"No. Listen, I can't make Nate do anything."

"Well, then maybe we should insist Nate move into your room, Mike, and you and Jamie can share his room."

"I don't think we can do that." Mike was fingering the offending zit again.

"I'll move into Mike's room. He can room with Nate."

"No way," Mike said.

Edie pulled her cell out of her pocket, along with a list of administrative offices and tapped in a number. Sam was walking right behind her and heard the message.

"Office hours are eight to five Monday through Friday. Leave a message after the tone and we'll return your call. For emergencies call..."

Edie ended the call and pushed in another number. On the fifth ring someone answered in a booming voice... "Peter Koskowski here. Can I help you?"

Edie proceeded to tell Koskowski what was going on in Jamie's room.

Koskowski cleared his throat loudly. "What building is this?"

She told him. Sam could hear every word on both ends. "Can he stay somewhere else till Monday?"

"Not really."

"Will it help if I send someone there to talk to this Nate?"

"Not in my opinion. You might scare him for a few days. He might also take it out on Jamie Carpenter, my nephew."

"I'll have to go in to the office to see if there is a room available. I'll take care of Nate and his girlfriend later. Meet me there." He gave Edie an address.

"Uh-oh," Jamie said, who could also hear.

Mike leaned against his doorframe, his fingers traversing his face.

Sam was in awe. She wanted to be just like Edie someday. She and Jamie trooped down the stairs behind her.

Jamie said, "Hey, Aunt Edie, can you hang around long enough for me to get my stuff out of the room? I don't have a car if I have to move to another dorm."

Sam knew he was more afraid of Nate than of carrying his stuff to another building. There were carts for that.

"We'll see what happens here."

Peter Koskowski stared hard at Jamie and cleared his throat. Like his voice, he was big. "This is true that Nathan Bloomburg's girlfriend, Betsy Schmidt, practically lives with him?"

"Yes, sir. They do things there that I don't want to watch."

"What happened to your face?"

"A guy in a black truck with license plate TRUCKIN 2 beat me up."

"Because?"

Jamie looked down. "He's been stalking me since we had an incident in a parking lot."

"What happened?"

"I nearly backed into him."

"Okay. I'll find you a room if you dye your hair back to its normal color. Then you won't have so much trouble. Deal?"

"Deal," Jamie said, looking down. Sam knew he didn't think that was fair. He believed his hair was his own to do with as he wanted.

Edie laughed. "Hey, it'll save you a lot of trouble, nephew."

Jamie pouted. When he was up against authority, he always balked. Sam gave him a shove. "You can be a blonde. They have more fun."

They left to investigate Jamie's new room, which was in the same building across the hallway from Mike's. It was a hidey-hole of a place that had been used for storage. It had a bed, a desk and a dresser shoved against each other. The closet was behind a curtain.

By the time they were done moving Jamie's stuff out of his old room, it was after eight and Sam was starved. They had not had to confront Nate, because he and Betsy were gone.

"Thanks for helping," Edie said to Sam.

"We can go to my place and eat my mom's leftovers," Sam said.

"I'll bring the rest of mine," Jamie offered.

"Okay," Edie said.

Nita was gone to work, Sam knew. She warmed up the last of the chicken and the butternut squash and green beans.

"Great leftovers," Edie said, but she ate little. "What are you going to do, Sam?"

Sam's blue gaze shot to meet hers. "Can you do something?" She blushed and dropped her eyes.

"Yeah Auntie, can you tell the landlord that there's another girl living here and not paying?"

"Sam can do that herself."

"Nita will hate me."

Edie smiled at Sam. "You could sleep at Jamie's when the girlfriend is here. Buy yourself one of those blow-up beds."

"I've got a sleeping bag," Sam said dispiritedly. She used it as an extra blanket.

Edie stood up. "I must go if I'm going to drive home tonight. Thanks for the food. Your mother is a fabulous cook."

"Welcome," Sam said, her appetite gone.

"And you, nephew, do as the man said. Re-dye your hair and try to stay out of trouble."

"You saved my life, Auntie. I'll be forever grateful." Jamie kissed her on the cheek and walked to the door with her. "Sure you don't want to stay overnight?"

Edie laughed. "And sleep where?"

When Edie's larger than life presence was gone, Sam wondered if Jamie felt as vulnerable as she did. She was at the mercy of Nita and her mouth. He was at risk from the man in the black truck and Nate. "We should hire her for protection," she said.

"Nah, we're good. Hey, I'm gonna go fix up my room. Want to help?"

She wanted to be anywhere but at the apartment when Nita came home. "Can I bring my sleeping bag?"

"Sure. Bring your books and stuff. You can bunk with me."

Maybe Nita would beg her to come back if she stayed away long enough, because she'd have to buy her own food instead of eating Sam's. She hastily crammed clothes in an empty bag and put her school stuff in her backpack, including her computer. Jamie carried her sleeping bag and her pillow.

Edie was sitting in the car with the motor running. They walked to the Focus, and Jamie pounded on the window. He laughed when Edie jumped. "What are you doing out here?" he yelled.

She rolled the window down a few inches. "Waiting for someone."

"You can wait inside," he said and turned to Sam. "You don't care, do you?"

"That's okay. It won't be long," Edie said. "Is Sam moving in with you?"

"Maybe."

"Well, be discreet about it, both of you. Okay?"

"I am the soul of discretion," Jamie said.

"Try anyway. I'll give you a lift, but I have to call someone first. Just wait a minute."

"Hey, we're used to hoofing it."

Sam was thinking she'd like a ride. She stamped her boots against the cold seeping up through the snow-covered ground.

"Bye, Auntie. Thanks for everything." He blew a kiss toward Edie and started off with Sam at a running walk.

When they reached the dorm, they took the steps two at a time to the third floor and Sam slipped off her backpack and set it in a corner in the crowded room.

"That's your side," Jamie said. "We'll have to get you something soft to put your sleeping bag on."

Later, when Sam was in the rather grim bathroom on the other side of the common room in the girl's wing brushing her teeth, one of the members of the LGBT group came out of a stall, zipping up her jeans. Sam watched her in the mirror, trying to place her. Her short cap of dark hair framed a heart-shaped face with bold blue-gray eyes and a wide mouth.

She turned on the water in the sink next to Sam. "Hey, how come we've never met here before?"

Sam smiled at her in the mirror, her mouth full of toothpaste. She spit in the sink and rinsed off her toothbrush. "Guess we didn't have to go at the same time."

"I thought you moved into an apartment with Nita Perez."

"I did. I'm staying here tonight with a friend," Sam said, assessing the girl in the mirror. *What was her name?*

"Hey, want to hang out with us tomorrow night—Toni and Lisa and me? My room is 317. Bring anyone you want. You could bring Nita." She grinned, and Sam felt a blush starting up from her toes for no reason at all. "What's your room number?"

What was it? She rummaged around in her mind and said, "It's the one by the stairs on the other side of the common room, but I've got to work tomorrow night." She shrugged and made a face, not sure whether to feel relieved or sorry.

"That's the men's wing," and the girl surprised Sam by touching her cheek with one wet finger. "What are you doing with a guy?"

"You know Jamie Carpenter, don't you? He's the friend."

"Yeah, I know him," the girl said. "Met him at an LGBT meeting."

When she left, Sam looked at her reflection. The blush was fading. Her eyes, the ones that felt like hot holes, were her best feature. Her mother had once said she could see the sky reflected in her eyes, but of course her mother would think such a thing. No one else would.

They had made some order in Jamie's room. The twin bed was pushed against the far wall. The desk was crammed next to it. The dresser stood in the closet with clothes piled on top. Her sleeping bag lay atop a cushion of dirty clothes.

Jamie was stretched out on the bed, watching the small TV on top of the dresser. He looked at her when she came in.

"Do you know who lives in three-seventeen?" she asked. "She came to an LGBT meeting."

"No, but I remember some of the girls. Lisa, Toni, Karen?"

"That's it! Karen! I saw her in the john and couldn't think who she was. She invited me to hang out with some other girls in her room tomorrow night, but I have to work." She put her toothbrush and toothpaste away and slid into her sleeping bag. It felt like she was lying on rolled up socks.

Jamie turned off the television. "Bet that feels a lot like the couch at your apartment."

"Feels pretty good to lie down anywhere after moving all your stuff." Her phone was buzzing next to her. She looked at the display. "It's Nita. Think I should answer?"

"Send her a text that you're not coming home tonight. Otherwise, she might call the cops when you're still gone in the morning."

Yeah, that would be bad, she thought and sent the text.

Nita wrote back, "Where are you?"

She passed this information on to Jamie.

"Tell her you're with a friend. Let her worry a little."

"She won't worry," Sam said but sent the text anyway and turned off the cell.

CHAPTER FOUR

Edie dug out Pam's card as she sat in her car outside of Sam's apartment. It had been a long week and she was too sleepy to drive to Point. Pam picked up on the second ring.

"Is this really you, Edie?"

Edie smiled at Pam's enthusiasm. "Yes, it's me. I had to come to Madison to help my nephew out of a bind. I know it's late, but I thought I'd give you a call."

"Hey, it's the shank of the evening as my dad used to say. Have you eaten?"

It was almost impossible to hear over the voices talking and laughing in the background. "I ate something with my nephew and his friend. I'm at four-thirty-five West Washington."

"We're at the Kabul on State Street. Don't move. I'll come and get you."

"Wait," Edie said, almost changing her mind, but Pam was gone. Did she really want to sit here waiting for Pam? Yes, she thought, just in case Claire was at the restaurant. She started the motor for warmth.

Pam knocked on her window, startling her out of a dream. She unrolled the glass a few inches, letting in the biting cold.

"Follow me," Pam said and hurried back to her car.

Edie followed the Jetta through a few intersections before Pam pulled into one of a double parking space around the corner from State Street.

"You'll be hungry when you smell this place," Pam said.

They half ran toward the restaurant. The warm redolence of the Kabul enveloped them with smells of garlic and ginger and onions and roasted lamb. They were led to a table for two. "Everyone was leaving for a concert when I came to get you," Pam said.

"Did I keep you from going with them?"

"Nah. I don't have a ticket."

Edie didn't believe her. She was surprised at how disappointed she was that Claire wasn't there. She wished she had headed for home despite the tiredness.

"Is your nephew all right?"

"For now he is, I hope." She told Pam how she went about getting Jamie another room. "His parents are in Mexico, so I'm his person of last resort." That wasn't completely true, of course. He always called her first when he needed help. She also told Pam about Sam and her dilemma.

"I wouldn't willingly be that age again, would you?" Pam asked.

"Probably nobody would. Oh well, I think he'll be okay now if someone doesn't beat him up again." She smiled fleetingly.

"Who beat him up?" Pam looked as if she was ready to take that person on.

"Some guy with a black truck. Jamie has violet hair and a big mouth." She was studying the menu. "I think I'll have the hummus. I am hungry after all."

"It's wonderful," Pam said. "I'll have dessert—the baklava with the fruit."

"You've already eaten, haven't you?"

Pam nodded.

"And you do have a ticket to the concert, don't you?"

Pam grinned and shrugged. Her pale eyes lit up. "Hey, I wanted to see you more than the concert. How often do I get to spend time with a famous author?"

"Well, that's nice of you," Edie said, wondering how to handle Pam's interest in her. She hated hurting people. "But I'm not a famous author." Was she one of those people who wrote the same book over and over? She hoped not. It always surprised her to see her books in drugstores and discount stores and grocery stores. There were so many better books out there.

"Why don't you stay in town tonight? I have room at my place."

It might be better to go to a motel than stay at Pam's and give her the wrong vibes. "Thanks. I'll see how I feel after eating."

"Listen, a bunch of us are going to meet at a bar when the concert is over. Claire will be there." Pam's eyes searched hers.

"Sounds like fun." She looked away, sure that Pam was using Claire as a lure to keep her here. Otherwise, why would she have mentioned her?

"By the way, I bought one of your books."

"Well, that was nice of you."

"Don't you want to know which one?" Pam leaned forward eagerly, a big smile on her face. "I haven't had a chance to start it yet."

She sighed. It was a terrible thing to be ashamed of what you did for a living. "Look Pam, I don't really like to talk about my books. They're romances about straight people." She was blushing. Had she ever told anyone that besides Lynn, who was always trying to get her to write a lesbian romance? Usually, when people asked her what she did, she sidetracked them with questions about what they did.

Pam's expression was almost laughable. She looked like what she'd tasted had suddenly gone bad. "Oh. Is it okay if I still read your books?"

"Sure, just don't tell anyone who I really am." She smiled. "I'd like to remain anonymous."

It was late when the concert ended and they met at a bar. Claire came in with another woman. She was even more attractive than Edie remembered. Under her black leather jacket she wore fitted jeans and a tight turtleneck sweater. Her hair shone as she leaned between Edie and Pam at the bar and asked for a Leinie's Red. She smelled wonderful.

Edie slid off her stool to be on the same level. "How was the concert?"

Claire gave her a bored half smile. "Okay. People were dancing in the aisles." She put her head back and drank from the bottle.

"Were you?"

"No." A slight frown appeared between Claire's brows. "That's not me. What brings you to Madison?"

"My nephew. He needed some intervention."

"Are you his guardian?" Claire looked away. She was losing interest.

"No. His parents are unreachable. He needed a room change and somebody gave him a beating." Would that interest Claire?

"Too bad. Are you staying with Pam?" She lifted an eyebrow, sending shivers across Edie's skin.

"I might. I don't want to fall asleep on the road."

Claire was turning away. Someone else was vying for her attention, the woman she'd been talking to when she entered the bar. "Well, enjoy your stay," she said.

Let her go, she told herself. She's got someone else, and then Claire swung back and introduced her to her friend.

"This is Janine Desmond." A dusky colored woman with dark brown eyes and a figure to die for put an arm around Claire and leaned into her.

"Hi." Edie extended her hand and Janine took it limply with slender fingers.

"Edie lives in Stevens Point. She came down here to rescue her nephew," Claire said with a smile.

"That true?" Janine said lazily in a smoky voice.

Edie felt big and awkward and out of place. Pam rescued her. "How you doing, Janine?"

Janine gave her a slow smile. "Good, Pam. You keeping us all safe from those homophobes?"

"I could do with some help from you two." Pam grinned suddenly. "But that's okay. Your job is to show the world that we're not all fat and ugly."

Edie looked at her in astonishment. She opened her mouth to say, "I'm not fat nor are you," and then shut it without uttering a word. She fervently wished she'd driven home or gone to a motel.

From then on she talked only to those who talked to her. Quite a few of the small crowd knew Lynn and asked if she did as well, sparking conversations about how much Lynn had done for gay rights, she and Frankie.

"Where is Frankie?" Edie asked.

"Out of town," someone said.

Edie's gaze kept wandering to Claire and Janine. After they left together, her desire to socialize tanked. She realized how tired she was and wanted to leave too.

As if reading her body language, Pam brought Edie her jacket and asked if she was ready. "Follow me," she said before they slid into their cold cars.

Pam's apartment was on the first floor of an elegant old house. It had a wraparound porch and Edie thought it unfortunate that it had been converted into rental units. A computer desk stood under a large window in the living room. Papers were strewn around the laptop and printer. There was a small TV and DVD on a stand against another wall. A chair that folded out into a single bed futon faced it, as did a small sofa and an easy chair. Papers and books and magazines were piled on the floor between the chairs and sofa. The kitchen was only large enough for appliances and a small table under another window. The other doors were closed.

"Hey, nothing fancy like your house," Pam said, apparently registering Edie's thoughts. "I didn't have time to pick up."

"It's homey, a great place to crash, which is what I have to do before I fall down." She was suddenly exhausted.

"I'll sleep out here. Just give me a chance to change the sheets on the bed," Pam said.

"No, I'll sleep here." Edie tapped the futon. "Just get me a blanket and a pillow and I'll be good to go."

Pam stood looking at her a moment. "I'm sorry, Edie. The place doesn't always look like this."

"I don't care, Pam." She smiled. "I'm just grateful to have a place to sleep."

When the lights were out, Edie found herself staring at the ceiling, unable to sleep. Finally, she turned on the light next to the futon and picked up one of the books off the floor. It was one she'd read years ago, a novel by Julie Alvarez, *In the Time of the Butterflies*, about the four Mirabel sisters, three of whom were murdered in the resistance against the dictator Trujillo in 1960 in the Dominican Republic. She got halfway through the book and fell asleep. She woke up when a yawning Pam emerged from the bedroom in the morning.

Pam saw the book lying open on Edie's chest and said, "Didn't you sleep at *all*? I *knew* I should have made you use my bed. That futon is *so* hard."

"I'm okay. Really."

While eating toasted bagels, she brought up Claire and Janine. "They make a beautiful couple."

"They fight constantly. If they lived together, they'd kill each other. They are opposites. Black and white." She laughed. "They *are* black and white in every way."

"Well, they seemed pretty cozy last night."

"I know, but I'll bet they were at each other's throats before the night was out."

"No kidding?"

"Nope. None. I agree that they make a stunning couple, though."

"They do," she said a bit too wistfully, then almost laughed. Was she lustful? Yes. She'd love to take either of those women to bed, but only if for some wild reason one of them wanted to go to bed with her. Their coolness toward her had been crushing.

"Can you stay for the day and let me show you Madison?"

Could she? Yes. Did she want to? She didn't know. Besides, she already knew Madison. "Let me call my nephew and see how he is doing."

Jamie answered his phone after five rings. "'Lo."

"I woke you up, didn't I? I forget that people your age sleep till noon."

"What time is it? Where am I? Ah, some sweet lady put me in this wonderful, little hidey-hole. I love it here and so does Sammy. Are you still in town, Auntie?"

"I thought I'd check on you before I left."

"With whom did you spend the night? I hope she was pretty."

Edie glanced at Pam. No, she wasn't pretty but she was nice—a whole lot nicer than Claire and Janine. "Don't get smart, kiddo."

"Sorry. I'm good, actually. Sam is better. She says hello and thank you."

"I'm glad. She's welcome and so are you. Try to stay out of trouble. Next time it might be your father who has to take care of things." Edie's baby brother had little tolerance for his flamboyant son.

"God forbid, if there is a God."

"See you next time."

"*Hasta luego*," he said and made kissing noises.

She laughed and put the phone away.

Pam was on her cell. "Today?" she screeched. "Why today?" She glanced at Edie and calmed down. "Okay, okay. I know I said I would. I'll be there in half." She snapped her phone shut. "I'm sorry. I promised to help with some stuff."

"Hey, that's okay. I need to get home anyway."

"I don't have time for a personal life anymore." Her phone buzzed and she looked at the display. "Give me a minute."

"Sure."

"Hi, Claire. What's up?" A pause. "Why do you need a ride? Can't Janine take you back to your place?" Another pause. "I can't."

Edie's heart leaped and she tapped Pam on the shoulder. "I can do it."

"Wait a minute." Pam put her hand over the mouthpiece. "You can?" When Edie nodded, Pam's eyes betrayed her disappointment. It had probably been the story of her life, and Edie felt badly for her but not badly enough. "Edie's here. She says she can take you home. You want to talk to her?" She handed Edie the phone.

"I'll need directions," she said, thinking she was a fool to do this.

"Pam can give them to you. I'll be out front, looking for you." Edie handed the cell back to Pam, who closed it.

Edie had trouble meeting Pam's gaze after Pam wrote down directions. She didn't like herself at the moment, but Pam seemed grateful. Maybe she thought Edie would get Claire out of her system.

"Thank you for letting me stay over."

Pam gave her a hug and said, "Good luck and, by the way, I started reading your book last night and could hardly put it down."

Edie paused to say thanks again before going out the door.

Claire was pacing back and forth on a street a few blocks from Pam's, which should have taken her only ten minutes to find instead of half an hour. She pulled up to the curb, and Claire slid in. Her hair was tangled and she looked mad. The tip of her nose was bright red.

"Sorry," Edie said. "The one-way streets are confusing."

"That's okay. Thanks," she said curtly. "Damn, I wish I smoked."

Edie laughed. "Why?"

"Doesn't it calm you down?"

"I don't know. I don't smoke." She smiled, thinking she must be trying to be funny. One look told her that wasn't the case. "Why do you need calming down anyway?"

Claire stared out the passenger window. "I should have known better than to go home with her."

"Janine?"

Claire's head whipped toward Edie, green eyes blazing. "Yes, Janine. I never learn."

"I hate to ask what it is you never learn."

"Well, don't then," Claire said rudely. "Sorry, I am so angry I don't know what to do with it."

They drove the rest of the way to Claire's home in silence, the only spoken words the brusque directions Claire gave Edie.

She parked in front of the duplex and was about to ask for directions out of town when Claire turned toward her. "Come on inside and have a cup of coffee."

Edie's eyebrows shot up in surprise. "You sure?"

"Of course, I'm sure," Claire snapped. "You gave me a ride. I owe you something."

She followed Claire into her home. The living room was light and airy with bright prints on the walls, which she wanted to look at, but Claire headed straight for the kitchen.

"Sit," she said and Edie sat, while she ground coffee and poured it in a basket in a four-cup coffeemaker.

"Look," Edie began uncomfortably as Claire tapped her fingers impatiently on the counter.

Claire spun toward her. "Fuck the coffee," she said, startling Edie. "Come with me." With surprising strength she pulled Edie out of the chair.

"Where..." Edie began, but shut up when Claire led her to a bedroom. Clothes were strewn over every surface.

Claire began throwing the garments off the bed, muttering something about not being able to make up her goddamn mind. She took her own clothes off, adding them to the pile. In a few shocking moments, she stood naked before Edie.

A flush climbed Edie's body, suffusing her face so that even her eyes were hot. "I can't..."

"This is what you want. Right?"

Edie said nothing for a moment, because Claire was right. This is what she wanted, just not this way. She stared at the beautiful body and briefly imagined it entwined with Janine's. She shook her head and when she found her voice, she said, "It's Janine you want, not me."

Claire gave her a knowing smile and took hold of the hem of Edie's mock turtleneck. "You're wrong. Take this off or I will."

It was as if she was rooted to the floor, unable to run or resist as Claire helped her pull off the shirt and unzip her jeans. Where Claire's body was finely boned, hers was the opposite with broad shoulders, large breasts, thighs that were muscular from years of skiing and hiking.

When Edie stood stripped of everything, red from head to toe, Claire threw back her head and laughed.

Edie looked at her long, pale neck and was overcome by lust. She buried her face in Claire's throat, her inhibitions gone. She backed Claire to the edge of the unmade queen-size bed and laid her down. As she hovered over her, she paused to look at Claire's face and what she saw she took to be desire. She held her weight off Claire with her strong arms and legs and asked, "Are you sure?"

Claire nodded and Edie kissed her eyes, nibbled on her brows, brushed her soft mouth with her lips, explored it with her tongue. She worked her way down Claire's body, caressing the silken skin with her mouth and tongue, leaving behind a trail of goose bumps, until she reached the joining of Claire's legs. Sliding onto her knees off the edge of the bed, she plunged into Claire's depths.

She would never have thought that this one-sided lovemaking could be so exciting. Attuned to the increasingly loud moans, she held the slender legs in a gentle grip. When Claire twisted out of her grasp and lay panting on the bed, Edie lay down next to her and kissed her on the mouth.

Claire responded with a rough and hurried touch that provoked more annoyance than desire. Edie was amazed that this woman knew so little about making love. She faked a climax in order to end Claire's half-hearted efforts.

"How was it?" Claire asked.

"Good," she lied and smiled into the clear eyes.

"Want that coffee now?" Claire asked as she put on a large shirt that barely covered her nakedness.

Edie dressed quickly. "Sure, I'll have a cup. Let me use the bathroom first."

"Be my guest." She nodded toward the open door in the bedroom.

Edie turned on the faucet before she peed. After, she washed her face and hands and left the room to find Claire coming out of a bathroom down the hall.

She drank her coffee quickly, wanting to be on her way. "I'll never get out of Madison from here without directions," she said with a smile, and Claire scribbled on a piece of paper.

As they said goodbye at the door, Claire shoved her fingers through her hair agitatedly before asking, "Are you coming back to town any time soon?"

"Not unless my nephew gets into trouble again."

Claire handed her a business card. "Call me if you do. What is your phone number anyway?" Her arms were crossed, hugging the shirt.

Edie reached into her pocket for a business card with her cell number on it. She was wondering if she should kiss Claire when Claire stood on her toes and gave her a peck on the cheek. "Thanks."

She raised her eyebrows in question. "For what?"

"You really are good in bed."

She smiled. "Well, thanks. I try to please."

Claire laughed and Edie stared at her throat, realizing that she could start all over again.

The drive home was a blur. She fought to stay awake and to keep her mind on the road rather than on bedding Claire. Although she was sure making love to Claire would be a one-time experience, she played and replayed the scene in her head—reliving Claire's warm, lovely body twisting under her large hands.

CHAPTER FIVE

Sam woke up in the dark room, disoriented. A siren wailed nearby and someone pounded on the door. She sat up, her heart banging loudly. She could barely make out Jamie till he switched on the gooseneck lamp on the desk. He looked ghoulish.

"Who is it?" he yelled in a high-pitched voice.

"Fire drill!" somebody hollered.

"You're shitting me. It's probably ten degrees outside," he screeched, but nobody answered. There was only the thrumming of feet in the hall and on the nearby stairs.

She wriggled out of her sleeping bag, wearing the sweatpants and an old T-shirt that were her pajamas. She grabbed her winter jacket and pulled on her boots. "Come on, Jamie."

"I'm not going," he said. "Do you smell any smoke? There's no fire. Some asshole pulled the alarm again."

She hesitated. "I'll go check." She shut the door behind her. The hall was empty. She went to the common room and saw Karen and another girl both in pajamas standing at the top of the stairs. She took a few steps toward them. "Are we going up in flames?"

Karen's hair stood pretty much on end. Sam ran her fingers through her own, sure it was flattened with sleep. The other girl frowned. "What the hell! They got us out of bed in the middle of the night for another phony fire drill."

Karen smiled her crooked grin. "You going outside?"

"Not until I smell smoke." Why would anyone pull the fire alarm? "That happened before?"

"A couple times," Karen said. "Right Lisa?"

"Yeah. I'm going back to bed. Wake me up if you see any flames." Lisa trudged past Sam, head down.

"Are you going to the meeting Wednesday?" Karen asked, walking toward Sam.

She thought she was going to walk on by too, but she stopped a couple feet away. "Meeting?"

"LGBT. It's at the Union." Karen looked Sam up and down and Sam fought a blush that was creeping up from her toes.

"If I don't have to work." She checked for sleep in her eyes and then dropped her hand.

Kids were coming up the stairs, surging past them, grousing about having to go out in the cold. Jamie ventured as far as the stairs. "I told you so," he said before retreating toward his room.

"Why are you staying with Jamie?" Karen asked.

How did she explain?

"You two must be really close."

"He's my friend. Nita…" she started and then couldn't finish.

"Nita what?" Karen wore pink flannel bottoms with cats on them.

She focused on the pajamas. "Those are cute."

"Yeah?" Karen smiled her sexy smile. "My grandma gave them to me for Christmas. Now what about Nita?"

"It's nothing." She made a move toward Jamie's room.

Karen took hold of her arm. "Hey, you can stay with Lisa and me anytime." She peered into Sam's face.

Sam looked away. Her vision blurred. "Thanks but I'm okay. I'm going to bed now. See you." She stumbled into Jamie's room, literally, falling over her sleeping bag and hitting the floor.

"Jesus, Sam." Jamie turned the light on. "Are you all right?"

"Goddamn it. Why'd you turn the light off?"

"Sorry. I wasn't thinking." He jumped to his feet. "Do you want to sleep in the bed?"

"No," she snapped and, holding her elbow, slid into the bag.

"Want some ibuprofen?"

"Yeah, if you got some."

He scrounged around in his backpack and came up with a couple. After she swallowed them, he turned off the light. "What did Karen have to say?"

"She wanted to know why I was here. I didn't want to tell her. She asked if I was going to the LGBT meeting next Wednesday."

"We'll go," he said.

She remembered Nita warning her that she'd never find anyone if she always hung around Jamie.

On Saturday she and Nita came to an agreement about the apartment. Carmen would no longer stay overnight when Sam was there.

Carmen had heavy black hair and black eyes with eyebrows that met between them. She also had a little mustache, but Sam guessed her great figure was the attraction. Nita and Carmen chatted together in bastardized Spanish that was difficult—impossible, if Sam was honest—for her to follow.

"Where did you learn to speak Spanish?" Sam asked Nita.

"My mother."

"You should take Spanish. You'd get an A."

"What would be the point of that?"

Already they were on the edge of a fight. "Is she going to be your roommate next year?"

"We're talking about it," Nita said, meeting Sam's gaze with unnecessary defiance.

It actually hurt to breathe. Being around Nita caused her physical pain. She thought she would be glad if Carmen took her place. She could move in with Jamie and maybe spend some nights with Karen, although her hips hurt and her back ached from sleeping on Jamie's dirty clothes. She lashed out, "Then why don't I move out? She can take over my lease."

A small frown appeared between Nita's brows. "I'll ask her."

She turned away to hide the hurt. "You do that." After slamming the door of her room behind her, she threw herself on the bed. The terrible part of all this was that she saw Nita at work, and they'd both be working tonight. There was no getting away from her. She picked up the text she was reading on learning disabilities. It would have put her to sleep had she not been so upset.

Her phone rang and she answered without looking at the display. "Hey," she said, expecting to hear Jamie's voice.

"Hey, you moved out."

"Who?"

"Karen. I asked Jamie for your number. That okay?"

"Sure." She stopped hurting for a moment.

"Want to hang out or study together or something?"

"That would be great, except I have to work tonight."

"What time?"

"Not till six."

"Lots of time. I'll walk you to work and maybe eat there and walk you home. Where do you live?"

She felt a sort of sick excitement—stunned by Karen's boldness, worried that Nita might give her a hard time. Wasn't that what she wanted, though, to make Nita jealous? She gave Karen directions.

"Cool. I'll come now."

She sat on her bed, trying again to study with no success. After reading one paragraph about five times, she put the book down and waited. When the doorbell rang, she ran her fingers through her hair and shook it out before going to the door.

Nita had let Karen in and was talking to her. She saw the

grin on Karen's face and thought who wouldn't smile like that at Nita. She was disgustingly attractive.

"Is Sam around?" Karen asked as Sam stood quietly watching.

"Yeah. Why?" Nita stammered.

Karen noticed her then, standing just outside her bedroom door, and said, "I was beginning to think I had the wrong place."

Sam smiled. "Let's study in my room."

Karen looked from Sam to Nita. "Sure." She went with Sam into the bedroom and Sam closed the door.

"So, what are you studying?" Karen asked, looking around the room as she set her backpack on the floor. The computer chair and the bed were the only places to sit. Karen chose the bed, pulled her Uggs off and crossed her legs under her.

Sam leaned back against the pillows mashed against the headboard. "I'm reading the most boring textbook in the world."

"Yeah? What's your major?" Karen asked.

"Education. What's yours?"

Karen grinned. "Mine too. I want to be a phys. ed. teacher and a coach and maybe a personal trainer."

"Cool! Do you ski?"

"Water ski? Love it. You?"

"I meant downhill."

"I was at Alta over Christmas vacation."

"Lucky you. I was at the U.P. and Granite Peak. I've been to Colorado but never to Utah."

"This was our first trip there." Karen's grin stretched. She grabbed her ankles and leaned forward.

Sam told her about skiing with Edie. "She's awesome. She got Jamie another room when his roommate's girlfriend moved in with them."

"You must be really good friends for you to stay overnight," Karen said.

"We are." She didn't want to tell her the real story.

Nita tapped on the door and opened it. "Hey, are you working tonight?" She hadn't shown any interest in what Sam was doing since she'd brought Carmen home.

"Yeah. Why?"

"Just wondering. I'm working too."

"I know. So?" Sam said rudely.

"Can I talk to you a minute?" Nita asked.

Sam sighed loudly as if this was an imposition, when in fact she was thrilled by the attention. "Excuse me," she said to Karen.

"Hey, I'm not going anywhere."

"What is it?" she asked after closing the door behind her.

"Is she going to be here all afternoon?"

"Carmen spends the afternoon here all the time," she pointed out.

"She leaves before I go to work. I want to talk to you about house rules."

"House rules. What house rules?"

"No one stays overnight. That's what we agreed on. Remember?"

Sam's face felt like it was on fire. For a moment her brain froze at the implications of this. "Oh, for chrissake, Nita, we're studying. Why do you care anyway?"

"I don't."

Karen opened the door. "Whoa, I don't want to cause problems."

"You're not." Her heart thumped.

"Maybe I should go," Karen said.

"No, no, don't go." Sam backed Karen into the bedroom and closed the door, hardly aware of what she was doing.

"I never saw Nita at any LGBT meetings."

"That's because she's always studying or working."

Karen looked at her. "You're not a couple, are you?"

She shook her head, staring back nervously. "No. She's got a girlfriend."

"Carmen?"

"Yes, Carmen with the single eyebrow." It was a mean thing to say and she was immediately sorry, even though it was true. She was better looking than Carmen, except for the figure.

Karen took a step toward her, close enough now for Sam to feel her soft breath on her face. She would have stepped away, but her back was to the door. Her heart hammered in her ears as Karen touched her cheek with the back of her hand, so gently she hardly felt it. She grabbed the hand awkwardly. "Let's sit down." She was panicking.

"Okay," Karen said.

Her cell phone rang, startling them both. It was Jamie, but she turned it off and dropped it on the bed.

"You don't want to answer it?" Karen asked with that crooked smile.

She shook her head. "Not now."

"Hey, it's Saturday. We can study tomorrow. Let's just get to know each other today. What else do you like to do besides skiing?"

"Bike, drive, kayak," she said after a moment of thought. "What about you?" She didn't mention the thing she liked to do best, which was read a good novel.

"Play softball and basketball and water ski. Stuff like that. I was on the girls' teams in high school."

Later, when they were getting ready to go to Chili Verde, Nita had already left. "Let's do this again," Karen said as they put their jackets on, "like tomorrow. We can really study then."

Sam smiled at her, wondering what Karen saw in her. She'd hardly come up with interesting answers when Karen had asked her what she liked to do. She'd said, "Drive." How dumb was that? But she loved to drive. She'd never played softball or basketball in high school except during P.E.

Karen leaned toward her. "I wonder what it's like to kiss you?"

Hardly able to breathe, Sam wished she'd forget the asking part and just do it. "I don't know," she managed to say.

"Would you like that?"

"Yes," she whispered, hoping her breath was okay.

Karen took her face between her hands and looked right into her eyes before kissing her.

It wasn't a first for Sam. She'd kissed Nicole a few times. Each time she'd been too worried about the process to enjoy the moment. When Karen said, "Mmm. You taste delicious," she laughed with relief.

When they were standing on the rickety porch outside Sam's apartment at eleven that night, Karen kissed her again, longer this time, and they sort of melted against each other. The door opened and they moved apart, but Karen kept her arm around Sam.

Nita's eyes flashed with what Sam thought was anger. "If you're going to kiss, do it inside. Haven't you heard of gay bashing?"

Karen smiled. "Don't you know we're in Madison, lesbian heaven? I'm going now. See you tomorrow, Sammy."

The heat of the apartment leaped out and embraced her as she stepped inside. She took her jacket off in sort of a trance. She could hardly believe what was going on.

"What happened to Jamie?" Nita asked with a hint of sarcasm.

"I've got to call him," she said and went into her bedroom.

"Hey, you called?" she said to Jamie.

"Yeah. Where you been all day? I almost came over to show you the new me."

"Karen was here." She told him what had transpired.

"No way. I'm jealous."

"I think maybe Nita is." She was whispering. The walls were thin. "And you know what? I don't care. Karen's coming over tomorrow."

"No shit?"

"None. What new you are you talking about?"

"I dyed my hair."

It was her turn to say, "No shit?" and then, "How do you look?"

"I'd come over but it's too late and too cold."

Carmen had arrived early Sunday afternoon and she and Nita were holed up in Nita's bedroom. Sam was sprawled on the lumpy sofa with the same old boring text in her lap when Karen showed up.

Sam opened the door. "Come on in."

Karen stamped her feet on the raggedy rug. Her backpack bulged as she set it on the floor. "It's goddamn cold out there."

"I know." The wind rattled the windowpanes, and the cold seeped through the glass. Sam picked up the backpack. It wasn't nearly as heavy as it looked.

"I packed some clothes and stuff. I thought maybe we could order a pizza and maybe I'd stay overnight. You know? Have a sleep-in, instead of having to walk back to the dorm." Karen met Sam's eyes and Sam glanced away.

"Nita won't like it," she said, her heart racing to nowhere. "See, we've got this agreement about no one sleeping over. It's because I didn't want to stay here when Carmen slept here."

Karen's eyes looked like smoke and a small smile played with her lips. "Rules are made to be broken."

"Come on," she said, going straight to her bedroom. Karen followed and Sam quietly closed the door.

"Let's study in bed," Karen said.

Wordless, Sam looked at her. Karen's nose and cheeks were red, her dark hair tousled. "Okay," Sam said. "I'm going to use the bathroom. Be right back."

She looked at herself in the mirror while brushing her teeth. Her blue as the sky eyes looked back at her. Did she want to do this? Yes, she did. She peed and washed her hands and hurried back to the bedroom, where Karen was dressed in worn gray sweatpants and a too big T-shirt.

"The towels are under the sink," she said, and as soon as Karen went to the john, she changed into a T-shirt and flannel pants. She was in bed when Karen slipped back in the room.

"Nita was coming out of the john when I went in. She doesn't like me, does she?"

"She doesn't like me either," Sam said. "She likes Carmen."

"Ah, Carmen with the single eyebrow." Karen slid under the covers and took Sam's hand, and again Sam could hardly breathe against the pounding in her chest.

She slid further down and so did Karen.

"This is perfect for kissing." Karen smiled sweetly.

They were facing each other. Sam inhaled shakily. She could smell toothpaste. "I brushed my teeth."

Karen laughed. "I did too, just for you."

Karen's lips were still cold, and Sam was thinking they weren't very good at this when the door opened. They jumped apart.

"No overnight visitors. Remember?" Nita stood in the opening her thin shirt backlit so that Sam could see the dark nipples.

"Carmen is here," Sam said.

"How about we change the rules when you and Sam both have someone over, so that we can all stay overnight?" Karen suggested.

"No," Nita said, "and you shouldn't be in bed together."

"Why? It's warm in here. You should try it," Karen said.

"Sam," Nita's voice was rising, "remember what we agreed to."

"Okay. I'll leave when it's dark," Karen said. "I just thought you ought to know that I can see through that T-shirt and if I can see through it, everyone can."

Sam was as shocked as Nita looked just before she slammed the door shut behind her. She giggled nervously, then put the pillow over her head and howled till she felt like she was going to throw up.

Karen lifted the pillow and grinned at her. "It wasn't that funny."

"I know. She's going to hate me." She was completely sober now and worried again.

"Hey, you have to live with her. I'll go in a couple hours. Next weekend my roommate Lisa is going home. You can stay in my room."

"I have to work weekends," Sam said as Karen snuggled closer.

"You can go to work from my place. I'll even walk you there." Karen kissed her on the nose and cheeks and then on the mouth. Her tongue snaked into Sam's mouth, and she pulled Sam against her. "I love the feel of you," she whispered.

Sam forgot about the test in her learning disabilities class on Monday.

"We'll study in a minute," Karen promised, reminding her. Her hand covered Sam's crotch and Sam felt an embarrassing gush of fluid. At first she thought she'd peed in her pants. "Hey, you are so wet."

Sam thought she was not ready for this, but Karen's hand slipped inside her sweats and the panties underneath. Her breath caught when Karen's fingers began stroking her.

"Come on, touch me." Karen's whisper tickled her ear.

She slid her hand into Karen's sweats. Karen wore no panties. Once set into motion the force of desire was unstoppable. They were both moaning, unable to stop despite Sam's worry that Nita might hear. The next moment, though, her entire attention focused in on Karen's fingers, which were sending her into frantic motion. She was in the throes of ecstasy when suddenly she climaxed and could no longer bear Karen's touch. Karen let out a startlingly loud shout and sort of collapsed on herself.

They lay on their backs afterward, breathing heavily. Sam's hand was drenched and she wiped it off on the sheets. Karen was the first to speak.

"Awesome, huh?" She turned her head toward Sam, who felt suddenly shy.

"Yeah." It had eclipsed years of masturbating.

"I know lots more ways to do it," Karen said after a minute. "I'll show you this weekend. Would you like that?"

Sam felt a surge of excitement and worry. Had she somehow been deficient in her response? She supposed so, but she could learn. She glanced at her watch. It was only four. "Maybe we should study now. I have a test tomorrow."

Karen laughed. "Okay." She laughed again.

At six they got up. Karen pulled clothes over her clothes. They shared the two chairs at the table with Nita and Carmen, eating Chinese food out of cartons. Nita kept glancing at Sam with a look that Sam couldn't decipher.

When Karen and Carmen left, Nita said, "What would your mother say?"

"About what?" Sam asked. They were standing in the living room near the door, and Sam's eyes shifted away from Nita's gaze.

"I'm not deaf. You did it, didn't you?"

"Didn't you?" Sam said.

CHAPTER SIX

Exhausted, Edie fell on her bed. She'd driven off the edge of the Interstate several times and only the ridged pavement had snapped her awake. She'd slept maybe two hours in the past twenty-four. She turned off her cell and when she woke up, hungry, the day had become night.

She listened to the messages—one from Jamie, one from Lynn, one from Pam and one from Claire. Her heart gave a painful blip when she saw Claire's name. What could she want? To tell her that their romp in bed was a mistake, which Edie already knew? She phoned Lynn.

"You'll never guess who is at this conference," Lynn said.

"I don't want to guess, Lynn. Anybody I know?"

"Remember Jamie asking me if I knew Dr. Julie Decker?"

She blanked for a moment before linking the name with Sam. "I thought Decker was a psychologist, not a professor." What she remembered most was Sam's obvious embarrassment.

"Someone at UW-O went on sabbatical, can't remember his name offhand, and she took his place. She's an absolute knockout. I told her Sam was looking for her. She knew her as Sammy and said that she isn't doing therapy right now, but she could recommend someone for Sam to see."

The "knockout" comment brought Claire to mind. Should she tell Lynn? Not yet, she decided. "I didn't get the impression Sam wanted to see anyone else."

"I didn't either. Julie gave me the name of another therapist at the clinic where she worked in Madison. One of us can pass that information on to Sam." Lynn took a breath. "I'm home, you know. The conference is here. Look, I'm going out to eat with some of my colleagues. Can I come over afterward?"

"How late?"

"I'll just slip into bed with you. I have to get up early, though. There's a speaker I want to hear."

She remembered Claire, and then decided it was foolish to think that what had happened between them was anything serious or lasting.

Lynn said, "How did it go with Jamie?"

"I'll tell you when I see you. I just got out of bed. I was up most of the night."

"Doing what where?"

She repeated, "I'll tell you when I see you."

"Tell me now."

"It's too complicated." That would spark Lynn's curiosity.

She showered, thinking of Claire even as she washed her off. After, while rummaging through the fridge looking for something to eat, she called Jamie. He answered on the fifth ring.

"You called?" she said.

"I re-dyed my hair. They didn't have any dishwater blond, so I became a real blonde." There was so much noise in the background she could hardly hear him.

"Where are you?"

"At Chili Verde where Sam works. I'm looking for a job

now that I'm so respectable looking. Got to go. Here comes the manager."

That left Pam and Claire to call. She chose Pam first but got her voice mail and thanked her again for giving her a place to sleep. She was holding the cell, trying to decide whether to call Claire, when the phone rang and Claire's name appeared in the display.

"Edie?" Claire said.

"Hi, Claire."

"Um, I guess you got home all right."

"I did. Is everything all right?"

"Are you alone?"

"At the moment. Lynn is on her way over."

"Is she your lover?"

She hesitated. "She's my best friend. Did I leave something behind?" Why the call? Why the questioning?

"No, it's just that I'd like to go skiing next weekend and I thought maybe you'd go with me."

Her heart lurched and she said warily, "Is Pam going?"

"I haven't asked her."

"I could ask her. I have a message to call her."

Claire emitted a big sigh and said with a touch of asperity, "No. I'd like to go with you and no one else."

Edie got the drift. Quietly exultant, she said, "Okay. Do you want to meet at my house and we'll drive together?"

"Yes, or we could stay there. Don't you have good places to cross country?"

"And downhill, if you do that too." How long had it been since someone made her feel so alive? Thirty years? She was cautious, though, not comfortable with putting her feelings out there for Claire to see.

She realized that Lynn would discover them if they stayed here. Lynn had a key to the house and a garage door opener. Of course, Lynn would also wonder at the strange car in her garage if she went away. She wasn't going to be able to keep this from her, but she could prevent Lynn from finding them in bed together.

"Listen, it will be better if we go up north." She refrained from asking why they were going at all. She could think of only one reason. *Was it too egotistical to wonder if the woman had never experienced good sex?* However, she realized that she didn't care why Claire wanted to be alone with her for two days and two nights, or even why this was ridiculously exciting. Right now, she decided not to look too closely at what she and Claire were doing. They were adults, after all.

"Tell me how to get to your house. I'll take the afternoon off." Claire's voice was low and gravelly and it sent chills racing across Edie's skin.

She heard the garage door open, signaling Lynn's arrival. "I'll send them. Lynn's at the door."

Claire said, "I've got company coming too."

"Well, if it's Pam, say hello." Lynn was calling her name.

"It's Janine."

She pictured Janine's dusky skin, her sexy voice and beautiful body, and her joy soured a little. Was Janine a reluctant lover? Lynn, still in a business suit, was mouthing, "Hello."

"I'll talk to you later." She snapped the phone shut.

"You're going to have to lend me a nightshirt." Lynn kept a toothbrush in a cup with Edie's. She smiled and her dark eyes lit up. "You look beat."

"Do I? I slept when I got home. I haven't eaten yet."

Lynn opened a bottle of cabernet that she'd brought with her. "My butt is sore from sitting." She stood on her toes and kissed Edie on the cheek.

"That's because you don't have any fat on your butt." Edie broke eggs into a small frying pan and put bread in the toaster. "When in doubt, fix breakfast."

"How was Madison? You must have spent the night there." Lynn was leaning against the wall next to the stove, sipping the wine. "Want a glass?"

"Sure. I spent most of the night staring at the ceiling on Pam's futon."

"Where did you run into her?" Lynn poured another glass and handed it to Edie.

"I called her after I left Jamie and Sam. I'll tell you the whole story in a minute."

She started talking when she sat down to eat. Lynn interrupted her once to ask if she'd met Frankie. She hadn't and wondered why. She admitted that she'd taken Claire home before leaving Madison but said nothing about what had transpired at Claire's duplex. She knew that Lynn would say Claire had used Edie to spite Janine, and Edie would have to admit that was probably true. Maybe Claire was telling Janine right now. Perhaps they were fighting or laughing about her and just possibly they'd end up in bed because of it. It made her a little sick thinking about it.

"There's a state meeting in Madison next weekend," Lynn said. "Do you want to go with me?"

She refocused. "I'll be up north communing with the trees."

"Alone?" Lynn was looking at her as if guessing something was being withheld from her.

Edie studied Lynn's almond-shaped eyes, made small and dreamy by thick lenses. She sighed. "I'm going to hit the sheets. I'm tired."

"You aren't going alone, are you?" Lynn said, mildly accusing.

"Don't I usually go alone?" she said defensively, cleaning up her dishes and heading for the bedroom.

"You didn't take long to find someone else." Lynn hurried to keep up with her.

"I haven't found someone else," she snapped, changing into a large T-shirt and getting under the covers. The flannel sheets and goose down blanket wrapped her in a cocoon.

Lynn slid in next to her. It had been months since they'd had any sex, which had occasionally bothered her before she made love to Claire. "Tell me about Dr. Julie Decker."

"Blonde, gray eyes, great figure, smart, fun. Whoever got her is lucky. She left late this afternoon. Said something about a horse show tomorrow."

"I always wanted a horse. Maybe every girl does."

"I wanted a dog."

Edie started drifting into sleep, jerking awake when Lynn spoke. Finally, she said "Good night," gave Lynn a kiss on the cheek and turned her back.

The week went by slowly. Every moment she wasn't preoccupied, she spent in anticipation of Friday. Claire and desire had become one. Why, she sometimes wondered, when Claire had proven to be lousy in bed?

When Claire pulled into the driveway Friday a little after three, Edie felt a rush of excitement that both thrilled and appalled her. She watched as Claire got out of the Escape, her bright brown hair flying. She looked around and hurried toward the front door. Edie opened it before she touched the handle, and they looked at each other briefly before Claire stepped over the threshold and Edie closed the door behind her, shutting the cold out.

"Where is the john?" Claire asked. She pushed her boots off in the small entryway and dropped her jacket on the carpet.

Edie pointed the way. "Down the hall on the right."

When Claire came out, Edie asked if she'd like coffee or something to eat before they left.

Claire smiled slowly. "You know what I'd like more than coffee?"

Edie's heart picked up speed as she asked, "What?"

"I want you to do what you did last time we were going to have a cup of coffee." Claire took her upper lip between her teeth, the smile gone.

Heat rushed to Edie's face. "It will give us a late start."

Claire appeared not to notice the blush. Perhaps she too was trembling inside. "It's only three fifteen."

She was glad that Lynn was already gone to Madison. "You're right," she said, switching gears.

In the bedroom, she hardly knew where to start. "I'll change the sheets."

Claire grabbed her arm as Edie pulled the comforter back. "I don't care about the sheets."

She looked at Claire's hand on her arm and Claire let go. Her heart was thudding in her ears, and she felt big and clumsy as she had that morning at Claire's before she realized what Claire wanted from her. She had thought they'd have a few hours to work up to this point. She lifted her gaze and saw Claire's face expectantly turned upward.

She bent to kiss her, gently, and Claire's tongue snaked into her mouth. Startled, Edie found the hem of Claire's sweater and pulled it over her head, breaking the kiss. She then tried to smooth the golden brown strands, which seemed alive with the same electricity that flared between the two women.

Edie kissed Claire's eyes and the lashes that curled on her cheeks. She bent further to nibble at her neck. When she unhooked her bra, releasing the small, firm breasts, Claire's pale nipples hardened under her gaze. Edie tasted them as she unzipped Claire's jeans and pushed them and her panties down to her ankles. She sat on the bed and turned Claire so that she was facing her, standing between her legs. Claire lifted one foot and the other, like an obedient child stepping out of her clothes.

Edie buried her face between Claire's breasts, breathing her scent. Her hands moved over Claire's body, feeling the smooth skin, the taut muscles, the curves of breasts and hips and buttocks. Her fingers slid between Claire's legs, testing. She stood up in one movement and laid Claire flat on the mattress.

For a moment, she gazed at Claire's body, wondering if she should take off her own clothes. Their texture would be rough on Claire's body, she decided, and quickly undressed. Carefully she placed her body over Claire's so that their skin touched, but she was so much taller that they did not connect at the right places. Her breasts were below Claire's, her ribs over Claire's belly.

Claire was sideways across the queen-size bed, which was where Edie wanted her. The tailboard would have made it impossible to slide off the bed onto the carpet as she had done at Claire's and as she did now after kissing and tasting her way down Claire's slender body. Claire was shaking when Edie spread her legs. She came quickly.

Edie climbed back on the bed and would have kissed Claire's mouth if Claire hadn't turned her head. Instead, when her breathing slowed, Claire put a hand on Edie's breast and said, "Wow."

Edie laughed, even though she felt big and awkward again and only wanted to put on her clothes.

Claire went right to the source. She did not use her tongue, but Edie was so turned on from her own efforts that she came quickly. When it was over, she said, "Shall we get dressed and go now? I have a room reserved."

They did not talk much on the drive north. The headlights made a pathway through the dark. Snowy banks and tall pines and alders flashed by as Edie's Focus parted the night. Claire had put the Escape in the garage, even though it had more room. Edie's and Claire's skis were bagged and tarp-hooked to the roof rack.

"Tell me about your job," Edie said.

Claire talked a little about the library branch where she worked. "There's not much to tell. I check in books, I check out books, I sometimes stack books, I work the reference desk when needed. Did you always want to be a writer?"

"Yes, actually. I lucked into a publisher and that sort of set my course." Now that the interstate had narrowed to two lanes, the headlights of passing vehicles flashed across their faces.

She glanced at Claire, who was staring straight ahead. She had not met her eyes since they'd left Edie's bed.

"Are you hungry?" Edie asked, because she was. "We could stop at Jacobi's."

"Sure."

Claire asked for a table in the far corner of the restaurant and sat with her back to the room. She ordered a glass of white wine.

Edie studied her quietly.

"Why are you staring at me?" Claire asked.

"Because you're across the table from me?" Edie was drinking water. She was afraid wine would put her to sleep. In her peripheral vision she was surprised to see Jennifer Gottschalk get up from a table of four. She hadn't noticed her when they were seated. She was always comforted by Jennifer's size, because there were few women as tall and big-boned as Edie.

"Hey, I must have missed your e-mail," she said with a smile as she approached. "Hello, Claire."

Edie glanced at Claire and thought, who would not remember her? "Sorry. This was sort of a spur-of-the-moment trip. Where are you skiing tomorrow?"

"Winter Park." Edie looked at Claire as if silently asking was this okay, but Claire would not meet her gaze. "And you?"

"The same." Jennifer had a warm smile, one that never failed to make Edie feel as if she were special. "You're doing the Birkie, aren't you?"

"Of course."

"How about you, Claire?"

"I'm not a great skier," Claire said with a slight frown.

"You don't have to be. We've had first-year skiers take on the Kortelopet, which is a lot shorter and geared more toward recreational skiers."

"You could come and watch," Edie suggested mildly. "It's an event as much as a race."

"Really?" Claire's smile was strained.

"Well, maybe I'll see you tomorrow on the trails," Jennifer said and returned to her table.

"The American Birkebeiner is the largest, most exciting cross country ski race in North America, and it's in northern Wisconsin."

"I know," Claire said as if bored.

Of course she knew, Edie thought, but she loved the Birkie. Over eight thousand skiers ranging from beginners to pros, from several states and countries would gather in the Hayward–Cable area along with some twenty thousand spectators. The Birkie was held in late February, and there was something for everyone. The fifty-four kilometer classic, the fifty kilometer freestyle, in which she would ski, the twenty-three kilometer Kortelopet for those not ready to tackle the longer races. There was even a separate race for kids.

Claire ate half her steak and was nursing another glass of wine before Edie was halfway through her shrimp scampi. Edie felt greedy and rushed and ended up asking for a doggy bag. The food would stay cold in the car.

"Ready?" she asked Claire, who jumped to her feet and pulled on her jacket.

When they reached the motel, Edie took the ski bag off the roof and carried it and her backpack to the main desk, while Claire hung back, studying the brochures. She started down the hall, and Claire followed. The door swung open when she slid the card through the slot. The room was identical to the one she'd stayed in when she met Claire and Pam while skiing.

Claire slipped past her and shut the door and slid the deadbolt in place. Edie tossed her backpack next to Claire's on one of the queen-size beds. Claire looked at it and said, "I sleep better alone."

"Okay." She threw her backpack on the other bed, too tired to even wonder at what she considered Claire's strange behavior. It was so contradictory.

They took turns in the bathroom and climbed into separate beds. Edie sighed at the feel of clean sheets. She was drifting off to the sound of snowmobiles when she thought Claire said something. "What?"

"I can't sleep."

"Sorry."

"I know something that would help."

"Really. What's that?" Edie asked, although she knew and wondered who provided this service when she wasn't around.

"You know how to make me relax."

She lay quietly for a few moments, letting the tension grow. Then she gathered herself up and closed the narrow space between them, her heart thudding with anger and desire. She wondered at the two emotions, so disparate, flowing through her, and the excitement that accompanied them.

When she lay down next to her, Claire whispered, "Cover me." When she kissed her, Claire murmured, "I still have my nightshirt on." Normally, the instructions would have turned her off, but for some reason, they had the opposite effect. She slowly worked her way down Claire's body as she had before, brushing her smooth skin with her lips, tasting it with her tongue. She paused. Claire was already moving, and Edie looked up to see her head thrown back, her neck exposed. She reversed directions and Claire grew still under her. When she kissed her neck and tried to kiss her mouth, Claire turned her head away.

In a grainy voice, she said, "Finish. Please." And so Edie did, her knees on the floor, her arms around Claire's legs, holding her as she jerked in response. When it was over, she pulled the covers over Claire and climbed into her own bed and slept.

When the morning light awoke her, Edie brought coffee and doughnuts back from the lobby. Claire was sitting up in bed and after eating, she said quietly, "It's better to do it before we shower. We won't be sticky then." Edie would have laughed if she hadn't been slightly appalled at the desire that immediately consumed her. They left the motel around ten.

Edie put on her boots and stepped into her bindings in the bright, cold morning. The snow was nearly flat in this expanse, and she dug in with her edges as she skate skied toward the beginning trail, pushing with her poles. Before she entered the woods, she realized that Claire was struggling to keep up. She paused and waited for her, knowing she was bigger and stronger. She did this several times, and while she was waiting at a juncture that led to the more advanced trails, Jennifer passed her, calling out, "Passing on the right, Edie."

Antsy to catch up with her, Edie took off, lengthening her stride, momentarily forgetting Claire. The sun's rays streaked through the trees, temporarily blinding her, and she was far along on the expert trial when she finally stopped to wait for Claire.

Snow-covered and furious, Claire caught up. "You could slow down for me," she snapped. "Don't just take off again. This is too advanced for me."

"Sorry. I got carried away." Moving kept her warm.

"Let's go back to the motel. I don't want to do this."

"Look, I'll get you off this trail and you can go back to the warming house. I have to ski if I'm going to do the Birkie."

She led the way to a crossover trail and told Claire to take it and follow the signs. She would deal with the anger later.

They ordered a pizza that night, because Claire was too tired to go out. Edie guessed she was furious, because Edie hadn't gotten back to the warming house until around four. She'd said nothing on the drive back to the motel and was sulking on the bed when Edie came back with the pizza.

Edie set the food on the small table. "Hungry?" she asked and when Claire remained quiet said, "Well, I am," and tore the greasy paper off the pizza.

"I don't want to sit in the warming house for hours tomorrow, waiting for you." Claire's voice was tight and low.

"Then ski with me. Isn't that why we're here?"

"You can ski with Jennifer What's-Her-Name next weekend. I don't want to waste my time trying to catch up with you."

The first piece of pizza was halfway to her mouth, and she sighed. "I think it was you who suggested we go skiing together." She took a bite out of the slice and it tasted so good that she kept eating till half the pizza was gone. "Come on over, Claire."

"I'm not hungry," Claire said, fury evident in every word.

"You gotta be kidding. You must be starving. Try some of this. It's good."

Claire sat up and looked at her. "You have to eat because you're so big."

She flushed. "Thanks for pointing that out. Why are we here anyway? Why did you call me?"

"I don't know. I won't bother you again. Let's go back."

"We'll go back in the morning. I'm not driving in the dark. I'm too tired." She stalked to the bathroom to wash her hands and when she came out, Claire was at the table.

She ate two pieces before going to the bathroom and back to bed, while Edie pretended to read.

"Come over here," Claire said.

Edie looked at her, trying to retain her anger. "Why?"

"Because I want you."

Of course, she went.

CHAPTER SEVEN

Sam and Jamie were walking home from Chili Verde after midnight. When Jamie's hair had changed from violet to blond, Bruce hired him. Nita had gone with Carmen to her place, and Karen was at the dorm studying for a test. A fierce wind tunneled toward them down the dimly lit street. Jamie stepped off the pavement to make a snowball, and a black truck pulled onto the sidewalk and blocked their progress.

The window on the passenger side slid down and the driver asked, "Want a ride? It's damn cold out there."

Jamie threw the snowball at the open window and nailed the white face leaning toward them. They froze as the door opened on the driver's side.

Jamie yelled, "Run!" They did, but Sam's jacket caught on the high bumper.

She heard it tear and paused to free it. The man's arms closed around her, and his hand clapped over her mouth. "Don't scream," he said in her ear. "I won't hurt you."

Paralyzed with fear, she wouldn't have been able to yell if her life depended on it, and she figured it did. She saw Jamie skid to a stop and run back toward them. The man let go of her mouth and shoved an elbow in Jamie's face and Jamie went down on the slippery sidewalk.

That's when Sam managed to scream. The man slapped her and her head snapped to the side. She couldn't believe this was happening, to her, to them. Her cheek burned.

"Git in the truck. Come on." He pushed her, holding her up at the same time, shoving her toward the passenger door.

Jamie scrambled to his feet and threw himself at the man, who kicked him in the shins, knocking his legs out from under him. When he was down, the man kicked him in the gut until Jamie curled into a ball on the icy sidewalk.

Sam looked wildly around for someone to rescue them, but the street was deserted. Her captor smelled of sweat despite the cold. He had to let go of her with one hand to open the door. She fought fiercely, finally spinning out of his clutch, and dashed toward Jamie, who was again on his feet. "Run, run, run..." she shrieked.

They dashed along the sidewalk away from Sam's apartment. The man in the truck followed them. He called out the open window. "Scaredy cats. You can run all you want, but I'll get you sooner or later."

When they came to an intersection, they sprinted toward a car idling at a red light. Out of control, Sam shouted, "Help, help, help."

The car was full of young guys in parkas, probably students. The windows rolled down and someone said, "Hey, what's happening?"

"Let us in," Jamie yelled, pulling on the back door. "He's gonna kill us."

"Hey, cool it," one of them said. Another asked, "Why are you freaking out?" The person in the backseat next to the window opened the door. "Get in. The girl can sit on your lap."

The one in the middle leaned over and said to Jamie, "Somebody kick you in the face?"

"Yes, the guy in the black truck." There were five of them in the backseat now.

"What black truck?"

It was about eighty degrees in the small vehicle, but Sam was shaking so hard her teeth chattered. The truck was gone, but she was sure it was just around the corner. "It's there, it's there," she said.

"Hey, get it under control. Who's gonna kill you?" the passenger up front asked.

Jamie started talking about the black truck and the driver. How he waylaid them and elbowed his face and kicked him till he couldn't breathe and tried to force Sam into the truck. How weeks ago this same guy had broken his nose. The others listened, although Sam thought Jamie's tale sounded jumbled as he mixed up the earlier beating and this one and the first time they'd encountered the guy in the black truck.

The driver interrupted him. "Where do you live?"

Sam got out with Jamie at the dorm. She and Jamie hurried inside, took the stairs two at a time, locked his door and huddled on his bed. Jamie rocked back and forth, clutching his midriff.

"I think he broke something," he said. "How does my face look?"

"Terrible." It was swollen again and already turning colors. "Now what do we do?" She held herself with both arms, trying to stop the shaking. How could they safely walk home from work at night? "I thought you gave the cops his license plate number?"

"No, I gave it to the doctor. Truckin something." He pulled out his phone. "What number do I call about an assault? Nine-one-one?" He posed the same question to whoever answered and then whispered to Sam, "I'm being transferred to the police department," where he launched into a detailed description of the assault. "I don't know what kind of truck. Hang on." He looked at Sam and she shook her head.

"A black four-wheel drive," she said.

"We can't come to the station. How would we get there? Can you send someone here? We'll meet them in the lobby. We're at Sellery Hall, one of the two towers. The other is Witte." He spelled their names.

Sam looked at him. "I don't want to go sit in the lobby."

"Why don't you call Karen? Maybe she's still up. She can go with us." His pupils were huge as she supposed hers were too. "I'll call her," he said when she didn't answer.

Karen had on her pink flannel pajama pants with cats on them and a rumpled T-shirt, and smelled of sleep. "Are you all right?" she asked, hugging Sam so tight that it almost hurt.

Sam thought of her mindless screaming, the waving of her arms in the air as she ran. "I'm okay," she said.

There were two officers in the lobby when they got downstairs—a young man and a woman who looked a little older. After giving them a recap of the assault, Jamie said, "Didn't anyone do anything about this last time it happened? I gave the license plate to the doctor. He said he'd report it. It's Truckin something."

"What was the doctor's name?" the woman officer asked. They'd given their names and showed their badges, but the names hadn't registered with Sam.

"I don't remember, but I'd know him if I saw him," Jamie said.

"It looks like you need some medical assistance," the woman said.

Jamie touched his cheek gingerly. "I'll go tomorrow."

"Call this number and give one of us the plate name or number when you find out." Again it was the woman officer who spoke.

Her partner tore off a copy of the sheet he'd been writing on and handed it to Jamie. He said, "Go in groups and avoid lonely streets."

A chill galloped across Sam's already cold skin. She tightened her hold on herself. Karen put an arm around her.

"Goddamn, my face hurts," Jamie said when the officers were gone. "Good thing I kept some of those pain meds." He'd taken a couple of Tylenols with codeine before they left the room.

"What if your cheekbone is broken?" Karen asked. "Shouldn't you go to UHS now?"

"There's probably no doctor there. I'll be all right till tomorrow. Besides, what do they do with a broken cheekbone? Put a cast on it?" His laugh was like a little yelp.

Sam was talking to Julie in her head. *He grabbed me. I knew he'd take me somewhere and rape and murder me and maybe stuff me under leaves. He'll come back. I know he will.* She was thinking how cold and lonely and humiliating it would be sprawled in the snow, naked from the waist down, even if she was dead.

Later, she lay in Karen's narrow bed, listening to Karen and her roommate breathe. Karen was curled against her, spoon-like, with an arm draped over her ribs. Sam was so incredibly tired and so wide-awake.

In the morning, while Karen showered, Sam put on yesterday's clothes, placing Karen's borrowed T-shirt on the bed. Karen's roommate, Lisa, had already gone to breakfast. Sam sat on the bed till Karen returned.

When she dropped the towel, Sam noticed how her nipples puckered, the tips resembling pink gumdrops. Water droplets glistened on the ends of the black patch of pubic hair. She was peeking without trying to peek. That would have been how she'd have looked, naked in the snow.

"I'm going to the apartment," she said.

"Should I come over tonight?" Karen asked.

Sam looked away. "I'm going to pack." And sleep, she thought, that too.

"What are you packing?" Karen stood before her, dressed in a black bra and dark red bikini panties.

"I'm going home."

"You can't go home. I just found you." She sat on the bed next to Sam and put an arm around her. "I'll keep you safe."

"How?" she asked.

"At least wait till Jamie finds out about the license plate."

"Jamie can't protect himself." Her voice was flat sounding. She could not think about last night without panicking. "I can go to UW-O."

Karen pulled Sam down with her on the bed. Her hand snaked under Sam's top and cupped a breast.

This evoked an image of the man with the black truck doing the same and Sam jerked away. "Don't. Please."

"I'll call Jamie," Karen said. "Maybe he can walk you back to the apartment."

"Hey, Jamie, where are you?" Karen asked, the phone to her ear. "At UHS? They're bringing in a doctor?" Karen turned her back to Sam, but Sam could hear. "Listen. Sam wants to go to the apartment and pack to go home. Will you talk to her? She's really spooked by what happened last night." She handed the cell to Sam, saying unnecessarily, "It's Jamie."

"Hey, Sam, don't do anything until I get there. Okay?"

"If you had your car, we wouldn't have been walking," Sam said accusingly.

"I know. I'll go get it."

"When?" she asked.

"This weekend. I'll get a ride home. Will you stick around till then?"

"I'll go with you."

"Look, I'm stuck here for a while. They're looking for the license plate info."

She handed the phone back to Karen.

"How's your cheek?" Karen asked and said after listening, "I'm glad it's not broken."

Sam hadn't even thought of his cheek. She got up and headed toward the door.

"She's leaving. I gotta go."

Karen's hand was on her arm, restraining her. "Wait a minute. Fuck my class. I'll walk you to your apartment. Okay? Let me get my stuff."

Karen did all the talking on the way back to Sam's apartment. "I'll take care of you. Just don't go away."

She realized, though, that there would be the one time when no one could be with her, and he'd find her. The only safe place was home, because he didn't know where home was.

When Jamie arrived, his ears and one cheek were red from the cold. The other cheek was so bruised it looked like mold gone amok on a peach. She stared at it. "You should never have made him mad." She felt like she was walking around in a bubble. Karen was sitting on her bed. All of them had skipped their classes.

"The doctor said he called in the license plate info, but the police couldn't find the truck. Next time we have to get the make and model and the license number. What are you doing, Sam?"

"Packing." Her suitcase lay on the bed. She couldn't bear to think of a "next time."

"You're not seriously thinking of leaving, are you?" he asked.

"Where are you going?" Nita was standing in the open doorway.

"What are you doing here?" Jamie asked.

"I live here. Remember?" she said with some asperity. "What's going on?"

"I can't stay here anymore," Sam said.

"And who's going to pay your half of the rent?"

"Carmen." Sam brushed past Nita on her way to the bathroom. She put her toothbrush and shampoo and toothpaste and all the other things she used in the bathroom into a plastic bag.

"What happened to your face, Jamie?" Nita asked.

She leaned against the sink as Jamie started to describe the assault in detail. When he got to the part about the guy grabbing Sam and elbowing his cheek, she sat on the toilet lid, her head in her hands. Her heart was pounding.

"You and your smart mouth started all this. What if he'd managed to kidnap Sam? What then?"

Sam suddenly couldn't stay alone. She grabbed the plastic bag and hurried back to her room as if she were being chased.

She felt their eyes on her as she dropped the bag in her suitcase and shut the lid. Nita put a hand on her shoulder and she jumped. "Don't sneak up on me."

"Sorry." Nita held her hands up. "Look Sam, I'll walk

home from work with you. So will Jamie, won't you Jamie? Maybe Karen will too. He won't dare attack us when we're all together."

Sam slumped between her suitcase and Karen, who put an arm around her again. The thing was, she didn't want to be touched. It reminded her of the attacker's grip and her helplessness. "Who do you think he'd grab, Nita? You or me? Look in the mirror. You're the one who's not safe."

Jamie said, "Hey, listen. I talked to Aunt Edie. She knows where Dr. Decker is. Decker gave her the name of someone at the clinic you can talk to." He pulled a piece of paper out of his pocket. "Sharon Arnold. She said Dr. Decker said for you to give her a chance, Sam."

She stared at Jamie, alert now. "Where is Julie?"

"I don't know. I didn't ask."

"What's Edie's number?"

"Sam, Decker's not doing therapy," he said gently.

She began crying softly and was unable to stop. Her throat hurt. Her chest ached. Her nose ran.

Karen dug a wrinkled tissue out of her pocket and handed it to Sam. "Hey, it's okay. You're safe." Her grip tightened on Sam's shoulders, but that only made Sam sob harder.

Nita set Sam's suitcase on the floor, plunked herself down and put her arm around her too. Their attempts to hold her were too much like the assault. Sam struggled to get away as they held on.

"I'll find out where she is. Okay? I'll call Edie right now," Jamie said in an alarmed voice.

Sam went still. "Will you take me there?"

"Yeah, sure." He put the cell to his ear and waited. "Call me ASAP, Auntie. We've got an emergency here."

"Look, I've got a class I can't miss," Nita got up. "Don't go anywhere till I get back. Okay, Sam?"

Sam nodded and curled up on the bed. "I'm so tired."

"Should I stay?" Karen asked.

"No, you better go to class too. Lock the door."

"I'll stay," Jamie said.

In her dreams, her mother came to take her home. They

loaded her luggage in the backseat. On Highway 41, a silver semi in the outside lane sideswiped her mother's car and forced it off the road. She and her mother screamed as they ran from the driver who was now chasing them. She woke up with a scream crammed in her throat. Jamie's cell was ringing.

He was asleep at the foot of the bed, his mouth agape in a snore. She poked him with a foot, and he sat up. "Huh? What?"

It was Edie. "Hi, Auntie," he said in a groggy voice. "Yeah, I was just taking a nap. I worked late yesterday." He looked Sam in the eyes. "Listen, that guy in the black truck found us last night."

Sam could hear Edie's voice but not what she was saying.

"He nearly broke my cheek and busted my guts and he tried to kidnap Sam. We were walking home from work after midnight. We got away, but Sam really needs to talk to Dr. Decker. And I really need my car."

Again Sam listened to Edie talking without understanding a word. Jamie thrust the phone at her. "She wants to talk to you."

"Hi," Sam said softly.

"Hi, Sam. Lynn was the one who talked to Dr. Julie Decker at a meeting. She took a teaching job at UW-O when someone went on sabbatical."

It was that easy. "I thought she didn't want me to know where she was."

"No, of course, not," Edie said gently, "but Dr. Decker isn't practicing therapy right now. Was this man who gave you trouble last night the same one who Jamie nearly backed into in the parking lot?"

"Yeah." He had to be. Why would another man in a black truck accost them?

"Listen, I'm coming down next weekend with Lynn. We can bring Jamie's car if that will help."

She was crying again and handed the cell back to Jamie without answering.

"No, Auntie, you didn't say anything wrong. Actually, you said something so right. We won't have to walk home from work if I have my car. Sam is just upset over what happened. She wanted to go home."

"So he couldn't find me," Sam whispered.

Jamie walked her to her next class at the Sewell Social Science building. He said before he took off down Charter Street toward Chamberlin Hall, "Wait for me afterward. I'll walk home with you."

She dozed off at the beginning of the lecture and never noticed when the room cleared out. Jamie shook her shoulder gently, and she awoke with a painful start, like an electric shock.

"Hey, come on. Pretty boring class, huh?"

"I couldn't stay awake. I tried." She closed her computer and put it in her backpack. His cheek looked even worse, like it was rotting. "Why aren't you scared? You're the one who keeps getting hurt."

"I am scared. Okay? I almost shit in my pants, but then I thought what a mess that would make."

"I've got it together now," she said.

"Good, because I hate to think of what you're like when you don't." He grinned. "I just met a dream man. Dark eyes, dark hair, great body."

"Yeah? What's his name?"

"I don't know. He's in my physics class. Maybe I'll ask him for help."

She threw her backpack over one shoulder. "You don't need help. I'm the one who needs help in math." She shuddered at the thought of having to study physics.

"You want me to call Karen? Find out where she's at?"

"I think I'll just go to the apartment."

"I have to work tonight."

"Don't go," she said, her bowels clenching.

"I'm done at ten. It'll be all right. I'll run all the way back to the dorm. He can't run fast enough."

"Call me when you get there."

"Okay."

"I mean it. Or I'll call the cops."

"Don't do that, Sam."

CHAPTER EIGHT

Edie hunkered down behind the wheel of Jamie's old Escort, embarrassed by the roar of the engine. Why hadn't her brother taken it to the Ford place and gotten the tailpipe assembly fixed or replaced? He was hard on his son, but she thought he'd forgive Jamie his youthful mistakes more easily if Jamie were straight. Sometimes she also thought he blamed her for his son's sexual orientation, as if he'd caught it from her.

She followed Lynn's Honda down the interstate, trying to keep up. Not only was the Escort loud, it didn't seem to have a lot of power.

When she told Lynn what had happened to Sam and Jamie, Lynn had looked as horrified as Edie felt. "I also told them that you'd met Julie Decker and she was teaching at UW-O."

Lynn said, "I doubt she can help Sam with this one. Only the police can do that by catching this guy. You'd think he'd stand out, cruising around campus."

"It's a big campus," she'd said.

They were on their way to Madison to a meeting. The only reason Edie was going was to see Claire. She and Claire had gotten back from Minocqua long before Lynn had returned last weekend, and Claire had gone home in a sulk.

She'd thought then that she was through with this foolishness with Claire. But as soon as Claire was gone, she began obsessing about her, reliving their times in bed, because those seemed to be the only good memories. This relationship was more like an addiction than a love affair. Claire did not love her. She didn't even seem to like her. Maybe she was the one who should be looking for Julie.

On Monday night Claire had called just as she was falling asleep. "Miss me?" she'd said as if she hadn't moped through most of the weekend, ignoring Edie until she wanted something from her.

She'd felt raw inside, sure she'd never see her again, and her heart leaped at the sound of her voice. "I thought you had plans with Janine. That's what you said before you left yesterday."

Claire had ignored the comment. "Will you be coming next weekend? There's a meeting on Saturday."

Fool that she was, Edie was doing as bidden. She would leave Jamie's car at Sam's apartment, then go with Lynn to the ERFA meeting where she was supposed to meet Claire.

She'd had to come clean to Lynn about Claire. She'd hardly been able to look her in the eye when she told her.

"Claire Bouveau?" Lynn had said, interrupting Edie. "When did this happen?"

Edie told her, and Lynn snorted a laugh. "And you were mad because I didn't tell you about Frankie."

"I know. I'm sorry. I understand now."

"Claire is a user," Lynn said in a soft tone.

"I know that too." She lifted her shoulders and grimaced. "I don't think she even likes me."

"Then why?"

"I can't seem to help it. Why Frankie?"

"You don't know Frankie. She's not like Claire," Lynn said gruffly. "Claire will hurt you."

"It hurts more not to see her." They were sitting at the table, drinking coffee. "I feel like an elephant around her."

"She wants you to feel that way." Lynn looked mad. "Think of yourself skiing. You're graceful. You're a gazelle. You're not heavy, you're just tall."

Edie laughed a little at the compliment.

Lynn leaned forward. "Don't let her put you down. Think of this as a midlife crisis."

"Is that how you think of Frankie" she asked.

Lynn had smiled. "No and you'll understand why when you meet her."

She parked the noisy car in front of Sam's apartment and Lynn pulled in behind her. Before they got to the door, it opened. "Heard you coming," Jamie said.

Sam was standing nearby, hands in pockets, looking tired. Her skin was pale except under her eyes.

"You two got a gay meeting?" Jamie asked.

Lynn said. "You should come with us, since it's all about saving your asses from the persecution of the wrongly righteous."

"And I thank you," he said with a little bow.

A girl joined them—cute with freckles and dark hair standing up in disarray. Her ears were studded with tiny rings.

"Hi, I'm Edie," she said, "and this is Lynn."

"Karen," the girl answered with a smile and put an arm around Sam.

So that's how it was, she thought, pleased. "Where is Nita?" she asked, wondering if she'd moved out.

"Working."

"Are you staying over?" Jamie asked.

Edie and Lynn exchanged a glance. "With friends."

"Your car needs work, Jamie," Edie said.

"I know. Maybe I can get it fixed now that I've got a job."

She placed two rolled up fifties into his hand and closed his fingers around them. She didn't want the car to break down while he was driving it. "It might not be enough, but it will help."

"Hey, thanks. Will we see you again before you leave?"

"I doubt it." She didn't want him to meet Claire, to know that his reliable aunt was not in control of her life.

Sam burst into the conversation. "Edie said you met Julie Decker, Lynn."

"I did. She's really cool."

Sam turned red and ducked her head. "She's gorgeous."

"Yes, yes, she is," Lynn agreed.

"She's more than that, though. She gets it," Sam said.

"I'm not surprised."

"What do you think she'd do if we went to see her?" Jamie asked.

"Not till you fix the car," Edie put in. "Promise you'll do that before you drive out of town."

He put a hand on his chest. "Cross my heart."

"I think before you go see Dr. Decker, Sam, you should e-mail her. Try JulieDecker@UWO.edu. She's got to have a mailbox," Lynn said.

They were late to the meeting, which started at ten. The large room was in the Union on the third floor and was hosted by the university's LGBT group. A crowd of people sat around a long table. Heads swung as she and Lynn walked in. They each grabbed a chair and squeezed in between Pam and another woman.

Claire was not there, and Edie quickly realized that she'd have to sit through the meeting even if Claire showed up. It would be rude to leave. Pam poured her and Lynn a cup of coffee and brought them doughnuts from a table near the door.

"Thanks," she whispered, smiling into Pam's eyes, pale as the early morning sky.

Pam leaned toward her. "I thought you'd be skiing,"

"I brought my nephew's car down." That was her excuse. If possible, she would hide her affair with Claire from Pam.

"If you need a place to stay, you know where I am."

People around the table shot "be quiet" looks their way, saving Edie from saying she thought she had a place to stay.

In charge, Todd talked about hate crimes and how some city councils were enacting ordinances against them. He also spoke about urging legislators to end "Don't Ask, Don't Tell" through letters and e-mails. On his right side, a woman next to Lynn stopped tapping on her laptop and spoke up.

Where Todd was ingratiating, she was commanding. "It's expensive to take on the state, and that's what we did, hoping to get the anti-gay marriage amendment repealed. I know how much you worked on this. It was heartbreaking to lose. Attitudes are changing, though, and there is the domestic partnership law. We need to create a stronger base from which to work to elect state and federal representatives and senators sympathetic to equal rights, because that's what we're fighting for." She smiled and her dark, soulful gaze roamed the room. "We're counting on you." She sat down.

Lynn nudged Edie and whispered, "That's Frankie."

To Edie's surprise, Frankie was not even remotely attractive. She was heavyset, and her "great hair" was bottle blonde with dark roots. Her eyes were her best feature.

When the meeting adjourned, Lynn introduced her to Frankie.

"You're the skier Lynn talks about." Her hand closed over Edie's and she gave her a big, friendly smile that almost won Edie over. "I wish I could ski. I can barely walk a straight line." She put an arm around Pam. "Here's the woman you want for a skiing companion."

"Oh, I know," Edie said. "I've skied with her." That was when she noticed Claire standing inside the doorway, and everyone in the room faded to background.

Claire was having an animated conversation with Janine, who had apparently arrived with her. Edie excused herself and walked over to them, but they continued talking as if she weren't standing nearby.

"Do you always eavesdrop on other people's conversations?" Claire asked, spinning toward her as if she'd just noticed her.

"I wasn't..." she began, but she was of course. Bruised, she slunk back to the people bunched around Frankie. Pam appeared at her elbow. "Are you coming back for the afternoon session?"

She hadn't known there was an afternoon session. "I don't think so."

"We'll break down into groups. You get to know more people that way."

"I guess I'm one of those members who just pays her dues." When Pam looked disappointed, Edie said, "I think it's great that you're involved, but I've been trying to change the way things are for a long, long time." She figured she'd done her part. She was watching Claire and Janine, fearing they would leave.

"C'mon with us for lunch. It's not the best food, but it's good enough and relatively cheap."

She filled a tray with an iceberg lettuce salad and a turkey sandwich and sat between Pam and Lynn, who was sitting next to Frankie. Claire and Janine were at another table, laughing it up with three guys, all of them gay. When her tablemates talked about gay marriage as opposed to domestic partnership, she said nothing at first.

She believed everybody should have domestic partnerships, gay and straight. She didn't want to tie her money up with someone else's. Maybe she'd been single too long.

Frankie said, "Like I said, it's about equal rights."

She took a deep breath, her gaze holding Frankie's. "I think everyone should have civil unions. That's what marriage really is, right?"

Frankie smiled. "Marriage is a sacred institution to most people. If nothing else we ought to enjoy the same rights as married couples—the right to our spouse's Social Security, for instance."

She paid, wondering what she would do with the afternoon. She was deeply sorry that she wasn't skiing. "I think I'll just check out the bookstores," she said to Lynn when the group headed for the elevators. "Where should I meet you?"

"Call me around four or I'll call you." Lynn was animated, full of smiles and laughter. Edie was trying to recall if she'd ever been this way around her. She felt lonely.

On State Street she ducked into shops selling souvenirs, into clothing stores that had no clothes that would fit her and into bookstores. She went to Room Of One's Own where she browsed the books and bought a coffee. She went to Borders and found a chair where she paged through a few books from the sales table. It was there that she looked up to see Claire standing in front of her.

A rush of adrenaline coursed through her like a small jolt of electricity. "I'd given up on you."

"What are you reading?" Claire asked, her eyes full of mischief.

"I'm just passing time," she said. She glanced at her watch but the time didn't register.

"Want to go to my place?" Claire gave Edie a wicked smile and Edie was lost.

"Where is Janine?"

She waved a dismissive hand. "I don't know."

They walked to a nearby parking ramp where Claire's Escape waited. Neither had spoken since leaving Borders. At the duplex a car was parked out front.

"It looks like Janine is here." Claire unlocked the door. "C'mon," she said when Edie hesitated. Grabbing Edie's hand she led her to the bedroom, saying when she got there, "What are you doing here?"

Janine was lying on the bed with nothing on. She smiled at them. "Waiting."

Edie took one look and her heart went wild. "I have to go," she said and whirled back toward the door, the image of Janine's dusky body implanted in her brain. She knew she'd never forget the slow smile, the dark breasts and darker nipples, the flat belly and black patch of curly hair sprouting between Janine's crossed legs. Her toenails were painted a bright red.

Claire darted ahead of Edie and stood in front of the door as if to bar Edie's escape. "Don't run away. It'll be fun."

Her face burned as her pulse raced without a beat. "Let me go, Claire. This is not my thing."

"You don't want me?" Claire said, her lovely mouth pushed into a pout.

"I don't want both of you." She felt big and hot and terribly uncomfortable.

Claire ran a hand down her arm and sidled closer. "You are so good in bed. Won't you show Janine your talent?" She stood on her toes to kiss Edie, who closed her eyes and let it happen. Reluctantly, she took Claire by the arms and set her aside. "Now I must go."

She was out the door, down the steps, striding away. The cold air soothed her hot skin. Where would she go, she wondered, and then realized that Claire was following her in Janine's car.

Claire called out the window. "Get in, Edie. I'll send Janine home. It's cold."

It reminded Edie of when she was a teenager and her best friend turned on her, riding in a car with her new best friend, taunting her as she walked home from school. She'd never understood why they bothered to follow her, much less mock her. It broke her heart, of course, and she never told anyone because she was so ashamed.

She kept going, even when Claire hollered that she was sorry. When she remembered her phone, she pulled it out of her jacket pocket and called Lynn. A glance at her watch told her it was close to four. "I need a ride," she said when Lynn answered.

It was Pam who picked her up and took her home with her for the night. Claire had long since turned around and gone back the way she'd come.

Pam talked about the meeting while Edie looked out the passenger window. She saw nothing and heard less. She ached so much that it hurt to breathe. Once in a while, she muttered a mindless response as Pam kept up a patter of words.

"Pam, do you know where I was?" she asked abruptly.

Pam shot her a nervous look. "With Claire?"

"Yes." Knowing that she might never be with Claire again was a stabbing pain in her chest.

"Are you all right?"

She snorted a laugh. How could she tell Pam what had happened? It made her look such a fool. "Yes. No. Thanks for picking me up."

"Hey, my pleasure."

She slept on Pam's futon, picking up *In The Time Of The Butterflies*, finding her place and finishing the book before falling asleep. Over coffee the next morning, she asked Pam where she had met Claire and how long she'd known her.

"At a meeting. Where else? About four years ago, I guess."

"Are you good friends?"

"As good as it gets with Claire. Any plans to get together might be cancelled at the last minute if Janine comes into the picture."

"But you went skiing together."

"Janine was out of town."

"Claire must like to ski. Why else would she go with you?" She was remembering the previous weekend.

"She had nothing else to do, that's why she went. Why?"

"She called me, wanting to go up north to ski last weekend, and when we got there, she didn't really want to ski at all." Pam looked away, and Edie knew she had hurt her because she hadn't invited her. "It was sort of a last-minute thing. I should have asked you. You'd have been more fun."

Pam smiled wryly, and Edie wondered what she wasn't saying. "I'm sorry, Pam."

"No problem. I completely understand. Whatever Claire wants, Claire gets."

The implication left Edie feeling both flattered—that Claire would want her—and insulted—that she was so easy to get. "Yeah, well," but she couldn't bring herself to say it was over. She found to her disgust that she was on the verge of tears.

Pam squeezed her arm. "Hey, I'm sorry."

She laughed, embarrassed that this conversation was even taking place. The ringing doorbell saved her from further humiliation. She was sure it was Lynn, but when Pam opened the door, Claire stood in the opening.

Edie pulled her phone out of her pocket and put in Lynn's number. When she got voice mail, she said, "Come get me at Pam's, Lynn."

When Claire walked into the apartment, she took up all the breathing space. "Aren't you going to offer me a cup of coffee?"

"I'll make another pot," Pam said.

She dropped her purse on the floor near the door and took a chair at the table. Propping her chin in her hand, she looked at Edie. "Want to have dinner together?"

Which meant a romp in bed, of course. "Lynn is picking me up soon. We're going home." The realization that it wasn't over with Claire came with great relief and as much shame.

Pam ground the coffee beans, while Claire stared at Edie. "Do you have to go home with her?"

"Yes. I don't have a car."

"Okay then," Claire said harshly. "It was a mistake, Janine being there. When are you coming back?"

Edie glanced at Pam, feeling her discomfort in a conversation that excluded her. "I don't know."

"Be that way," Claire said, getting up and striding toward the door. "I try to do you a favor," she said with her hand on the doorknob, "and you blow me off."

With surprise, Edie realized that looks really could be daggers. She felt the sting. Claire opened the door and nearly ran into Lynn.

"What was that all about?" Lynn asked when she was inside and Claire was gone.

"Much ado about nada," Edie said. With Claire gone, the tension in the room fizzled, but along with it went the excitement.

"Whew," Pam said, and Lynn laughed.

Edie smiled, although it was painful. She was miserable and Lynn was happy. Maybe she should look for a Frankie like Pam, but the vibes weren't there. It wouldn't be fair to her or Pam.

On the way home Edie asked, "Do you think I'm a prude?"

Lynn glanced at her. "Why?"

"Did you ever go to bed with more than one woman at a time?"

Lynn said, "I sometimes take the wrong road right around here. I need to pay attention or we'll end up in Baraboo."

"You did, didn't you?" Her face was hot with the thought of

what she might have done had she known that Lynn had already crossed that ground. A moment of regret came and went. What were the logistics? How did you make love to two women at once, especially if they only wanted to be on the receiving end?

"It's not something I want people to know. You have to promise to tell no one." The two of them alone in the car created an intimacy.

"Who would I tell?"

"Promise," Lynn insisted.

"Only if you 'fess up," she said.

"It was long before I met you, when I was coming out. My roommates and I had been smoking dope, and it just sort of happened. I remember thinking at the time that it was more fun with two than three. It was sort of awkward, but it worked." There was a pause before she asked, "So what happened?"

"I walked away from Claire and Janine."

After a pause, Lynn said, "How could you let that chance slip away? Sex with the awesome twosome?" She laughed.

Edie forced a laugh. "I couldn't do it."

"What I wouldn't give to have that opportunity." Lynn shot her a grin, which quickly faded into concern. "I'm sorry. I didn't know." Lynn reached over and patted her hand. "She must be a good lover."

"She's a terrible lover, but for some goddamn reason I don't care."

"Is this really serious?"

"It is right now. I didn't know anyone had that much power over me. I hate it and I think she does too."

"How's that?"

"I don't think she wants to want me, but she can't help it either."

"Wow. I don't know what to say to that."

"Yeah, well, I don't know what to do about it." She stared moodily out the window.

"Want some advice?"

Edie was pretty sure she knew what that advice would be and she was right.

"Don't answer the phone when she calls. Don't go to

Madison. Don't invite her to Point. You'll get over it. Ski your ass off, instead." Lynn grinned and continued, "Or screw her as often as you can till you're sick of her."

Surprised, Edie laughed. "So, I have your blessing?"

"I won't go that far. I won't hold it against you, though."

She smiled. Not sure she would be able to take the first advice, she was glad for the second—that is if Claire ever made contact with her again. When she got home she e-mailed Jennifer.

Want to ski next weekend?

CHAPTER NINE

Nita only had so much patience, it seemed. She wouldn't hang around with Sam, who was waiting for Jamie to collect his car from where he'd found a parking space two blocks away. She walked ahead, saying they could pick her up on the way if she didn't get back to the apartment first.

Sam stood in the doorway of Chili Verde. It was the beginning of February and there was just a hint of warmth in the air. She clutched her jacket tightly around her and stomped her feet to fend off the cold. She had wanted to go with Jamie to get the car, but Nita had still been there then so she stayed with her, and then Nita suddenly decided to leave. She'd watched her worriedly until she disappeared from view, agonizing about whether she should run after her. In the end, she waited for Jamie.

He'd gotten the muffler repaired, so that the Escort sounded like most cars. When he turned the corner and parked in front of the restaurant, she hurriedly climbed in the front seat.

"Nita wouldn't wait. She's walking home. We better catch her."

Jamie goosed the car and they burned tire for a few hundred feet in the otherwise quiet night. Pinned to the back of the seat, Sam tried to fasten her seat belt. She shivered as she perused the sidewalk for signs of Nita.

The day after Edie had brought Jamie the car, Sam and Karen and Jamie had tried to remove the bumper stickers without much success. After hours of washing and scraping when there were still pieces of sayings stuck all over the vehicle, Jamie covered them with new stickers—*Escape to Wisconsin, UW-Wisconsin, Badgers On Board.* The idea had been to make the car less obvious. What they'd done was make the car inoffensive. Other students blew their horns or shouted and gave them thumbs-up as they passed.

At the apartment, he and Sam piled out of the car and raced to the door. Sam fumbled with her key. Nita opened up before the lock turned and they fell inside.

"I made it home," she said, looking pleased.

"That doesn't make you safe, Nita," Sam said, as they stood crowded together.

"Maybe *you're* not safe, but *I* probably am. I doubt if he connects me with you or Jamie." She put her hands on her hips. "I'm going to bed now. Don't wake me up in the morning."

"Do I ever?" Sam asked, wishing Karen were there with them. Her one weekend alone with Karen in the dorm had been a learning experience. Her crotch tingled when she thought of those two days. There'd been little opportunity since for anything but quickies under the covers at Sam's apartment. They never knew when Nita would burst into the room. Once she'd caught them in mid-sex, and they'd had to pretend nothing was happening. It really put a damper on the act.

Before Sam fell asleep, her hands wandered over her body, reliving that weekend. She dreamed of sex awake and asleep. When Karen smiled at her in a certain way in public, she turned bright red, sure that everyone knew what the two of them were doing when they were alone. Karen had gone home this weekend to take care of her younger brother and sister while her parents went to some conference.

Nita was always annoyed with Sam now, nagging her for stupid things like leaving books on the living room floor, as if she never did that. She watched as Nita disappeared into her bedroom before whispering to Jamie. "You better go."

"Okay," he whispered back. His so-called dream guy hadn't worked out. When he closed the door behind him, he yelled, "Hey," and a chill of pure terror swept through her.

She flung the door wide and yelled, "Get in here, Jamie. Quick!"

Instead, Jamie ran toward his car, screaming, "Call nine-one-one and lock the door."

With the door still open she pushed in the numbers on her cell with shaking fingers. Nita ran out of her bedroom and called for Jamie to come inside. When he kept hollering for her to shut and lock the door, she did.

Sam was crying on the phone and Nita took it away from her. "Yeah, four-thirty-five West Washington. Hurry! He's beating on the car with a tire iron, and he just hit the owner with it. We're trying to get him inside. He won't come."

But then Jamie was banging on the door. Sam unlocked it and he stumbled inside. She slammed the door shut as tires spun on icy pavement, then caught and squealed away. Sirens filled the night air.

Jamie was holding his right arm carefully with his left hand. It looked crooked, and he stared at it a moment and then staggered to the couch. Sam sat next to him, wondering how they were going to get him to UHS or to the hospital.

"My car looks like a piece of crumpled aluminum foil. I don't think it can be fixed." The color had drained from his face. "My dad's going to kill me."

"It's not your fault that a lunatic is after you," Sam said, telling Nita with a glance not to say he'd pissed this crazy man off.

"I think I'm going to throw up," he said, and Nita ran for a vessel.

She hurried back with the dishpan and Sam held his head, as her mother had done for her, while he retched into the pan.

Hammering on the door startled them. Nita and Sam shot fearful looks at each other. Someone said, "Open up. Police."

"Don't open it. We don't know they're police," Sam said, when Nita bounded to let them in.

Nita peered out the window and then opened the door.

The police were the same two officers who had questioned Sam and Jamie at the dorm. The woman officer said, "Another squad stopped a man in a black truck. He had a tire iron with him. He's being transported to the police station." Her gaze honed in on Jamie. "He needs medical attention."

"I know," Sam said. Jamie was leaning heavily against her, his head lolling on the back of the couch.

"I'm going to call an ambulance for the young man. I think one of you should notify his parents."

"No," Jamie said, sitting upright, still leaning on Sam. "Take me in the squad car. I'll be all right." He looked at Sam. "Call my mom, Sam. The number is programmed in my phone in my pocket."

Sam called from the police car, the siren rising and falling eerily at intersections as they drove through red lights and stop signs.

The two police officers helped Jamie out of the car, bustling him through the doors and into a wheelchair at the emergency entrance to University of Wisconsin Hospital. Sam and Nita followed—Sam worried and Nita grumbling.

"How did we get caught up in this, Sam? Jamie will always lead to trouble."

Sam gave her an outraged look as the doors opened and they walked into the emergency waiting room.

"What did his mother say?" Nita asked with a sigh.

"They're on their way. She sounded scared, even though I didn't really tell her what happened."

They found a couple of chairs. Before Nita fell asleep, she said, "I'm going to fail everything."

Sam thought it was an accusation. It was more likely she and

Jamie would fail. She'd gotten a D on the learning disabilities test. Her mom would have a shit fit. She too fell asleep and was awakened by the woman police officer.

"Come on, we'll take you home."

"Can we see him?" Sam asked.

"He's out cold. His arm is badly broken. They had to put it back together. The collarbone was a pretty clean break. You can see him tomorrow, but you need to come to the police station Monday morning."

"How am I going to get there?"

"I can arrange to have someone pick you up." The police officer's name was Dana Talmadge. This time when the two had shown their I.D. badges, Sam had paid attention. The policeman was James Delacourt. She had repeated the names to herself in an attempt to remember them.

Dana was tall with short hair and pretty features. Delacourt was the same height as she was with a crew cut and pitted skin. He looked younger than the woman and seemed in a hurry to leave. Maybe their shift was ending.

She went alone to the hospital the next morning and said she was Jamie's sister. He was pale, his eyes huge with dark skin around them. His damaged arm was in plaster and fixed somehow against his chest, so as not to move the broken collarbone, he said. The rest of him looked long and skinny.

She said, "I have to go to the police station tomorrow to identify him." Him was the guy who had assaulted them, the one who sent ripples of terror through her. "I never got a really good look at him. Did you?"

"Older guy with a ball cap and greasy hair. Shorter than me."

"That's a real good description, Jamie," she said sarcastically and then was sorry because he looked like he was in pain. "Does it hurt terribly?"

"It aches, but hey, I've got my own morphine machine." He nodded at a bag filled with a solution dripping through a tube into a needle in his hand. "Nail him, Sam. We can't let him get out of jail. Who would've thought this would happen."

She left then. His mom and dad were on the way from the hotel where they'd spent the night, and his Aunt Edie was driving down for the day.

Karen came to the apartment that afternoon. She looked from Sam to Nita and said, "What happened?"

After they told her, she took Sam into the bedroom and lay down with her. "This will help you forget, she said, getting under the covers and touching Sam in those places that made her gasp with pleasure. Even as she hovered on the verge of coming, Sam could not forget the man she was supposed to identify in the morning.

There were several men of about the same age and size. She looked from one to the other behind the one-way window and was unable to pick one out and say for certain that this was the man who had grabbed her. She said instead, "He always wore a black ball cap."

The guy in charge left the room and next she knew the men behind the window took turns wearing a ball cap. It made them look even more alike. Desperate to identify the right man and have him jailed, she was close to tears. The thing was if she identified the wrong man, then the guy who had been harassing Jamie and her would be set free.

"Will they turn him loose?" she asked Dana on the drive home.

"I don't think so. He was found with the tire iron right after your friend and his car were attacked. The arresting officers will no doubt say he's dangerous. Can you identify the truck? It's been impounded and has a stolen plate."

"I don't know. It was nearly always dark when I saw him and the truck." Except for the first time in the parking lot, and she only remembered that the truck was black and four-wheel drive, not the make or model.

"Why was this guy after you and your friend?" Dana's profile was clear in the morning light without the police cap she had always worn when on duty. Her chin-length hair had a nice flip at the ends.

She told her the story. "I know Jamie made him mad." She was thinking that she would never see Julie now that Jamie's car had been impounded as evidence too.

"That's no excuse for harassment and assault." Dana's deep voice resonated with conviction. She threw Sam a quick look. Her eyes were a golden brown. Her hair was dark blond like Edie's and Jamie. She seemed a lot like Edie to Sam, confident and in charge.

By some miracle there was a parking spot in front of the apartment and Dana eased her car into it. "My partner, Jim, and I'll be in court during the trial. We'll be on your side."

"Thanks." Sam got out of the car.

The man's name was Charles DeWitt. It was strange to give this person who terrified her a name, like he was a regular person. "Sorry I didn't recognize him." She felt this was a monumental failure. If DeWitt was released for some reason and came after them, she would be responsible.

"That's not uncommon," Dana said. "You can always reach me if you need to. It's always okay to call."

Nita was at the apartment, studying with her bedroom door open. "Hey, how did it go?" she asked.

Sam leaned against the doorframe. "There were five guys and they all looked alike."

Nita's dark eyes bore into her. "So you couldn't ID him?"

"No." Sam's phone was ringing. She pulled it out of her pocket.

"Hi Sam. This is Edie. I'm at the hospital with Jamie. He wants to talk to you. How are you anyway?"

"Me?" she asked with surprise. "I'm okay. I just got back from the police station." She told Edie about the lineup and how she couldn't pick Charles DeWitt out of the five men.

"Most people can't, I hear. I wanted to thank you and Nita for getting Jamie to the hospital."

"Are his mom and dad there?"

"Yes. We're all here. I'll give you to Jamie."

"Hey." Jamie's voice was weak. "I'm being released today."

"Do you think you can recognize the guy and his truck?"

"I've been thinking about this, and I don't know if I want to anymore. What happens if he gets out?"

The fear was palpable. She shrank from it. "But you said we have to keep him in jail. You're going to have to testify at trial."

His voice dropped to a whisper, "My mom keeps trying to take me home."

She was thinking maybe that was a good idea.

Edie looked at Jamie's pasty face and the white cast and sling that held his collarbone in place and felt a helpless anger laced with fear. This person who had attacked him three times was unpredictable and dangerous and likely to be on the streets again soon. If the judge set bail and he could come up with the cash, Jamie would become a target again.

She glanced at her sister-in-law, who looked bewildered and sort of lost. She and her husband—Edie's brother, Dave—had not been kept apprised of the situation. Her brother was pacing the floor, looking furious. He glanced at Edie and jerked his head toward the doorway.

Out in the hallway, hands on hips, he asked, "How did this happen? Why would someone use a tire iron on Jamie and his car?" He was a big man but had never grown the belly many men develop with age.

She was silent for a moment, wondering how to make him understand. Then she told him the story as briefly as possible.

"Only Jamie could make someone mad enough to try to kill him."

"The man not only attacked Jamie three times, but tried to force Sam—you know Sam—into his truck. He's anti-social." That's what Lynn would call him. "No one has the right to attack another person because they're annoyed with him."

"Wouldn't you be pissed if some kid with purple hair nearly ran you down and then mouthed off at you?"

She lost patience. "Leave the hair out of this, will you? You had long hair when you were young. Dad hated it. Have you forgotten?"

He stared at her and the ghost of a smile jerked at his mouth. "I did, didn't I? Do you think he'll be safe here? His mother wants to take him home."

"I think we should find out if this guy gets out on bail."

"You shouldn't keep things from me, Edie." Her brother's hands were still on his hips.

"You're always so hard on him, Dave. Why? Because he's gay?" she asked, surprising herself. She'd never talked about sexual orientation with him.

Dave looked away and mumbled something.

"What?" she asked.

"It didn't come from me," he said defensively.

"Maybe it came from me," she admitted, like it was a disease or something. He walked away and she watched him for a few moments before going back in the room. He was her baby brother. When she'd left for college, he was six years old. He'd seemed more like her son than a brother, and she'd loved him with all her heart. Over the years, he had morphed into their father, disapproving and rigid. She supposed their father had once been rebellious himself. Why did all memory of what it was like to be young seem to evaporate with the years? She could remember being eighteen and defiant. Maybe it was the gay thing he couldn't swallow. She thought, as she had before, that it might be different between Jamie and his father if he'd been a girl.

Jamie was reaching for his mother with his good arm when Edie returned to the room. "Hey, Mom," he said.

Jean got up and put a hand on her son's unhurt arm. "It must hurt terribly, Jamie."

"Nah. I'm okay. I can't wait to get out of here. Are you and dad going to stick around?"

"How are you going to do anything without help?"

"I'll have plenty of help. There are people lots worse off than me. There's a guy in one of my classes who has MS and is in a wheelchair."

"I think you should come home for a week at least to recover," his mother said.

Edie jumped in. "I agree. You've just had surgery, Jamie."

He caved then. He would ride home with his parents and if they didn't take him back the next weekend, Edie promised she would.

Edie drove home without calling Claire or Pam. She was worried about the book she was writing—*Midnight Magic*. She had around one hundred and sixty pages of what she considered crap and she was stuck. Whenever she wrote a romantic scene, Mary Ann, the protagonist's best friend, popped into her head in the form of Claire. Her deadline was April first. She had never been so far away from the finish with less than two months left, nor had she ever disliked writing as she did now.

At home, she forced herself to sit down in front of her computer. Don had just proposed marriage to Elizabeth when Mary Ann came in the back door and called Elizabeth's name.

"Hey, woman, how about a cup of coffee?"

Elizabeth smiled at Don and shrugged helplessly. "We'll have to talk about this later. Besides, I can't answer without giving it some thought, can I?"

Shaggy dark hair hung over his eyes. His gaze burned through it as if he might convince her by staring at her. "All right. I have to go now." The UPS truck was parked out front. If his boss found out he'd gone out of his way to stop at her house, he'd probably lose his job.

"Oh," Mary Ann said from the doorway. "I didn't realize you had company. I'm sorry."

Elizabeth smiled at her friend, certain that she wasn't sorry. "Let's go have that cup of coffee." She put an arm around Mary Ann and smiled into her eyes.

She shouldn't write that, she knew. Women didn't smile into other women's eyes, not in Horizon Romances, but at that moment the story came alive.

In the kitchen Elizabeth started decaf and the two women sat at the table, waiting for it to drip through the grounds. "Are you going to accept?" Mary Ann asked.

"I don't know if I want to share everything with him."

"Well, there you go." Mary Ann *made a palms-up gesture as if everything was solved. "You should trust your instincts."*

Elizabeth smiled. "You don't like him, do you?"

Mary Ann shrugged and dodged the question. "It doesn't matter whether I like him. He's been here weeks and I still don't know him. Do you?"

"He doesn't talk much about himself."

"You can't marry someone you know nothing about."

She knew a few things, which she'd passed on to Mary Ann. He was divorced with no children. His father was dead. His mother had Alzheimer's and lived in a nursing home. He had a brother on the west coast whom he seldom saw.

Edie stopped. What about this guy? He was the hero in the book, not Mary Ann, and she still hadn't fleshed him out in her head or in words. She took a break and looked at her e-mail.

Jennifer's name leaped out at her, and she clicked on it. It was a reply to her message. *You name the place. I'll either meet you there or we can drive together.*

She shot back—*Standing Rock, Iola, Winter Park, American Legion. Pick one.*

Jennifer responded immediately. *Winter Park. Meet me at my place at seven a.m. Saturday. We can ride together. Chip might come with.* She gave directions.

See you then, Edie sent. She thought she'd made a move to put Claire in her past and was proud of herself. Then she remembered her promise to take Jamie back to Madison and called his mother.

"Jean? Will Jamie be ready to go back to school on Sunday?"

"I don't know. He sleeps all the time. The pain meds, I guess. We can take him back when he's ready. That makes more sense, Edie. You've done enough, getting his room changed and all that when we were gone."

"Is that okay with Dave?"

"Of course. Want to talk to Jamie? His eyes just opened."

"Hey Auntie. I hope your life is more interesting than mine." His voice was still weak.

"Your mom said they're going to take you back to Madison."

"I'm their prisoner. They're going to keep me here forever. Right, Mom?" Jean said something in the background. "No, just joshing. Dad is ready to get rid me."

"The truth, Jamie?" She was smiling.

"Actually, he's treating me like a human being. They're going to take me back on Sunday or Monday or Tuesday. What are you doing?"

"Working." Before she went back to writing she made coffee.

Don knocked on Elizabeth's door at five. She was grading papers at the kitchen table. Mary Ann, who taught at the same middle school, had gone home long ago to also grade papers. She got up with a sigh and went to the door.

No bells and whistles blew when he grinned at her. She was thinking she should tell him to get on with his life, when he walked inside and kissed her hard. It was such a surprise that she neither responded nor resisted.

He leaned back to look at her. "Isn't it about time?"

"Time?" she repeated.

"Why don't you show me your bedroom?"

"Oh. Okay." Maybe it was time.

When they started down the hall, Mary Ann burst through the door without knocking.

"Does she live here?" Don asked.

Elizabeth looked from one to the other. If she had to make a choice, it would be Mary Ann, she realized. A good friend is indispensable.

Mary Ann said with a smile, "Would you two like to come over for a cookout?"

"Not now," Don said.

"I've got some leftover slaw in the fridge." Elizabeth jumped at the invitation.

She should have gotten Elizabeth and Don in bed pages ago, but every time they got near the bedroom, Mary Ann showed up. Doggedly, she made Mary Ann leave and Don and Elizabeth continue toward the queen-size bed down the hall.

When Don started to remove Elizabeth's clothes, she said, "Let's just lie down together for a few minutes."

He glanced at his watch and she at hers. They had about an hour before going to Mary Ann's house. Elizabeth lay on her back, her arms folded over her chest. She was thinking about the ungraded papers.

Don put an arm over her and pulled her toward him. He kissed her again, this time deeply. One of his hands was resting on her breast, when the kitchen door opened.

"Come back here, Riley. Elizabeth, it's me and Riley. I came to get the slaw," Mary Ann's eight-year-old daughter, Jane, called.

Elizabeth jumped to her feet as Riley, who was all paws and wagging tail, jumped on her and knocked her back on the bed. She pushed him away with a laugh and got up quickly. Before she shut the door behind her, she heard Don say, "If it's not Mary goddamn Ann, it's her kid and the dog." She smiled and hugged Janie.

Edie looked out the window. A light snow was falling, clinging to the two blue spruces in her backyard. She abandoned the computer, put on her warm clothing and went outside. She'd deal with Don and Elizabeth and Mary Ann later. The tracks along the trail were only lightly coated with snow, and she stepped into them and began to pick up speed. Skiing always cleared her head.

The day was fading quickly through thickly falling snow when she cut back to her house.

CHAPTER TEN

Officer Dana called Sam late Monday afternoon to tell her that Charles DeWitt had been released on bail. She was walking with Karen toward the Union. A strong wind was blowing off the lake, and her ears were freezing. The wind and passing traffic made it difficult to hear.

"But you said they wouldn't let him go." A rush of adrenaline left her weak. She'd been so sure he was off the streets. She'd almost gotten used to feeling safe.

"The arresting officers missed court."

"Why?" she yelled in angry frustration.

"They had an accident."

"But he's going to kill Jamie and me." She truly believed that.

"He never saw you. That was one-way glass. All he knows is that no one identified him. He has to come back for trial."

"When's that?"

"Eight weeks. You can get a restraining order against him."

"That will really keep him away." She knew how effective restraining orders were from her Women's Studies Class.

"I'm sorry, Sam. Call me if you even think you see him. Okay?"

"Yeah, sure." She shut her phone and shoved it and her hands in her pockets.

"What happened?" Karen asked as they climbed the steps of the Union and pushed inside.

"He's out on bail. There was some fuckup."

"Maybe you better get out of that apartment."

"I can move into Jamie's room till he gets back." Angst made her edgy. DeWitt could be anywhere.

"Okay," Karen said. "Let's get your stuff and move you."

They turned to go outside just as Carmen came inside. "Hi. Where are you going?"

"Back to the apartment. I have to move."

Carmen looked surprised. "How come?"

Sam was trying not to focus on Carmen's one eyebrow. "Listen, Nita needs to get out of the apartment too."

"Isn't that guy in jail?"

"No, he's out on bail."

Karen took her arm and urged her toward the door. "It's getting late. Let's go."

"I'll come with you," Carmen said. "Nita can stay with me."

The three of them ran down the steps and arrived at the apartment breathless.

"What's happening?" Nita said, looking alarmed.

It was unusual for Carmen to be with her and Karen as if they were friends, Sam realized. "You need to get out of here. DeWitt was released on bail. There was a screwup."

Nita stared at Sam. "Where are you going?"

"I'm staying in Jamie's room. Carmen says you can go with her."

Nita paused only a moment. "Okay."

Sam called Jamie from his room where she was sitting cross-legged on his bed wrapped in his blanket. "Hey, guess where I am?"

He sounded sleepy. "I don't know. My head is all fucked up with drugs. Don't make me play games."

She told him about DeWitt being out on bail and how she'd moved into his room and Nita had moved in with Carmen. There was a long pause.

"You're shitting me. This guy is out on bail? He'll fucking kill me."

"I know. I think we should transfer to UW-Oshkosh."

"So you can see your therapist. Right?" He let out a big sigh. She pictured him falling back on a pillow in bed. "What are we gonna do about this guy, DeWitt? Is that his name?"

"Yeah, Charles DeWitt. Are you going to be ready to come back on Sunday? Maybe you shouldn't."

"I'm a one-armed fucking target," he said.

A long silence fell between them. "I'm going to buy a can of Mace."

"Good idea. I could do that too, but I don't know if I can run. It hurts to walk."

Karen slipped quietly through the door and sat on the bed next to her. She took one end of the blanket and wrapped them in it together. "Hey to Jamie," she said.

Sam repeated it.

"You lucky bitch," he said. "No fucking in my bed."

"C'mon, you're no fun." She wanted to make him laugh, and he did.

"It's okay if you do, just don't mess up the sheets."

"As if they're not already a mess."

"I could hire a bodyguard," Jamie said, "some handsome gay guy who works out a lot."

"You know someone?" she asked.

"Yeah, but he's not handsome. He needs money, though. Thad Young. He lives in Witte. Can you find him?" Jamie actually sounded excited. "Tell him I've got a job for him. My dad will pay. Mom will make him." Jamie's dad owned Instant Printing.

"You're serious?"

"Goddamn right I am."

She and Karen found Young on the fourth floor of Witte. The door to his room stood open. No clothes were strewn on any surface, books were stacked neatly on desks or shelves and the beds were made.

Young was no looker. His ears stuck out and his eyes were small and close together, topped by jutting brows. He had a thick neck and a muscular body, which towered over them. She had just given him a short history about Jamie, and he was staring at her with disbelief.

"He needs someone to protect him. He'll pay minimum wage. All you have to do is walk places with him. If you've got a class, he'll wait till it's done so that you can escort him home or vice versa."

"What happened again?" he asked, his voice unusually high for someone so big.

She gave him an abbreviated version and added, "He's not a sissy. He just can't defend himself."

Thad sat on a bed, on sheets and blanket tucked in tightly. He motioned for them to sit down on other bed.

Sam and Karen exchanged glances. "We can't stay," Sam said. "Can you do it? He's coming back Sunday." She gave him Jamie's cell number.

"How does he know me?" Thad asked.

"He said he saw you at a LGBT meeting."

Thad turned red and studied the floor between his huge feet.

"Hey, we're members too," Karen said.

"My roommate doesn't know. I could get kicked out of ROTC."

Ah, that was why he was such a neatie, Sam thought. "We won't tell anyone."

He looked at them. "What about you? Didn't you say this DeWitt guy attacked you too?"

"Yeah," Sam said, "but he's really after Jamie." She couldn't afford to pay someone to follow her around, and she didn't want to ask her parents for money. If they thought she was in danger, they'd probably make her go home.

"I'm her bodyguard." Karen smiled.

Thad scribbled a phone number on a piece of paper and thrust it at Sam. "Okay. I'll do it."

"Hey, thanks," she and Karen said at once.

They went back to Jamie's room, scrounged for clean sheets, and put them on the bed, placing a towel over the middle. Sex was something Sam was still learning, but she no longer came with the slightest touch as she had at first.

She raked her fingers through Karen's short hair, making a mess of it as they stretched out on the bed, already kissing, already naked. She squirmed closer as Karen's hand moved over her—slow, teasing—making Sam gasp and forget what she was doing. Karen's fingers slid between her legs and began that gentle caress, creating a pleasure that was almost painful in its intensity. Lost in the exquisiteness of it all she could only copy Karen's moves. She thought, when it was over, that she had been a poor imitation.

"I like having this room," Karen said, "no one barging in to see what we're doing, no hiding under the covers."

Sam tingled with pleasure. Her only regret was that the act was so short-lived.

Karen sighed and stretched. "We'll give it the taste test next time. Okay?"

Sam had been horribly worried the first time they had done it that way. All those jokes about smelling fishy had made her cringe, but she hadn't noticed anything except the nearly unbearable pleasure and her inability to hold off climax. She had thought until then that there could be nothing more exciting than Karen's touch.

Afterward, she and Karen tried to study, but they both fell asleep. At midnight they got up and ate Jamie's store of Twinkies and potato chips. Sam kept track, so that she could replace the hoard.

When she felt her phone vibrating against her ribs the next morning, she answered without looking. "Hey," she said sleepily. Karen was gone from the bed. She'd had an early class.

"I forgot something and went back to the apartment to get it. Someone had broken in," Nita said in a rush. "All of our drawers were dumped, like he was looking for something. I couldn't get out of there fast enough. You took your computer, didn't you?"

She'd snapped awake. She went nowhere without her computer. Chill bumps scurried across her skin and fear momentarily paralyzed her mind. What had been in her desk drawers? Any ID? Were there any letters from home with the return address? Usually, she corresponded with her family via the web, but she thought there had been a card from her mother.

"I grabbed everything and put it in a bag, but he could have gone through the stuff. Look, I'm coming to the dorm now. Call that policewoman. Okay?"

She felt a little thrill that Nita had called her, that she was coming over, that there was this connection between the two of them. Rummaging through her backpack she found her checkbook and credit card and her driver's license—all safely in her wallet. She did her banking online.

Nita knocked once and opened the door. Carmen was with her, and Sam's joy at possibly forging a new bond with Nita vanished. She wondered why she had even been excited. She'd assumed that Nita was history for her.

"That fucking Jamie," Nita said. "Did you call the police?"

Sam nodded. She'd left a message for Officer Dana.

Dana phoned as they stood in Jamie's bedroom. She said they wanted to comb the apartment for fingerprints. If they found DeWitt's prints, there would be a warrant out for his arrest. Could Sam or Nita meet them at the apartment?

"Now?" she asked, glancing at her watch. She had a class in less than an hour. The learning disabilities class she couldn't afford to miss after nearly flunking the last test.

Nita tossed her dark hair and said, "If you can't go, we'll meet her there."

Edie spent the week working. She added fifteen pages, but there were more scenes between Elizabeth and Mary Ann than Elizabeth and Don. Her editor e-mailed to ask how the book was progressing, and she admitted there were problems. She didn't like Don. Make him more likeable, her editor said. She decided that Mary Ann would have to move away to give Don a better chance.

Claire called when she was leaving to meet Lynn for Friday night fish. As always, she felt a rush of excitement.

Claire said, "Pam told me you were in Madison. Why didn't you call?"

"Jamie was hospitalized. I went to see him, then came back home to work."

Silence. "When are you coming back?" No questions about what had happened to Jamie. Maybe she knew. Lynn had probably told Frankie and one of them had told Pam. "What are you doing this weekend? I think there's a meeting."

"I'm skiing on Saturday."

"Alone?"

"No. With Jennifer and Chip. You met Jennifer."

"Who is Chip?"

"I think he's Jennifer's husband."

"Oh, well, break a leg as they say."

"Claire? Are you there?" But she had hung up, and Edie resisted the urge to call her back, to ask her to come with them. She knew where that would lead.

On Saturday morning she awoke when the radio turned itself on. She made coffee, showered and ate breakfast before putting her ski bag and backpack in the car. When she reached Wausau, night had turned into day. She found Jennifer's house easily.

Chip flung the door open. "Hi. Great day for skiing, huh?" His grin was contagious, but what caught her eye was how much he looked like Jennifer—the same light brown eyes and reddish brown hair. He was tall, too, maybe six foot two.

He called, "Hey, Jen, Edie's here."

"Hi, Edie. Come in and have a cup of coffee," Jennifer hollered.

She walked ahead of Chip into a large kitchen with big old windows, a yellow linoleum floor and white painted cupboards.

"Hey," she said with a big smile, shaking her head at the coffee. "I'm already floating."

"Okay, we'll take it with us." Jennifer poured the contents of the glass pot into a thermos. "You know my brother, Chip, don't you?"

Edie smiled. "I always thought he was your husband till today when I took a good look at him."

"No, there's no husband." Jennifer smiled wryly.

"She's the only one who can almost keep up with me. That's why we usually ski together," he said.

"What do you mean almost." Jennifer punched him lightly on the arm.

Chip drove. Jennifer sat in the front of the Subaru. Edie stared out the window at tall pines and alders and blinding snow under a cold blue sky. Last night at dinner, Lynn had suggested she surround herself with other people, when not writing, as a way to fill the empty spot Claire had so quickly created. Claire was an ache that she wouldn't even admit to Lynn. She'd never get over her if she kept calling.

The sun shone brightly without warmth. She and Jennifer followed Chip through the wooded trails. She shed outer clothing as she went—stuffing her hat into her windbreaker pockets, then tying the jacket around her waist. She thought of nothing but the terrain as they skated up and down hills. At lunchtime, they stomped into the warming house, the snow from their boots pooling into steaming puddles. It was a late lunch and they found a table to sit at with two others.

Edie had worried that she wouldn't be able to keep up with them and was exhilarated that she was skiing right on their heels. When they went outside again, the cold energized her.

They quit when the ski area closed, and after equipment and backpacks were loaded, Jennifer climbed behind the wheel. She stopped in Minocqua for gas and Edie tried to give her money, but she waved it away. "Next time you can drive," she said and asked, "Do you want to ski somewhere local tomorrow?"

Edie was pleased. She was planning to go to Standing Rock and said so, "Unless you'd rather go elsewhere?"

"No, that's good. It's enough of a challenge."

On the way home when Chip's head lolled against the window and Edie started to drift off, Jennifer said, "I know you write books, which I think is awesome, and I don't use that word often. Where can I find one to read?"

Edie came fully awake and met Jennifer's eyes in the rearview mirror. She had been dreading this. Her book covers, which often were a man and woman in embrace, embarrassed her as did the dramatic jacket copy, but she answered as she always did, "I write under a pseudonym—Lauren James. You can find my books just about anywhere."

"That's really cool. Are you in the library?" Then, "No, I should buy one."

"Try the library first." That was also what she told everyone who asked. She didn't want anyone spending money on something she might not like. Ninety-nine percent of her audience was women. To change the subject she asked about Chip.

"I'm a pharmacist, like Jennifer." He apparently hadn't been asleep at all, and he turned and smiled at her. "Boring, compared to being a writer."

She said, "What I do can be stupefying. How did it happen that you do the same thing?"

"Coincidence or maybe it's because we're twins," Jennifer said, glancing at her brother.

At ten the next day Edie was in the warming house at Standing Rock, putting on her boots and talking to people she knew, when Jennifer came through the door. She raised a hand and Jennifer strode toward her. She was a striking woman, Edie thought—the commanding stature and reddish hair, even her wide smile made heads turn.

"Where's Chip today?" she asked as Jennifer sat down next to her.

"He went to Granite Peak with some friends. He actually likes downhill better than cross-country."

"Do you?" Edie preferred cross-country to the often-crowded slopes and lifts of Granite Peak.

"Not really. How about you?" She slipped out of her Sorrels and put on her ski boots.

Edie shook her head. "This is so much cheaper and there are no lift lines, although I do go downhill on occasion."

After skate skiing around the wide trails twice, they put on diagonal skis and stayed in the tracks. When the ski area closed and they were again in the warming house, taking off their boots, Jennifer said she had bought one of Edie's books that morning—*The Beach House*.

"I couldn't wait till the library opened." She was smiling.

Edie noticed a sprinkling of freckles on her cheeks and nose. "I hope you're not disappointed."

"Want to ski next weekend? We can talk about your book." She lifted eyebrows that were the same color as her hair.

"I don't think there's that much to discuss." Edie got to her feet. "I write to entertain." And to pay the bills, but she didn't say that.

"Hey, don't put yourself down. I think writing three hundred pages about anything is amazing," Jennifer said as they walked outside.

There was a feel of impending spring in the air. Too often the snow turned soft and sticky or melted and froze, taking the fun out of skiing. They both paused and looked at the darkening sky. Stars were beginning to appear.

She said, "I think we need a good snowstorm."

"A blizzard." Jennifer agreed.

"That would be awesome," Edie said with a laugh.

"I'll call you later in the week now that I have your cell number. Okay?"

At home, Edie turned on the lights and built a fire. She picked up *The Beach House* and paged through it. She considered it one of her better books. Actually, it was pretty hot stuff, even for her, but sex was in the mind. All you had to do was create the right venue. Now if she could just do that with *Midnight Magic*.

She had been getting vibes from Jennifer. Even before she found out that Chip was Jennifer's brother, she had wondered. She was pretty sure that Jennifer had some interest in her. Why else would she to want to ski with her two weekends in a row? Would she even call after reading *The Beach House?* Edie sighed. She hoped she hadn't shot holes in their fledgling friendship, but she couldn't lie about her books. That would be denying what she did.

The next day she was at her computer early, trying to make Mary Ann say goodbye to Elizabeth.

"But you're my best friend," Elizabeth said *with tears in her eyes.* Too corny, she thought and deleted the *tears in her eyes.*

"I'll miss you more than you know," Mary Ann replied, *"but I've always wanted to be a principal. You can visit."* She dropped the *more than you know.*

"Won't you miss teaching, the hands-on molding of kids?" She searched Mary Ann's eyes. Edie deleted the last sentence and then did away with *the hands-on molding* bit, thinking also too corny.

Let Mary Ann go, she told herself. It'll be easy without Mary Ann around. She should never have put her in the story. She packed Mary Ann and her daughter up. Elizabeth watched as they drove off in a U-Haul. The dog's head hung out the window, looking toward the future. After they were gone, Don showed up and comforted Elizabeth.

Edie stalled and made more coffee. She could hardly believe she was missing Mary Ann with her blazing blue eyes and blondish hair, as if she'd been her best friend.

After several more pages of Don wooing Elizabeth, Don turned into a scoundrel with a real wife and a child in Chicago. Elizabeth had accidentally read an e-mail he'd stupidly sent on her computer. She called Mary Ann.

Edie got up and walked around the house. She'd have to invent another hero, one she liked better. She decided to transform the neighbor, to whose door she'd sent Don, the one who owned an auto shop. She'd have to go back and bring him to life. He would be an unassuming man, one who respected Elizabeth's independence.

Her cell rang. She seldom answered when she was working, and she let the call roll into voice mail without even glancing at the display. Later, when she listened to her messages, Claire's voice electrified her.

"Call me."

Just like Claire to give her an order and just like her to obey it, she thought, as she returned the call. "You phoned?"

Claire said. "Why don't you phone?"

"Because I'm busy. I'm working. Aren't you?"

"Look outside. It's dark."

"What is it you want, Claire?" she asked, tired of the caustic tone.

"I thought we had something special, but apparently not."

Her heart was pounding annoyingly in her ears. "If you want to do threesomes, you'll have to find someone else."

Claire's harsh laugh startled her. "Is that all that's wrong?"

Irritated, she said, "No, that's not all. It seems as if all you want from me is sex."

Silence. Then, "You don't like sex with me?"

Edie sighed. She was sweating. The trouble was she loved sex with Claire. "I do," she admitted.

This time Claire's laugh was real. "Come here and show me how much."

"I have a deadline to meet."

"I'll make it worthwhile."

"I work during the week." Of course she could take an afternoon off, but it broke her concentration.

"Come on the weekend."

"I'm going skiing."

A silence followed and she pictured Claire pouting, which made her stubborn. "Look, maybe this isn't a good idea—you and me. I think Janine is the one you want." There, she'd said it. But the continuing silence made her anxious.

"I'll see you tomorrow. Wednesdays are best for me. I'll be home by three thirty."

Edie stared at the phone. She wasn't sure what amazed her more—Claire's rudeness or her own willingness to put up with it. A tingle of excitement began to dissipate her anger. Tomorrow. She could write in the morning and leave at one. If she were a little late, it would make Claire worry. She let go of her determination to give Claire up and latched onto Lynn's idea that seeing a lot of Claire would surely cure her.

When she went back to her computer, she worked Al, the widowed neighbor, into the story.

Snow started falling mid-morning on Wednesday, which she could have used as an excuse to stay home. Snow was what she wanted, lots of it, and it had seldom kept her off the roads. She shoved a change of underwear and the kit with her bathroom stuff into her backpack and headed toward Madison. Tiny flakes that froze as they hit the pavement made driving dicey. When she took the ramp onto the interstate, she knew she was a fool to drive in this stuff.

Just before she got to the Plainfield exit, the Focus went into a slow-motion, heart-stopping skid. She tapped the brakes and steered into it, as the car turned slowly toward the median strip. A pile of snow reared up, and she braced herself as the car rammed into it.

As the adrenaline drained away, she began to shake. When she calmed a little, she put the driveshaft into reverse and tried to back out. The tires spun on the icy snow. After a few attempts at freeing her car from the snowbank, she called Lynn.

"I'm stuck in the median strip near the Plainfield exit."

"Where were you going? The roads are dangerous."

"I think I found that out."

"How near are you to the exit. There are two gas stations there."

"I know. I can see the ramps. I guess I better start walking."

"Give me a call and let me know how it's going. I'll be worried."

With difficulty she pulled on boots and stuffed herself into her jacket before struggling against the wind to open the door. Her hood blew off her head and icy pellets stung her face. The car door ripped out of her hands and slammed, and she started toward the exit. Holding her hood in place she crossed the snowy median strip, peered down the road for oncoming traffic and ran across the northbound lane. She lost her balance on the other side and fell into the snow. Back on her feet, she walked along the edge of the road toward the ramp. The wind was at her back, pushing her up the incline. When she reached the top, she looked both ways and ran across that road. The gas station was at the end of a long drive, and she took a shortcut, plunging through the snow, turning her head away from the icy pellets, till she was on the tarmac of the station itself and then safely inside the warm building.

"I need someone to pull my car out of the median strip. I skidded off the road," she said to the kid behind the counter, who looked like he should be in middle school. His name was stitched on a oval patch on his shirt—Phil.

"The tow truck is out. There's a bunch of people off the road."

Bits of snow fell down her neck when she pushed the hood off. She shrugged out of the jacket and gave it a shake.

"We got coffee and stuff over there," he said pointing. "There's a Subway on the other side, but the woman who works there couldn't make it in." He lifted his thin shoulders. "So, no Subways, but you can sit down there."

She looked around the gas station and realized she'd forgotten to grab her book, the one thing she told her friends and family to go nowhere without. There was a newspaper stand, however, and she put a *Milwaukee Journal Sentinel* on the counter. It would help pass the time. She paid for the paper and a cup of coffee and took them to the empty Subway.

An hour later she was still sitting in a booth, having long since finished reading the paper. She cursed herself for forgetting *The Girl with the Dragon Tattoo*. After a while, she put her head in her arms on the table and fell asleep.

"Hey, ma'am. The tow truck is back."

She awoke with a start and glanced at her watch. It was exactly three thirty, the time Claire said she'd be home. "Thanks," she said, sitting up.

A man with a stubbly chin and tired eyes was standing in the hall between the station and the Subway. "You in the ditch, ma'am?"

She felt like apologizing. "I am, just north of the southbound exit." Why hadn't she made it to the other side of the overpass? Now they would have to double back.

"C'mon. We'll get you out." He looked at the boy. "You all right, son?"

"Yeah."

"Goodbye Phil," she said as she went out the door. Her voice was snatched away by the wind, and she hunched into her jacket. When she stepped on the running board, she slipped before climbing into the truck.

"Smutty day to be on the road," the man said, sliding in behind the wheel. "It looks like snow, but it's more like ice."

"I found that out," she said.

When he parked behind her car to let her out, he said, "Best to get off the road."

"I'm going back to Point, if I can get there," she promised.

It was scary driving up the exit ramp to State Highway. 73 and even scarier taking the ramp back to the interstate, going north. Her heart leaped into her throat every time the car hit an icy patch. It took her nearly an hour to drive the normally twenty-minute distance.

Her phone had been ringing most of the way, but she hadn't dared take her eyes off the road. When she stepped into the warm kitchen and closed the garage door behind her, she checked her voice mail. She talked to Lynn first.

"I'm home. I will never do that again. It's a skating rink out there."

"Good. You could have called me back earlier. I was worried."

"Sorry. I fell asleep waiting for the tow truck, and I couldn't drive and talk at the same time." She slipped out of her jacket and pushed off her boots. "Home never felt so good."

When she phoned Claire, she expected a tongue-lashing. Instead, she got silence as she told her why she wasn't in Madison.

"When are you coming?" Claire asked.

"I don't know. Maybe next Wednesday."

"Better call first. I might be busy."

"Why don't you call me?" She had no patience with this passive-aggressive behavior.

"If I can."

"Do you care at all, Claire, that I might have been in an accident?"

"You weren't, though, were you?" And then she was gone as if there were nothing else to discuss.

CHAPTER ELEVEN

Sam and Karen turned their backs to the driving sleet and walked toward Sam's apartment. Jamie's parents had brought him back the day before, Tuesday. The apartment now had two locks, both new, one a deadbolt, which Officer Dana told Sam never to forget to use.

Sam thought the police officer felt responsible for DeWitt's release on bond. Not only had she told Sam to change the locks before she moved back in, she had stopped by to check them out, which had made Sam even more aware of the danger she was in.

She and Karen had spent the previous night at the apartment. The old house creaked as if it were complaining, and Sam awoke at every noise. Once she shook Karen awake when she thought she heard someone outside. They had crawled to the window and peered out through the frosted pane, but the noise came from the storms banging against the rotten window frames. To Sam it sounded like someone hammering at the door. Cold radiated through the glass panes and wood floor.

"Hey, it's okay, Sammy," Karen said. "I know what will help you sleep. C'mon, let's go back to bed." Once there, she worked her way under the covers, but Sam pulled her back up.

"I like it better when we do that together."

"Me too." Karen was a thoughtful lover.

The touch of her tongue took Sam's mind off anything else. DeWitt could be banging at the door and she'd never hear him.

They were nearly to the apartment now. Sam was scheduled to work that night, and she dreaded going out, not just because DeWitt might be in the vicinity but also because the weather was so shitty.

"I'll go with you," Karen said. Karen sometimes worked shifts when Chili Verde was short-staffed. Otherwise, she sat in a corner and studied or talked to customers till Sam was done.

"I couldn't make it without you." This was true, but her grades were sinking and she knew it was because Karen was always there to distract her. "I have a paper due Friday and I haven't even started it and now I have to work."

"You want me to work for you? I think Bruce would be okay with that."

She'd be home alone, which was not an option. "I'll get it done. It's Women's Issues. You know, gender and society. Should be easy." She was shouting to be heard and was glad when they came to a stop in front of the apartment.

That evening Chili Verde was empty except for the staff, which hung around the hostess's booth and chatted, until Bruce sent them all home and closed early due to the weather. It was a lucky break for Sam, who tapped out her paper on the computer.

The web was her source of information. She wrote about how women always have had lower status than men—that it was demonstrated by the jobs they often held despite their education, jobs like receptionists and data processors instead of managers and CEOs. She pointed out that women in 2000 made about seventy-six cents to a man's dollar. Pregnancy and child bearing had a direct effect on women's ability to attain and keep jobs, of course. What might it be like if men bore the children? She quoted from Alan Wolfe's, *The Gender Question*, "Of all the ways that one group has systematically mistreated another, none is more deeply rooted than the way men have subordinated women." She quoted the passage in Leviticus where God told Moses that a man is worth fifty sheikels and a woman worth thirty—about the same as the present day difference in pay. She concluded with a 1980 summation by the United Nations Commission for Women of this unequal burden: "Women, who comprise half the world's population, do two-thirds of the world's work, earn one-tenth of the world's income and own one-hundredth of the world's property." But she couldn't answer why the world was this way today, why women, who were the daughters and wives of men, continued to be held in such low esteem by these same men.

She printed what she had written and gave it to Karen to read. Karen looked up afterward and said, "Wow. You are so smart. This is really good. It's a real turn-on, and it's time for a break." She got up and gave Sam a big kiss and backed her toward the bed.

These "breaks" were what kept her here. Where Karen went she would follow. As Karen lowered her onto the unmade bed, already unzipping her jeans, the front door opened.

"At it again, huh?" Nita said, standing in the bedroom door. "Like a couple of rabbits."

"Jealous?" Karen asked, standing up and straightening her clothes and hair. "Not getting enough from Carmen?"

Nita stepped forward and raised her hand to Karen. Carmen, who had been standing behind her, grabbed her arm.

Sam jumped to her feet. "Stop it! Just fucking stop it! You said you'd walk to work and back with me, but it's Karen who does it. You're fucking nuts if you think I'm going to give her up!"

"I didn't work last night," Nita said.

"That's what I mean. You're not always there."

"Hey, cool it down," Karen said, touching her cheek.

Carmen jumped into the fray. "Shouldn't we hang together? I mean no one should go anywhere alone."

"Sorry," Nita mumbled, turning away, looking like she might cry. "You're right. I'm just so fucking scared all the time. You know?"

"Hey, it's going to be all right," Karen said. She put a hand on Nita's shoulder and Nita moved out from under it.

Sam said, "I'm sick of being scared. We should have some friends over. What do you think?"

"I think you're fucking nuts," Nita said, slumping on the sofa.

Sam plopped down next to her, feeling a kinship in fear. "Hey, it might be fun. We've been living like fugitives for weeks."

Nita's voice broke and she began to cry. "College is supposed to be fun, not a nightmare. My grades are in the toilet." The words were enunciated with sobs.

Sam put an arm around her. This was the closest she'd ever been to Nita, so near she could smell her shampoo. When Nita only cried harder and tried to move away, she said, "I'm tired of living like a goddamn mouse, scurrying from hole to hole."

The sobs ceased. Nita turned her gaze on Sam. Even reddened, her eyes were beautiful, set in a perfectly oval face. Sam backed off. She didn't want to want Nita. She had Karen, who was kind and fun and great in bed.

"So, what do you want to be? The cat that chases the mouse?" Nita said sarcastically. "We have a party and invite Jamie, who is a magnet for DeWitt. You think he'll crash our party, don't you? And somehow we'll catch him. Stupid but tempting."

Although baiting DeWitt with a party hadn't entered her head, she said, "We'll tell Officer Dana to stick around."

"No beer then, you know. Who is going to come to a party without beer?" Nita's dark eyes hypnotized her. She found it impossible to look away.

"They can bring their own."

"And get arrested?"

"Maybe they'll come for the excitement. So, you're okay with a party?"

"Who are you going to ask to this beerless event?"

Jamie, she thought, and Thad for protection. "People from Chili Verde, from LGBT, Karen's roommates."

"I'll donate," Karen said, raising a hand.

Nita ignored her. "When?"

"I don't know. Saturday?" Her pulse quickened, although she seemed to be less scared than she had been. If DeWitt tried to grab her again, though, she'd pee in her pants like the first time.

Carmen sat down on the other side of Nita and put her arm where Sam's had been, pulling Nita close. The hypnotic eye contact was broken. Sam stood up and Karen wrapped her in her arms.

"So, are you never going home, Karen?" Nita asked, eyeing her.

"Not unless Sam goes with me." Karen grinned at Sam, apparently unfazed by the attempted slap.

Nita gave up the argument, and began to issue orders. "We can all spread the word. You two get the chips and stuff, since you want this thing."

Sam started to protest the cost and then thought better of it. Nita might change her mind, and besides, Nita had less money than she did and Karen had promised to pitch in. A tiny bit of excitement, the good kind, niggled at her. The only fun she had these days took place in bed with Karen. She would call Jamie as soon as she got away from Nita. He knew how to get the word out.

"Got to go. I can't miss this class. It's the only one I've got an A in," Karen said, looking at her watch.

"Want me to walk with you?" Sam asked.

Karen crinkled her nose and gushed, "Aw, aren't you sweet. Yes and no. I'd love the company but I'm safe. Call Jamie."

She pushed in his number and waited through seven rings before he picked up. "Don't hang up, even if it takes twenty rings. Remember, I've only got one hand."

She asked if Thad was with him. He was. She told him about the party. "Invite some people. How's it going with Thad?" She heard cars passing through slush.

"He's my main man. Couldn't do it without him, even if I

didn't have to worry about someone trying to kill me. My dad's going to sue that fucker for medical costs."

"What's he like?"

"Who? My dad?"

"No, Thad."

"Don't ask questions I can't answer. Meet me in my boudoir tonight. I've got something for you—one of Aunt Edie's books. Remember you said you wanted to read one?"

"I do. I've been looking, but I forgot her writing name."

"Well, I picked up her latest at Walgreens when I was getting my street meds." He meant his oxycodone.

People started showing up for the party around seven. By nine they filled the rooms—shoulder-to-shoulder, swigging beer, chomping down handfuls of chips, spilling dip, shouting and laughing. The neighbors in the rest of the house followed the noise and joined the party. Sam leaned against the counter in the kitchen with her arms crossed, watching. Jamie was glued to Thad who acted as a barrier between his arm and shoulder and anyone who came too close. His voice was as loud as the others, his words slurred by a combination of meds and beer. "I was so fucking mad—I mean my car looked like it had a bad case of acne—I went running outside, thinking I could grab that tire iron out of his hand. I heard my own bones breaking." He basked in the sympathy, loved it when someone fawned over his mending collarbone and broken arm.

Karen was on his other side, talking to her roommate Lisa. Nita stood near the door with Carmen, letting people in. It was Sam's job to open new bags of chips and containers of salsa and put them on the table, which was the hot spot in the apartment, and the apartment was hot. She'd shed her sweater long ago. Chips and salsa and beer were ground into the old carpet. Eight people were sitting on the couch, four of them in someone's lap. Who knew how many were in the bedrooms. Everything had quickly spun out of control. Why would DeWitt walk into this noisy trap?

Jamie said loudly, "Sam couldn't ID him. I'll have to do that at trial."

She wished Jamie would shut up or tone it down. The three beers she'd guzzled had given her a headache. Small talk was not her thing. It had been her idea to hold this party, yet all she wanted to do was retreat to her bedroom and read Edie's book. Of course, her bed was probably in use. She reached down and pulled the paperback out of her backpack, which was leaning against her leg. The cover was of a small white cottage, surrounded by sand. She turned her back to the crowd and began to read.

Lila Bentley had spent all her summers in a small white cottage on Lake Michigan, the one she was walking through right now. She hadn't agreed to sell it out of the family, but she'd been unable to come up with the money to buy it. Her grandparents were dead, her parents divorcing. She had come today to say goodbye, and right now she wasn't sure that was a good idea.

When someone tapped her on the shoulder, she threw her hands in the air, the book falling onto the counter.

"A little nervous, are we?" Jamie said, laughing.

"Jesus, don't sneak up on me."

"What are you doing reading at your own party?"

"I can't resist your aunt's book. It is a good party, isn't it?" She wasn't sure she knew a good one from a bad one. Would she be having fun if it were someone else's party?

"Any party is a good one." He leaned on the counter, breathing heavily.

"You don't look good," she said, wondering why his eyes were so bright and realizing it was because his face had no color. "You want to lie down for a while? We can chase everyone out of the bedroom."

"No, I'm going back to the dorm. I'm not ready for so much fun."

"Is Thad going with you?"

"Yeah." He smiled wanly. "This is taking longer than I thought it would. I'm always tired."

"Well, the beer doesn't help," she said dryly.

"I know. That's probably why I feel so shitty. Talk to you tomorrow."

Thad cleared a path and she trailed them to the door. She even looked outside, hoping to see Officer Dana hanging around, thinking Jamie could hitch a ride with her, momentarily forgetting the police officer would know he'd been drinking. She'd be glad when they turned twenty-one. The rush of cold air felt good. She stepped out on the porch.

Thad and Jamie were walking slowly away. The wind tugged at her hair and she was turning to go back inside when someone grabbed her arm.

He covered her mouth with a bruising hand and dragged her through the pile of melting snow to the side street a few feet from the porch, where he slammed her face down on the backseat of a large, old car and fell on top of her.

How could this happen when her apartment was swarming with people and Jamie and Thad were walking down the street less than a block away? She bit at his hand, but couldn't get her teeth in it. Panic threatened to take away all reason.

He whispered in her ear. "Listen, you stupid cunt. You think you're so smart, don't you, college student?"

She tried to shake her head no, but he had a death grip on her head and she was having trouble breathing. She concentrated on getting enough air.

"I'm gonna tell you this once, and you better listen good, because you're going to get hurt otherwise, like your kinky boyfriend. You listening?" His body lay heavy upon her.

She attempted to nod, but that too was not possible. She smelled alcohol and cigarettes.

"You keep quiet about this. You hear?" He shook her and again she tried to nod but couldn't. "You're never going to identify me, or I'll find you and do things like this to you." He shifted his weight and grabbed her crotch. She squirmed frantically and he let her go.

Exhausted from struggling to get away, she went limp under him, hoping someone would come outside and see the old car and investigate. She also knew that wasn't going to happen.

His cold hand flattened against her backside, working its way into her jeans. "You like this? Yeah?"

Frantic, she came to life, biting at the hand over her mouth and twisting so that he had to use both of his hands to hold her in place and cover her mouth.

He shook her. "Remember what I said. Don't identify me, no matter what your queer boyfriend says. Otherwise, you'll always be watching your back. I'm going to let you go now. If you scream, I'll take you somewhere and finish what I started." He backed out of the car, grabbed her wrist, wrenching her shoulder, and threw her into a dirty snowbank.

Whimpering, she wiped her face with the back of her hand and staggered toward the porch as he drove away. She thought the car was an old Cadillac. The Wisconsin plate had the letters one and four and nine on it.

When she shut the door and leaned against it, flattened by the heat and soothed by voices that filled the small apartment and spelled safety, at least for now, she began to shiver.

"Sam," Nita touched her shoulder. "You're so cold. What's the matter?"

Sam shook her head as Karen put a possessive arm around her.

"Where's your jacket?"

"I was hot," she said. "I'm okay now." Her teeth were chattering.

"I'll get a blanket," Nita said.

"Okay." She'd peed her pants. She needed something to cover the wetness.

Karen put somebody's jacket over her shoulders. It smelled of cigarettes. Her mind was churning. Could she tell anyone what had just happened?

Wednesday afternoon Edie rang the bell at Claire's duplex. She felt a fool for being here, for giving in to Claire's whims. However, when Claire opened the door and smiled, she forgot everything she had been determined to say.

"Want a cup of decaf?" Claire asked.

"Sure." She stepped inside and followed Claire through the living room to the kitchen, watching her backside swing in black leggings.

"How have you been?" she asked, like she might have asked anyone she hadn't seen for a while.

Claire shrugged. "Why?"

"It was just a conversation opener." She sipped the coffee, which tasted like it had been in the pot for hours.

"How have I been?" Claire repeated, sitting down opposite Edie. She hadn't poured herself a cup and Edie understood why. "Busy."

"Me too." Edie set the cup back on the table.

"Don't you like the coffee?"

"I guess I'm just not thirsty. What's new?" she tried again.

"Work is a drag."

This wasn't a conversation. It was a prelude. She gave it another try. "What are you reading? Anything good?"

"Why are we talking about this stuff?"

"Because that's what people do. They talk. I'd like to be a librarian. I love books."

She smiled wryly. "I've read some of your books."

Edie felt a flush starting to spread over her.

Claire laughed. "I like the way you blush. I never would have expected you to be a bit of a prude. Come on. Let's go to bed. Show me how Mark made love to Tawnya."

She searched her mind for a Mark and Tawnya without success.

"You don't remember? He licked her ear and kissed her all over while she squirmed with pleasure."

Edie stood next to the bed, trying to recall these characters, suspecting that Claire was making fun of her.

"You don't remember, do you?" When Edie shook her head, Claire laughed. "I made them up. I should be a writer." She pulled her top off and shook her head. Her hair crackled with electricity.

Edie looked at the breasts pushed up by the white bra, creating cleavage and bent to kiss the smooth skin. She unhooked the bra and let it slide off Claire's arms while she knelt to bury her face in the freed breasts. With a hand on each she held them while she breathed in Claire's odor—a hint of cologne, soap and Claire's own scent.

She pulled down Claire's leggings and sat her on the bed while she worked them off her feet. This time she started at the toes and moved slowly upward—kissing, tasting—until she reached Claire's mouth. She buried her fingers in Claire's hair and kissed her. Claire had scrambled back onto the bed, and Edie reversed direction.

When it was over, she lay beside Claire, staring at the ceiling, breathing heavily. Claire climbed on top of her. They did not fit well together, and Edie rolled them onto their sides. She smoothed Claire's hair back. Her green eyes looked sleepy. She smiled.

"Do you want me to do that to you?"

If Claire had to ask, Edie was sure she didn't want to perform that particular act. "It's okay," she said, and it was. She had gotten what she wanted.

She stayed the night. It was the first time she'd slept with Claire. Claire curled up tightly on one side of the queen-size bed and she on the other. In the morning, Edie awoke to Claire's touch. "There's time," she said.

After, while Claire was showering, Edie made coffee. She would shower when she got home.

"When am I going to see you again?" Claire asked. They were eating toast.

"I don't know. Next Wednesday?" She looked at Claire in a fitted top and slacks and wished there were more time. It was as if she couldn't get enough of this woman, and it shamed her.

She fought to stay awake on the drive home, despite the cup of coffee. She'd been afraid she'd stray onto Claire's side of the bed, incurring her displeasure, and hadn't slept well. She hadn't forgotten Claire saying she slept best alone, although she certainly seemed to sleep soundly—mouth open, periodically emitting little snores.

Thursday evening, when Edie was convinced she was never going to hear from her, Jennifer called. "Hey, is our ski date still on?"

Surprised at how relieved she was, she asked, "Where do you want to go?"

"How about Northern Highlands and Escanaba? We probably could do both."

"I'll pick you up. Is Chip going with us?"

"Maybe. What time?"

"Is seven early enough?"

"Sure. We should be skiing by nine. I've got to go. We'll talk on Saturday. Okay?"

Not a word about the book—whether she'd read it, whether she'd liked it, whether she'd hated it. What had she been expecting anyway, a rave review? Had anyone ever raved about her books? She went through an inner dialogue like this whenever someone she knew was reading one of her novels.

Jennifer came out the front door as she drove into the driveway on Saturday. They loaded her ski equipment in the car. She threw her backpack in the back and climbed into the passenger seat. "Saw you coming," she said with a grin.

"You must have been hanging around the front door."

"I was. I'm a little worried about trail conditions. I hope it's not gummy."

"Or frozen, although that's better than sticky." She smiled. "How was your week?"

"Busy and a little boring. How was yours?"

"Busy too." She had worked long days around her trip to see Claire and was pleased with her progress. Writing these books for some reason never got easier. She tried to build sexual tension between the main characters and at the same time create a story that kept the reader reading. In *Midnight Magic*, it was uncovering the deception of Don, Al coming to the rescue and Elizabeth's discovery of her own inner strength—with Mary Ann's help, of course.

"You've been writing, I suppose." Jennifer was looking straight ahead. She said in a quiet voice, "I couldn't put your book down. I never thought romances could be so interesting."

How easy it was to make her happy. Why couldn't Claire say things like that? She smiled as a mixture of relief and happiness suffused her. "Thanks."

"I mean it. How do you do it?"

She shrugged and glanced at Jennifer. "I start with a character and go from there. There is sort of a formula, though. Guy meets girl, guy and girl are attracted to each other, something keeps them apart, the guy and girl overcome the odds against them and get together in the end."

"You make it sound so easy." Jennifer said. Her smile was hesitant, and Edie was guessing the book had thrown her, that she had expected something different.

With a laugh more like a snort, she shook her head. "It's not easy, but it feels good when someone likes a book I wrote. I don't get much feedback."

"Well, I liked it. I'll have to read the rest. How many are there?"

"About twenty-five. You better go to the library." She laughed a little again. "Look, don't feel as if you have to read my books unless you really want to. I won't care, one way or the other." Not true, she thought. She'd be a little miffed, but she'd understand.

"No, I want to read them."

"Okay, that's great. Have you been watching the weather forecasts? It might snow tonight or it might rain."

"I know. Speaking of snow would you like to bunk with us during the Birkie? Chip and I've got a cabin rented with Tom and Mike. We go up Thursday. Gives us time to look things over, meet old friends and have some fun. The only thing is you might have to share a room with me."

"I have a place rented, but it's a dormitory sort of thing, where I might end up on the floor. I'd much rather go with you and Chip."

"Okay. Sounds good."

The snow was packed and slick, the diagonal tracks close to the surface. Edie seldom worried about steep hills and sharp turns, but she felt as if she was a little out of control. They ate lunch on their way to the Escanaba Trail.

"We better get some snow, not rain, next week," she said as much to herself as to Jennifer.

"They'll bring in snow if they have to."

"I know."

The Escanaba trail curved along lakes. It was a fast course, up and down hills. Halfway through their run a cold drizzle began to fall. Jennifer, who had taken the lead, picked up speed. Edie tucked her head and followed.

They were packing up Edie's car by three thirty. Both were quiet at first on the way home. Finally, Jennifer said, "Well, that sucked. They probably should move the date of the Birkie to the end of January."

"Winters are getting warmer."

"Climate change, I suppose." Said wryly. "What are you doing for dinner tonight?"

Edie shot her a surprised glance. "I don't have plans."

"Would you rather go out to eat or eat leftovers at my place?" Jennifer hastened to add, "You don't have to do either, of course, but it would be nice to have company."

"I lean toward the leftovers." She liked this woman, who was so friendly and open. Claire, who was anything but friendly or open, popped into her thoughts.

"Great."

The sleet had turned to light snow that melted when it hit the pavement. When she parked in Jennifer's driveway, she grabbed Jennifer's backpack, while Jennifer carried her ski bag inside. "I'll just throw the backpack in my room and turn up the heat. Be right back. If you need to use the facilities, there is a bathroom down the hall to the kitchen."

She used it before going into the kitchen. Jennifer was already there. She'd changed out of her ski pants and into jeans. Her hair curled around her ears and glowed red under the ceiling light. "Would you like something to drink? We have beer, vodka, gin and more."

"A beer would taste good." She was thirsty.

"Dark? Light?"

She laughed. "You're well stocked."

"That's Chip's doing. He and his friends could arrive any

minute. So be prepared. They take up a lot of space and they're noisy."

"Dark sounds good."

"This was our parents' house. They moved to Florida and left me in charge. Chip was still married then, living in his own place." She smiled, her face lighting up.

"It's a lovely house." It was two stories with oak woodwork and wood floors.

"It's too big even for the two of us, but we grew up in this house and I've always loved it. Besides, Chip has two kids, who are often here on weekends—a girl and a boy."

She had wondered about Chip, who seemed to have no wife or girlfriend. "How old?"

"Eight and ten. They're good little skiers and hikers. They're fun to have around."

"I bet." She thought of Jamie, who was twenty. He'd been a fun little boy, too.

"Pasta campanella and salad and bread. How does that sound?"

"Wonderful. Can I help?" she asked.

"Nope. I just have to warm up the pasta. It's better fresh and there's no meat in it. Hope that's okay."

"I like pasta without meat." Edie thought she'd eat anything right now, even Claire's stale coffee and toast. She wondered if Claire made a fresh pot for Janine. Her cell was vibrating for the second time since her arrival. She ignored it.

She loved the pasta and said so.

"It's easy. I'll send you the recipe. It's on my computer."

Edie helped clean up the dishes. "I'd better go now," she said afterward.

"Let's just check out the weather." Jennifer turned on the backyard light and peered out through gathering snow. "We were just saying we needed snow. Right? We could ski tomorrow at Nine Mile if you stayed the night. The roads are probably pretty nasty by now."

The garage door opened and three men spilled into the kitchen. They brought in the cold and snow on their jackets. "Mike, Tom, this is Edie," Chip said. "She writes books."

The two men came forward to shake Edie's hand. "Hope you don't mind us barging in," one of them said to Jennifer.

"I'm used to it." Jennifer smiled.

Chip took three beers out of the fridge and gave two to his friends. "It was icy at Granite. But now it's snowing like crazy."

"It was icy up north, too. How are the roads?" Jennifer asked.

"You could skate on them. The snowplows are having trouble keeping up with the snow." Chip opened the fridge and took out two frozen pizzas. He turned and grinned. "It's awesome, isn't it?"

Edie laughed. "If you mean the snow, yes."

He raised his beer. "Thanks to whoever sent it."

Jennifer smiled at Edie. "You must stay."

She smiled back, said, "I have to go outside and see how bad it is." She grabbed her jacket and went out the front door. Her car already wore a thick blanket of snow—light, fluffy stuff. She stood for a moment, looking up, tasting the flakes.

Jennifer joined her, her jacket open, her arms spread wide, her face turned upward, too, in welcome. "I can't let you to drive off in this."

She looked at Jennifer, wondering how young she was. Thirties would be like robbing the cradle, but Claire had to be in her thirties. She nodded. "Okay. Thanks." She didn't want to end up in another snowbank. "I'll get my backpack."

When they went inside, Chip was building a fire in the huge fireplace that took up most of one side of the living room. They joined him and his friends and talked about everything and nothing till Edie was fighting sleep. She awoke to Jennifer's hand on her shoulder.

"I'll show you your room." Her face was rosy in the firelight.

Edie looked around. Chip and his friends were gone. "I'm sorry." How rude to fall asleep in the middle of everything.

"I'm the one who's sorry. If we're going to ski tomorrow, we better get some sleep."

When she climbed under the covers in one of the upstairs bedrooms, she lay awake for what seemed a long time. She heard snoring from somewhere down the hall. Outside her window, the snow fell silently. It was too late to call Lynn back, but she knew Jamie would be awake at eleven o'clock, and his earlier call might have meant another emergency.

"Hey," he said sleepily. "Where you been?"

"Skiing, talking to people. I thought you'd be awake."

"So did I. I left a party before it was over. That's a first."

"Well, you're healing. It takes time."

"Did I tell you DeWitt—he's the one who hit me with the tire iron—is out on bail? And someone broke into Sam's apartment. The police couldn't find any fingerprints, but I'm sure he did it."

Stunned, angry and fearful for Jamie and Sam, she said, "Why was he released? He's dangerous."

"Somebody screwed up. I've got a bodyguard now. His name is Thad and he follows me around like a bloodhound. Dad is paying him."

"Why haven't you told me any of this?"

"You've been out of the loop. Where are you?"

"At a friend's house. It's snowing like crazy, and we're skiing again tomorrow. Keep me informed. Okay, Jamie? How is Sam?"

"She was the one who had the party. I think she thought DeWitt would crash it and we'd nail him. She couldn't ID him, you know. That's one of the reasons they let him go till the trial."

"When is the trial?"

"Early April, I think."

"I want to be there."

"Are you staying with some sexy woman?"

"She's a great skier, she and her brother."

"She can be sexy and a great skier."

"Go back to sleep, Jamie. If something else happens, let me know. Okay?"

Someone tapped on her door in the morning, wakening her. She had dropped off after talking to Jamie and felt groggy. She looked out the window. The snow had stopped, but clung in mounds on trees and bushes, looking like a Christmas card.

After using the bathroom and dressing, she went downstairs. A few coals still burned in the fireplace as she walked in her socks through the living room to the kitchen. Chip and Jennifer sat at the long table. Jennifer got up, coffeepot in hand.

"Ready?"

"Am I ever!"

Chip pulled out the chair next to him. "Sit." He was eating a bowl of cold cereal.

"Where are your friends?" she asked him.

"They went home. They live nearby."

"What would you like?" Jennifer asked, handing her the cup.

There was a bowl of scrambled eggs with chunks of bacon and a plate of toast.

"I'll eat what's on the table," she said.

"Cereal is my dessert," Chip said. He had a smudgy growth of beard, which made him look like a young Brad Pitt.

"This will be enough." She scooped out some eggs and took a piece of toast.

"We're arguing about where to ski today. Jennifer thinks we should stay close to home, which means Nine Mile or Granite Peak. I thought Iola would be fun."

Edie thought so too, but that meant driving back roads. "Hey, Nine Mile is good. I don't have my downhill skis." She took a bite and looked up. Jennifer was smiling at her—eyes soft, expression unguarded. She looked away quickly when she realized Edie was looking back. Edie concentrated on her food.

Jennifer and her brother began discussing the pros and cons of downhill as compared to cross-country.

"So what do you prefer, Edie?" Chip asked.

"She prefers cross-country," Jennifer told him.

"She can't talk for herself?" he asked.

Edie cleared her throat. "I do like cross-country better. It's more environmentally kind and less expensive." In case she sounded preachy, she added, "I like downhill almost as much."

Jennifer rode with Edie, after Edie convinced her that it was better to take one car rather than two, even though she would have to drive Jennifer home before leaving for Point. Chip had decided to pick up his kids and ski at Granite Peak.

The snow was blindingly beautiful against the dark hardwoods and the green of pines and spruces and firs. Even with sunglasses, Edie squinted. "Thanks for letting me stay overnight."

Jennifer's eyes were hidden behind wraparound dark glasses. "I made you stay. I think you would have gone home if I hadn't insisted."

"Probably. It was a fun evening, though, even if I fell asleep in the middle of it. I like your brother and his friends."

"Chip moved back home after his divorce last year. It's nice to have company, but I wish he'd stayed with his wife. She and I were good friends. We're still friends, but there is always a choice to make. I hate that, and the kids badly wanted their parents to stay together."

"That must be hard," Edie said, "especially for the kids."

"His wife has a high-powered job. He was always spending the money. The kids love him, though, because he's so much like a kid himself. He likes to play."

"Does she like to do the things he does?"

"Yeah, but you can't play every minute you're not working. You have to shop and take care of the house and make sure the kids are doing their homework. It's a good thing I never got married. I like to do my own thing too when I'm not working."

Jennifer switched topics before Edie could comment. "It must take a lot of self discipline to do what you do. You don't have the constraints of the workplace."

"That can be a problem." Like going down to see Claire when she should keep her butt glued to her computer chair.

On the trails, Edie's long strides loosened up her muscles, aching from yesterday's ski. After a short while, she tied her Windbreaker around her waist. A hush settled over the trails, making audible their breathing and the sound of their skis moving against the fresh snow. Then a blue jay screeched overhead. In the woods, chickadees called and nuthatches muttered. Edie heard a deer snort as if in surprise. It was an incredibly beautiful scene—the pristine whiteness, the stark trees, the evergreens bending under the heavy weight of snow. She would hate for this day to end.

Around two the women loaded their equipment and ate the lunches Jennifer had packed for them on the way back to her house.

"Chip and I will drive to Cable. Okay?" Jennifer said before she got out of Edie's car. "It'll be fun sharing the Birkie with you."

"These two days have been fun," Edie replied. She was reminded of Claire and how fun didn't seem to be in her vocabulary, at least fun with Edie.

The interstate had been cleared. Snow was piled along the edges. When she pulled into her garage, she was already thinking about the book she was writing and where the plot should go now.

After blowing the snow off the driveway and before booting up her computer, she called Lynn.

"Where have you been all weekend? I know you weren't in Madison, because I was there and I saw Claire."

"Where else? I was skiing."

"With whom? Yourself?"

"With Jennifer Gottschalk. You know her, don't you?"

"Yeah. She's a tall lady. You must match strides. You didn't answer when I called."

"I spent the night at her house in Wausau. The roads were really bad and we were going to ski again today. So I stayed. Her brother lives with her."

"Does he? They're both giants."

Edie laughed. "She's no taller than I am. What did you call about?"

"Just to talk. Seeing Claire made me think of you and wonder how Jamie is."

She told Lynn about her last phone conversation with Jamie. "I'm scared for them both." Meaning Sam and Jamie.

"I think Julie Decker is doing therapy once a week in Madison. I heard it through the professional grapevine. Maybe you could tell Sam that."

"Or you could send Dr. Decker a message for her."

CHAPTER TWELVE

Julie Decker read the message twice. Dr. Lynn Chan had sent it and for a moment, Julie tried to recall who she was. The e-mail read—

Dear Dr. Decker,

We met at a conference in Stevens Point a couple months ago. At that time you recommended a therapist for Samantha Thompson at the clinic where you once worked in Madison. Sam has had a number of life-threatening experiences beginning the day she tried to set up an appointment with you. They are too numerous and confusing for me to explain in an e-mail. You are the only person Sam will talk to. I understand that you're seeing clients again in Madison. Sam can be reached at the following number. I know this is an extraordinary request, but I respect the person who asked me to make it. Her name is Edie Carpenter. If you want to talk to her, she can be contacted at the following number. Thanks in advance.

Julie phoned Edie Carpenter. She leaned back in her office chair, listening to the rings. She would be driving to Madison on Saturday for the day. She had enough to do preparing and giving lectures, grading papers, counseling students and going to meetings. How tired she was of meetings. She much preferred therapy. She'd chosen Saturdays, when she was alone in the office with the phone workers, because those were the days her ex-husband was usually in Madison, wanting to see their daughter. Besides, Julie's partner, Peg, was either showing horses or giving lessons on most Saturdays.

When Edie picked up, she said, "Hi. This is Julie Decker. Dr. Lynn Chan asked me to contact Samantha Thompson at your request. She did not go into details."

"Hi. I did ask Lynn to send you an e-mail. I'm worried about Sam. I haven't seen her for a while, but she is my nephew's best friend. Do you have time to hear the story?"

"Of course."

Julie listened with growing horror. It was not difficult for her to believe this man, DeWitt, would assault two kids because one had angered him. She had met too many people like this—abusive husbands and boyfriends and, more rarely, women. People with anger management problems. She had only a few questions when Edie finished talking.

"Are you sure Sammy wants to talk to me or anyone?"

"Yes, I'm certain of it. Jamie, my nephew, said she wanted to transfer to UW-O so that she could see you."

Julie chuckled. "When you last talked to her, how did she sound?"

"Worried. She'd been unable to identify DeWitt."

"Thanks, Edie. I'll call the clinic and ask them to contact her. If she wants, she can set up an appointment."

"Thank you."

Julie snapped the phone shut and swung her chair around to look out the window.

This had been one of the snowiest winters. She'd grown

up in Chicago and remembered how she'd loved the snow and the lights on Michigan Avenue. She'd liked the snow when she and Peg had lived on Murray Street in Milwaukee in that attic apartment.

She drove every weekday from their country home to UW-Oshkosh, sometimes on snowy roads, and now she traveled on most Saturdays to Madison. Although lovely to look at, snow was one of the hazards of living in Wisconsin, like the deer that sometimes jumped in front of her car.

She swiveled back to her desk and sent a message to the clinic in Madison, asking someone to contact Samantha Thompson. Then she pulled on her coat and headed for home in the darkening day.

Peg was in the kitchen. Peg's daughter, Charlie, sat in her high chair, eating Cheerios from the tray. She banged her little feet against the chair and laughed when she saw Julie. Julie's daughter, Peggy, had met her at the door and was telling her about her day at kindergarten.

Julie put her arms around Peg and kissed her neck. "What's for dinner, sweetie?"

"Spaghetti." Peg turned her face for a kiss. They ate spaghetti at least once a week, sometimes more often, but Julie never complained when someone else did the cooking. "Ready to eat?"

"Sure." She would change after dinner.

Peg gave Charlie a bowl with cut up spaghetti. Charlie dug into it with both hands and tried to shove it in her mouth.

Peggy laughed and started to do the same thing.

"Hey, you're not a baby. Use your fork," Julie said.

Peg smiled sweetly at her. "How was your day, Doctor?"

"Are you a real doctor, Mama?" Peggy asked.

"I'm not the kind that listens to your chest." Julie was tired. It had been a long day and it wasn't over. She had to finish off a lecture.

"Your mama helps people who feel sad," Peg said. "Don't you think that's just as important as the kind of doctor who fixes you when you're sick?"

Julie smiled at Peg. "Hey, you're better at this than I am. You talk and I'll eat."

When the kids were in bed, Julie worked on her laptop. Peg went out to the barn to check the horses one last time. The house they'd had built in the hayfield next to the barn was quiet. She put the finishing touches on her lecture and shut the computer down as Peg came in from the barn and went to shower.

In bed Julie asked about her day, and Peg talked about working with a new horse and its young owner. "I rode him today. He's four and a little spooky. I wish parents would choose older horses for their kids to ride. It would be easier for everybody. Nice looking animal, though."

Peg had gone into partnership with her brother. They trained and showed horses. Peg gave the lessons and usually rode the youth and amateur horses, while Cam showed their young stallion and judged horse shows.

"I'm taking Peggy with me to Madison Saturday. Her dad will be in town."

"Say hello to him for me."

"I just found out today that one of my student clients from UW-Madison has been looking for me. A concerned colleague told me about her. She's going through something really harrowing. I asked the Madison office to give her a call."

"I'd be looking for you, too, if you disappeared. Didn't you give a forwarding address?"

"Yes, but not on the web. I didn't want ex-clients calling me, since I wasn't doing therapy. Now that I have to take Peggy down there anyway, I suppose I should change that."

"What's going to happen when you start working at Family Care full time, when the sabbatical is over?"

"I'll be on Family Care's Web site, but I'll still have to go to Madison when Joe's in town." Joe, Peggy's father and Julie's ex-husband, was a Congressman. "I really thought this girl was going to be all right." She felt some guilt about that assumption.

Saturday morning she wakened Peggy at six. Peg got up at the same time and fixed breakfast for the girls. Charlie was an early riser and was eating Cheerios off the tray of the high chair when Julie came into the kitchen.

"Want some oatmeal?" Peg asked from the stove.

"You're a talented cook," Julie teased. She kissed Charlie's dark hair and sat down next to Peggy. "Good morning everyone."

"Juwee," Charlie shouted. She banged a spoon against the tray and Cheerios flew in all directions.

"Hi, baby," Julie said.

"I'm your baby," Peggy said grumpily.

"You're my big girl." Julie smoothed her daughter's flyaway blond hair.

After breakfast, Julie told Peggy to get her backpack and kissed Peg and Charlie. "See you tonight."

"Drive safe," Peg said, cleaning up Charlie's face and hands. She would take her to her mother's house next door while she worked with horses and clients. Peggy ran back in the kitchen, dragging her backpack.

"Okay, kiddo, let's go," Julie said.

Peggy slept most of the way to Madison, so Julie had time to think. She had several appointments that day. Three of them were students who, like Sam, were there because they'd in some way threatened suicide.

How do you make kids understand that the present is just a blip in their lives? How do you convince them that getting dumped by a girl or boyfriend is not the end of the world? With some kids it was about loneliness. With gay kids it was often about fitting in or being bullied. Always, it was about family. More and more, alcohol and drugs and abuse were part of the picture.

She parked outside Joe's apartment around eight forty-five and walked with Peggy to the door. On her toes, Peggy pushed the buzzer and when Joe said, "Who is it?" she shouted "It's me, Daddy."

Joe met them in the front hall. Peggy leaped into his open arms and he smiled at Julie, who smiled back. He loved his daughter, that much was obvious. "How you been?" he asked.

"Okay. And you?" Gray had crept into his hair.

Peggy kissed him on the cheek. "You're bristly, Daddy."

He lightly rubbed his cheek against hers and growled, "I just got up."

"I'm good," Julie said.

"Want a cup of coffee?"

"No, thanks. I'll be back around five. Is that soon enough?"

"Yeah, sure." He winked at her. "Save the world."

"That's your job." She leaned forward and kissed Peggy. "See you later."

She used her card to let herself into the back door of the clinic and walked to the office she used on Saturdays. Taking off her coat, she went to say hello to the phone workers, who doubled as receptionists on Saturdays. One of them gave her the schedule with her appointments on it. She saw Sam's name opposite three o'clock and was glad.

She went to her office. One of the phone workers would unlock the main door and let her know when a client arrived.

At three she went to get Sam, who was reading. She noticed the studs in her ears and the tiny one in her nose, all that were left of the many she'd worn when Julie first met her. Her hair was cut so that it fell softly around her face. She'd always been thin, but now she appeared almost gaunt. When she looked up, Julie saw that she was also tired. Her gaze landed on Julie and a flush crept over her neck and face, coloring the pale skin. Her lips trembled when she smiled, which tore at Julie's heart.

"Hi, Sammy," Julie said with an answering smile. "Come on in."

Sam followed her to the same office she'd used when Sam was a regular client and sat in the same chair she had used then. She asked, "When did you come back?"

"A few weeks ago. No one told me you came in looking for me."

Sam began to cry. She leaned over and sobbed into her hands.

"Hey," Julie touched Sam's arm, and the girl jerked away. She pushed the tissues on the desk closer.

Sam grabbed one and wiped her face. She raised bloodshot eyes and met Julie's gaze. "It's been bad," she muttered.

"Maybe I can help."

"You're the only one I can talk to, because you can't tell anyone else." She held Julie's gaze. "You won't, will you?"

"What you say here is confidential, unless you are in danger," Julie said.

"If you tell, I'll be in danger." Sam began at the beginning and told a long rambling story about DeWitt's abusive behavior. Julie had heard much of it from Edie. However, Edie had said nothing about a party. Sam's voice dropped to a near whisper, and Julie leaned closer in order to hear.

"I went outside when Jamie left, and DeWitt grabbed me off the porch and threw me facedown in this filthy car. I could hardly breathe with him lying on top of me and covering my mouth. He grabbed me between the legs and then he put his hand in the back of my jeans and said if I identified him, he'd find me and finish what he started."

No wonder the girl looked exhausted. She was probably afraid to sleep. "You didn't tell the woman police officer about this?"

Sam shook her head. "I didn't tell anyone till now." Her blue eyes shimmered. "Jamie has a bodyguard. I have Karen."

"Karen is your girlfriend, the one who walks everywhere with you? She sounds like a wonderful friend."

"She's my lover." Sam lifted her chin.

Julie nodded, smiling. "Good. Look, if you still want to transfer to UW-O, maybe I can help with that."

"How did you know I wanted to transfer?"

"From the person who told me you wanted to see me."

"Jamie's Aunt Edie." She said it as a fact, not a question.

Julie smiled.

"He'd find me there if he wanted to."

"How did you get here?" Julie asked when the hour was up.

"I walked."

"Alone?"

Sam nodded. "Yes."

"I'll take you to wherever you want to go."

Julie said goodbye to the phone workers, and she and Sam left by the back door. The lights in the parking lot created isolated pools in the darkness. Sam looked around before stepping outside. Snow had been piled in the center of the blacktop. Parked close to the building next to Julie's car were the phone workers' vehicles. The doors of Julie's car clicked open as they approached it. Sam was walking backward, her hands stuffed in her pockets.

"What is it, Sam?"

"There's an old car parked on the street." She nodded.

Julie glanced in that direction. She thought it odd that a car was parked after hours among the office buildings that dominated the block. Seeing Sam so apprehensive raised the hairs on the back of her neck.

"Maybe someone is working late." However, all these buildings had parking lots of their own. "Come on. Jump in."

Sam pulled the door shut behind her and locked it. Julie did the same. When she left the parking lot, she could see no one in the parked car, but it was several parking spaces away. She turned the corner. Sam was looking out the rear window.

"Is there anything I can do, Sam?"

"Can I come back next Saturday?"

"I think I have something else scheduled that day. Check with the clinic. I will be back the following weekend." There were headlights in the rearview mirror about a block back.

"That car turned the corner. It's following us," Sam said.

"How do you know it's the same car?"

"He's checking up on me. He probably thinks I told you about what happened at the party." Sam was craning her neck.

Julie parked in front of Sam's apartment. The old house reminded her of the one she and Peg had rented in Milwaukee. "Which floor are you on?"

"First," Sam said. "Thanks."

It would be much safer to be on a higher floor. "I'll wait till you're in the house." A car had passed them and pulled into a parking space half a block ahead. Julie strained to see if anyone got out. In the minute or two while she watched Sam run to her door and disappear inside, someone could have left the car and gone into one of the buildings.

She drove slowly, peering into the parked cars. She saw no one in any of them. When she turned the corner, she picked up speed as she negotiated through traffic to Joe's apartment. He came out the door, holding Peggy's hand. She glanced at her watch. It was five o'clock. She was on time.

The danger that this man, DeWitt, represented to Sam hung like a pall over her as she and Joe exchanged a few words and she settled Peggy into the car seat in the back. Even Peggy's chatter on the way home could not dispel it.

CHAPTER THIRTEEN

After locking the apartment door behind her, Sam went straight to the kitchen. She was foraging through the fridge when her cell rang. Without looking at the display, she answered.

"Did you tell that bitch?"

"What?" she stammered, her heart thumping in her ears so loud she could hardly hear.

"Did you?" The voice was low, threatening.

"I don't know what you look like." She stumbled over the words, wondering if he was sitting in a car outside the door. Her legs had turned to mush. She said, "I can't identify you."

"I'm watching you and your queer friend."

She said nothing. The fridge door hung open, its compressor humming. Fear had hijacked her words and thoughts.

He hung up. She climbed into bed with her clothes on and shivered under the covers.

Karen and Nita found her there. "Hey, you okay?" Karen was shaking her shoulder. She had fallen asleep.

"You saw your shrink, didn't you?" Nita asked, like she should be better now.

She sat up and ran fingers through her hair. "She brought me home. He followed us."

"How do you know?" Nita asked, looking scared.

"Because he called me. I can't go anywhere without him knowing."

Karen sat down on the bed and kissed her. "Hey, baby, they'll put him away."

"I can't ID him. I don't know if Jamie can either," she said.

"Would you if you could?" Nita asked, her dark eyes flat.

She looked away. No, she thought, no she wouldn't. If he got released, he'd come after her.

"I thought so," Nita said and left the room.

"Thanks for taking my shift," she said to Karen.

"Hey, no problem." Karen got up and began undressing. "Come on, get your clothes off. What are you doing in bed with them on?"

"I've got homework. Don't you?"

"Yeah, but I think we need to get close and personal."

Sam, who had been willing to do whatever Karen wanted before DeWitt put his hand down her pants, said, "Close but not too personal."

Karen paused, one leg halfway out of her pants, and looked at Sam. "You didn't used to push me away."

She shrugged. Anyone's hand on her ass made her want to run, even Karen's. "It's not you."

"Yeah, you keep saying that, but what difference does it make? If it's not me, what is it?"

Sam got out of bed and put on a big T-shirt and sweatpants. "Why do you like me?"

"You're damn cute." Karen stood in the puddle of her pants and stroked Sam's arms. "You're one hot chick."

A smile crept over her face. "You're the hot one. Let me brush my teeth."

"I'll come with you. That's one of the great things about

being a lesbian, you know. You can go to the john with your girl even in public places."

Sam laughed. "Yeah, that's a real perk."

Nita had disappeared, probably into her bedroom.

They tiptoed with exaggerated steps to the tiny bathroom, where they peed and brushed their teeth. On stealthy feet, they hurried back to the bedroom. Cold drafts swept through the room, and they huddled under the covers. Karen put her arms around Sam and pulled her close.

"I love the smell of toothpaste," she said, kissing Sam.

Sam tried to put DeWitt out of her mind. She desperately wanted to forget the smell of his breath and the touch of his hands. After all, nothing had really happened. She kissed Karen back. Karen was a noisy lover, worrying Sam when she moaned loudly, startling her when she climaxed with a shout.

"You have to be quiet," she whispered when she slid her hand between Karen's legs and Karen moaned.

"But that feels so sweet."

She didn't want Nita bursting through the door. However, Karen's gentle touch felt so good that she heard herself making little sounds like whimpers.

When it was over, she lay back to catch her breath. Karen's arms were wrapped loosely around her as she nibbled at her neck. Maybe this was the way to forget about DeWitt. She certainly forgot everything else when they were doing it.

She imagined him barging through the door while they were in the bed. He'd broken in before. What would happen then? She thought of all the ways that scenario could work out. Some of them excited her and made her ashamed.

Sunday morning she awoke hungry and remembered she hadn't eaten since noon the day before. She wolfed down two big bowls of Honey Nut Cheerios, while Karen ate toast with jam, their laptops open on the small table.

Nita came yawning and stretching into the room. Karen looked at her, clad in flannel pants and a T-shirt, and asked, "Where's Carmen?"

After pouring herself a cup of coffee, Nita leaned against the counter. "We're not together anymore."

"When did that happen?" Karen asked.

"Last night."

"Hey, I'm sorry."

Sam was staring at Nita. Even wrinkled and rumpled with sleep, she was gorgeous. Her thick black hair hung loosely around her shoulders. Her dark eyes looked soft and sort of unfocused. "Me too."

"Want to talk about it?" Karen said.

"She's fucking scared when she's here." She shot an angry look at Sam.

"You know, it's bad for you to be mad all the time," Karen said.

"Sam's friend Jamie is the reason Carmen is afraid to hang around with me."

"He was your friend too," Sam said.

"Yeah, well not anymore. You're sitting in my fuckng chair, Karen." There were only two chairs at the table.

Karen went to Sam's bedroom and rolled her computer chair into the kitchen. "Which fucking chair do you want, Nita?" With a hand on one hip, Karen looked Nita up and down. "You are so pretty till you open your mouth."

Sam ducked her head and continued eating.

Nita sat down in the rickety chair across from Sam. "You wouldn't be laughing, Sam, if you lost your girlfriend." Her lower lip was quivering.

"Sorry, Nita." She reached across the table and covered Nita's hand, but she couldn't resist adding, "Karen's not afraid of anything."

Nita went to her room. Karen shut her laptop after a while and said she needed to go to the dorm to get clothes.

"Want me to come with?" Sam asked, looking up from her computer.

"Nah. You stay and study." She jerked her head toward Nita's room. "Maybe you better check up on her."

She knocked on Nita's door after Karen left. No answer. She knocked harder and turned the knob. The lights were off. She walked toward the curled up figure on the bed. Nita was asleep. In her hand was a bottle of pills. Sam gently loosened the container and read the label. Vicodin.

She shook Nita's shoulder, startling her awake. She sat up on the bed and glared at Sam.

"I thought maybe you had taken too many," Sam blurted.

"They're to help me sleep."

"Did Carmen get these for you?" The labeling had been in Spanish and English.

"Yes, if it's any of your goddamn business." She ran her fingers through her luxurious black hair, rearranging it.

"You scared me," Sam said, looking into her dark eyes.

"I didn't think you cared." Nita flopped back on the bed and yawned. "What's it like with Karen?"

Caught off guard, Sam shrugged. "Like it is with Carmen, I suppose."

"Carmen doesn't do sex. She's a good Catholic girl."

Sam wondered what to say and ended up with, "Maybe you should be seeing Julie."

"Maybe you should show me what it's like. Hmm?" Nita took her hand and pulled her onto the bed.

"I can't," she said and then realized that she could and she wanted to. She'd always had a thing for Nita. She kissed her, something she'd longed to do for years, and Nita put her arms around Sam and pulled her down.

Sam didn't waste time taking off clothes. In the back of her mind she knew Karen could return anytime. She pushed Nita's shirt up and buried her face in Nita's breasts. The nipples were dark. She smelled like soap. Nita gasped when Sam slipped a hand in her sweatpants. She came quickly and quietly, quiet enough for Sam to hear the door open and know that Karen was back.

She pulled her hand free and turned over in time to see Karen turn her back. "Don't go, Karen." She jumped up and rushed into the kitchen where Karen was shutting her laptop and into the bedroom where Karen grabbed her things and shoved them into her backpack. "I didn't mean to. It just sort of happened."

Karen raised her chin, and Sam got a look at the pain that screwed up her face and turned her gray blue eyes stormy. "Please, Karen. It was a mistake."

Karen shoved past her toward the door, dropping her key to the apartment on the floor. In a minute she was gone.

"Was it a mistake?" Nita said, coming to the door of her bedroom. "I don't think so." She leaned against the frame, her dark hair tousled, and crossed her arms. She looked incredibly sexy.

On Tuesday Edie called Claire to say she couldn't make it on Wednesday. "We're leaving for the Birkie." Which was a half lie. They were leaving on Thursday, but she was feeling a little frantic about how the book was going and felt she needed those two days to work.

A long pause ensued, while Edie waited. She was hooked on this woman. It didn't seem to matter that Claire was rude and had no interest in Edie's life. It was all about sex, which must have been why Edie couldn't let her go. Even now, with Claire on the phone, she longed to lay her down on the bed.

"Are you going with Pam?"

"No, I didn't know she was going," she said.

"Well she is, with Donna Hesselmeier."

This was one of the most informational conversations she'd had with Claire. "Maybe I'll see them there."

"You won't see me. I may have to start working Wednesday afternoons."

"Then I should call next Tuesday and make sure you're going to be home Wednesday." She held her breath, thinking maybe it was over.

"If you want. I have to go now. Janine is on her way."

She failed to understand the relationship between Janine and Claire. They should be lovers, and she felt a pang thinking about them together. She called Pam whom she knew she had neglected.

"Hey, I thought I was never going to hear from you again."

"I'm sorry, Pam. I'm trying to finish a book."

"I'm trying to finish one of your books too. I've been reading them."

Edie had to ask, "And?"

"Oh, I love them. A romance is a romance, you know."

Meaning, Edie supposed, that it didn't matter if the hero was a hero instead of another heroine.

"Claire said you're skiing the Birkie."

"I'm doing the Kortelopet with a friend. I think I'm not ready for the Birkie. I should have called and asked if you wanted to go with us."

"I am going, actually, with Jennifer Gottschalk. She came to our table at Jacobi's."

"You'll be well matched," Pam said. She sounded happy. "I think you met Donna. She's going with me. Are you coming to Madison tomorrow?"

So she knew. "No, I need the day to write."

"Well, I guess I'll stay out of Claire's way then."

"Why?"

"When you don't come, she's not fit to be around."

"Really?" she said with a grin, "I had no idea."

"Well, that's how Claire treats the most important people in her life. She doesn't want to let you know how much you mean to her. I don't know why."

"She doesn't even seem to like me," she blurted.

"Well, right now you are one of those important people. I think you outrank Janine. Janine is her default person. The one she falls back on when she loses someone."

"No kidding." She was amazed and delighted and disbelieving.

"Trust me. Do you want to meet somewhere?"

"I'm riding with Jennifer and her brother, so I'm not in charge. If we see each other among the thousands of people, I'll buy you a drink after the race."

"Sounds like a plan. Good luck."

"You too."

She went back to the book but had trouble picking up the thread. She had changed Al's name to Tony and given him a distinguished look with threads of white in his dark hair. He had rescued Elizabeth from loneliness when Mary Ann had moved away. He encouraged her to create an exciting life of her own. She opened a store next to his auto shop where she sold trendy clothes from California. One night someone broke into both the auto shop and the clothes store. Tony went back to his place of work for something he forgot and was shot. Elizabeth found him on the cold floor of the office. He was rushed to the hospital where emergency surgery was performed. Mary Ann hurried to Elizabeth's side to offer support.

"I don't think I could have faced this alone," Elizabeth said.

"Well, you don't have to. I'll stay the night."

"Where are Janie and Riley?"

"I called the babysitter." Mary Ann smiled.

Elizabeth studied her face. *"I've missed you terribly."*

"And I you." Mary Ann took her hand. *"That must have been a terrible thing to see."*

"The floor was covered with blood. I thought he was dead."

When the surgeon talked to Elizabeth, he gave a guarded prognosis. She was allowed to go into Tony's room. Tubes crossed his body, feeding him fluids and morphine and oxygen and carrying away urine. She held his limp hand and spoke to him in a soft voice, telling him he'd be all right, until the ICU nurse told her he needed to rest and so did she.

At home, she asked Mary Ann to keep Tony's side of the bed warm. When Mary Ann comforted her with an embrace, she said, "I'm not sure I'm up to losing Tony and you."

"You don't have to be. I've been offered the principal position at Harrison." It was the middle school where they had taught together. *"I'm moving back here."*

Edie had over two hundred fifty pages. She couldn't afford to kill off Tony and introduce another hero. The best she could do was let Tony recover and keep Mary Ann as a best friend.

She looked out the window. The snow on the Green Trail was soft and sticky. Water dripped from the gutters. Now that she had a vision of how the book would end she could go to Madison on Wednesday. She quickly put that thought out of her head. What she didn't need was Claire messing with her emotionally before the race. Instead, she worked the next day, adding another twenty pages.

On Thursday she arrived at Jennifer's house a little after four, the agreed upon time. The garage door rose as she got out of her car.

Chip walked to her open window. "I'll back my car out and you can put yours in."

Jennifer carried her ski equipment to Chip's car. Her backpack was slung across her shoulder, her jacket open. Chip put the skis and poles in the Thule roof rack on top of the Subaru.

At first they chatted excitedly. The Birkie was one of the most thrilling events in Edie's life. Darkness fell swiftly, leaving a smudge of yellow along the horizon. Edie was riding in the back. The radio was on low, and they fell into a comfortable silence.

Around six they stopped at Phillips, more than halfway to Cable, and picked up subs, which they ate in the car. Edie was paying little attention to where they were, but when Chip turned off State Highway 77 onto a local road, she knew they must be near the rented cabin on Lake Tomahawk.

The smell of wood smoke greeted them. The A-frame log building was dwarfed by the larger lake homes around it. Mike and Tom, Chip's skiing friends, had turned on the cabin's heat and lit a fire in the fireplace.

"You ladies can have the bedroom," Chip said.

Edie tossed her backpack on the double bed and switched on a small lamp. The walls and ceiling were cedar as were those in the rest of the cabin. There was a dresser and another lamp on the other side of the bed.

The sleeping loft had been built over the bedroom, the bathroom and small kitchen. The great room stood alone with large windows that faced the lake. Snowmobiles sped across the snow-covered ice, their bobbing lights leading the way.

The five of them sat around the fire for a while, exchanging stories about past Birkies. Edie was the first to say "I'll see you tomorrow." She took her backpack to the bathroom where she removed her contacts, brushed her teeth and washed her face with her hands. Back in the bedroom, she stripped down to long underwear and slid between very cold sheets.

Shortly after, Jennifer joined her, also getting into bed in her long underwear. "Yipes!" she said. "I thought you'd have it all warmed up."

Edie marked her place in *The Girl With The Dragon Tattoo*. "I tried," she said. "I always have to read before I can sleep." She put the book down on the table and folded her reading glasses on top of it.

In the night they rolled against each other. Edie's eyes opened as she felt the warmth of Jennifer's body, but she couldn't stay awake long enough to move. She slept soundly and awoke in the morning pressed up against Jennifer.

Jennifer turned her face toward Edie. "You're better than an electric blanket."

"Thanks. So are you."

Tom had turned up the heat and the main room was a whole lot warmer than the bedroom. After hurriedly dressing and taking turns in the bathroom, she went into the kitchen. She had brought granola for breakfast.

"I felt I was sleeping near a couple of chainsaws," Tom said as they ate.

"I think that was coming from the bedroom," Chip teased.

"You're a hoot," Jennifer shot back.

They crammed into Chip's car and joined a stream of vehicles heading toward Telemark Lodge. Many of the license plates were from out of state, but most were those of Wisconsin, Minnesota and Michigan.

Flags of the participants' countries hung outside the lodge. Huge ice sculptures adorned the entrance. The sculpture of the historic rescue in 1206 of Norway's Prince Haakon stood in the doorway. The baby was in enemy territory when two Birkebeiner soldiers skied him to safety during a snowstorm. King Haakon later united Norway.

They walked past dozens of vendors into the huge room where registration tables were set up. The perimeter was littered with large plastic gear bags, each marked with the participant's bib number. In the bags were promos and the timing chip that skiers wore around the left ankle. The white bags were for Birkie participants, the yellow for those doing the Kortelopet. Jennifer's and Edie's bags were with the third skate wave. Chip was in the second skate wave. She thought Tom and Mike were in the same one.

After getting their bags, they went to the Expo and studied the waxes on offer. The right wax was everything when it came to speed. Familiar faces filled the hall and they stopped to talk to others.

After piling into the Subaru again, they drove toward Hayward joining a stream of traffic going both ways. Massive ice sculptures of skiers and Birkie scenes marked the towns of Cable and Seeley on the drive south. Main Street was covered with packed snow. Dogs in harnesses pulled skiers back and forth in Hayward, demonstrating the sport called skijoring. After their display, elite ski sprinters raced each other down Main.

Edie wanted to browse her favorite ski shops—Outdoor Ventures and New Moon—both packed with pre-race shoppers. New Moon's wax counter was a must see. There, wax experts answered questions, and as every skier knew, waxing was the biggest concern. After eating lunch at a crowded coffee shop, they bought fresh bread at a bakery and made a stop at the grocery store. They stopped to admire the Birkie flame and to take each other's picture sitting in an ice chair with American Birkebeiner carved in the high back.

Edie was thrilled to be with Jennifer and Chip and even Tom and Mike. Like herself, they were Birkie regulars and interested in the same stuff she was. Back at the cabin, they waxed their skis, consulting each other on which waxes to use. She helped fix supper—spaghetti and garlic bread and a salad. Carbs were a must before a race. Conversation concerned the weather and the condition of the snow—slightly soft due to warming temperatures—and past Birkies.

After cleaning up, they sat around the fire. The talk was about the race, about what time they should leave in the morning. Edie and Jennifer laid everything out for the next day—socks, boots, Under Armour, ski jacket, bib, hat, sunglasses, gloves, Gatorade and water, timing chip, backpack with change of clothes, white bag to hold everything not needed during the race. When she and Jennifer climbed in bed, Jennifer told her how much she enjoyed having her with them.

"I was the only woman before you joined us."

"Hey, I feel lucky to be here," she said.

They talked for a few minutes more before turning their backs on each other. For a few moments Edie lay awake, worrying. Then she closed off her mind and slept.

She awoke at six. Jennifer was already dressed. She consulted her about clothes—long underwear or just the ski tights, a vest or a jacket.

"I've just got the tights on. I get hot when I start moving," Jennifer said.

She decided to wear her ski tights with Under Armour. She pulled a wick-away top over an undershirt. She would wear a Windbreaker. It was better to be cold at the beginning of the race than hot once she began to ski.

They all ate a breakfast of oatmeal and piled into Chip's car, putting their skis in the carrier on top, and headed to the nearest field that was used as a parking lot.

School buses were dropping off skiers behind Telemark Lodge. Chip unloaded skis and poles, and she and Jennifer took theirs and made their way through masses of brightly colored skiers to the giant tent ringed by dozens of Porta Potties. Lively rock music filled the air. Big heaters roared in an attempt to beat back the cold.

Edie was hyped. Who wouldn't be? The announcer's stand was on the airstrip behind the lodge. Flags from every participant's country lined the strip. Slightly away from the starting area were box trucks with signs, one for each of the ten waves. She and Jennifer threw their white bags with everything they needed after the race into their designated truck. Some of the skiers were dressed in silly costumes. They too would race the distance.

The elite waves were ready to go and she and Jennifer joined the dozens of people lining the starting area. The national anthem filled the crisp air and the governor gave a brief speech welcoming the racers and wishing them a speedy and safe race. The very first skiers to go were the re-enactors, dressed in authentic furs and birch leggings, striding out on wooden skis. The husband and wife and their baby symbolized the Norwegians carrying

Prince Haakon to safety. They would ski the entire classic race of fifty-four kilometers.

The elite skiers lined up along the starting flags. After the countdown, the starting gun fired and up went the flags. The skiers sped away, disappearing into a distant line of trees in minutes. Those in the next wave, who were kept behind a plastic line with little flags, moved into starting position.

Edie had eaten the banana and drunk the Gatorade and water she had brought with her. She and Jennifer had stood in line at the Porta Potties. They cheered the second wave as it left and moved into place. The wind bit through Edie's scant clothing. Ten minutes seemed like forever. The skate skiers no longer used the same trail as the classic skiers. They skied fifty kilometers, but skate skiing required enormous energy. Not only did they skate down the hills, they skated up them.

Edie was ready. She had positioned herself in the center front next to Jennifer. The anxiety in the pit of her stomach disappeared as the wait ended. The announcer's encouragement and the cheers of the crowd barely registered. The countdown began and when she heard the gun, she skated out with the others. Pushing with her poles, gathering speed with every thrust of her strong thighs, she disappeared into the trees. On the other side were the dreaded power line hills. She had managed to avoid colliding with anyone among the hundreds in her wave. The bane of ski racers was the skier who went down in front of them.

Now she skated up, up, up the wide, clear area with the giant power lines, only to fly down the backside and climb again. Her heart rocketed into the anaerobic zone. The spectators, shouting encouragement, the skiers around her and the sheer excitement of the race pumped her into a steady, sustaining pace. Drummers lined the route, keeping a beat as she and the others climbed. Jennifer forged ahead, urging her on. She climbed the killer hill. Amazingly, no one in front of her fell on the steep curve at the bottom.

Most of the trail ran through the lovely northern hardwood forest with rolling hill after rolling hill. Edie's heart settled into a steady one hundred sixty beats per minute. She was cruising.

She bantered with the other skiers, shouting encouragement to those she passed.

After about nine kilometers the first food stop appeared. The many volunteers held out Gatorade, bananas and orange slices. She grabbed a cup of Gatorade, downed it and tossed it aside as she kept up her pace. She knew how important it was to take some kind of nourishment at each of the food stations. It was true she felt new power after a few minutes. Her muscles needed replenishment.

Halfway through the race she came to the infamous Bitch Hill, where crazily dressed "bitches," both men and women, accosted the skiers as they climbed the seemingly endless hill, yelling for them to "keep moving." Edie avoided getting pinned with an "I got pinned by a Bitch" pin.

She skated to the top of the big hill where snowmobiles were lined up, their riders holding up signs with scores, yelling out the best (meaning the worst) fall on the harrowing downhill side. She had fallen once and thought her fall should have rated a higher score.

So far, she had been following Jennifer, sure that Jennifer would avoid anyone who took a spill and just as sure she would not fall. They had passed Burma Shave signs, telling them to keep going. They were closing in on a little over three hours when they came out of the woods, went over a little bridge and skied into a field, which led to a barren, windy lake.

Edie was running out of steam, but she kicked it into high gear and managed to pull alongside Jennifer. Jennifer grinned at her and surged ahead. The last few hundred yards they raced against each other along the "Mashed Potato Street" and onto Main in Hayward. The adrenaline was pumping when she crossed the finish line with Jennifer next to her. The announcer called out their names and the number of Birkies they'd participated in, and she and Jennifer raised their arms in the air while the crowd roared. They were standing now, coasting to a stop.

Volunteers pinned their Birkie year pins on—thirteen for Edie, fourteen for Jennifer—and took off their timing chips. Chip and Mike and Tom were cheering with the other spectators, some of whom rang cowbells, most of whom held beers up in salute. The men, who had already finished the race, walked with them to the tent where they retrieved their bags and changed their outer clothing and boots. There they consumed a bowl of much appreciated chicken noodle soup and drank a beer.

The exhilaration that had carried Edie the fifty kilometers was still with her, along with a sense of power. She was on a high and wouldn't come down until exhaustion caught up with her.

Jennifer grinned at her. "You were on my tail all the way."

"The only safe place to be," Edie said. "I knew you'd keep us out of trouble."

"Yeah, but then you caught up with me in the end."

Edie raised her eyebrows and smiled. "Of course. That was the plan."

"You are a fox, you know."

Edie smiled and tuned in to the sights and sounds around her. Chip was talking as was Mike and Tom. They were rattling on about the race. She wasn't sure anyone was listening. Outside the tent it was one huge party, and they joined in for a while, cheering as skier after skier crossed the finish line.

Later, at the cabin, Mike fired up the gas grill on the deck overlooking the frozen lake. The guys cooked brats and burgers. Edie brought out the pasta salad she had made at home and put the dressing on it. Jennifer whipped together a huge fruit bowl. They feasted, cleaned up and sat around the fire for a while. When they were talked out, they went to bed.

Edie said just before she went to sleep. "Now I'm ready for spring."

"Maybe we can hike or bike together when we can't ski anymore," Jennifer said.

"Sure." Edie fell into a deep sleep. She awoke only once in the night, when Jennifer rolled against her. Her body was warm, her breath soft against Edie's cheek.

The next morning they ate breakfast, cleaned up the cabin, made sure the fire was out and left in separate cars. Chip was talking about next year's Birkebeiner. He wanted to bring his kids to do the Barnebirkie, which would mean coming a day earlier.

"Think you could do that, Edie?" Jennifer asked.

Pleased to be included, she said, "You bet."

CHAPTER FOURTEEN

A week and a half passed. A week and a half when Karen didn't answer Sam's calls. A week and a half when Karen looked away if she saw her. Sam had sought advice from Jamie.

"Ms. Snotty seduced you?" He had sounded astounded.

"Yeah. I think she did it because she knew Karen was coming back and might catch us."

"Didn't you know that?"

"She came back sooner than I thought she would," she'd said glumly.

"I can hardly fucking believe this. Did you do it again?"

"Once or twice. It wasn't my idea, though."

"I don't think Karen would know the difference."

"Okay, Jamie. Whose fucking friend are you anyway." But she knew he was right.

"Listen. You better walk with me and Thad."

"Thanks," she'd said dispiritedly, and that's what she'd been doing ever since.

Now she and Jamie were on their way to work. Thad trailed along behind them. He and Jamie were getting it on. Jamie said he was hot, despite the fact that he hardly ever said anything.

Saturday she had an appointment with Julie, and she would have to walk alone. Jamie was working. Nita was hostessing, and Karen was out of her life. DeWitt didn't like her talking to a counselor. He had said so. She'd reported his calls to the police, but she knew Dana couldn't protect her. After he grabbed her off the porch, she realized no one could.

"I miss Karen. Will you tell her?"

"I did. She won't talk about you, but I'll say something to her again—like you're desolate without her."

"Thanks." She kicked a pile of snow by the sidewalk. It was rock hard and filthy. Most of the snow was gone, but this chunk was on the side of the street where the sun rarely shone.

"Talk to Julie about it," he said.

"DeWitt doesn't want me to see her."

"You gonna let that fucking nut rule your life?"

"You gonna protect me from him?"

"I am. You're walking with me and Thad, aren't you?"

"Yeah, but you can't walk with me Saturday."

"Maybe Thad can at least go over with you, and if Julie can't take you home, give him a call."

DeWitt would know where she was. She'd told him she couldn't identify him. If he kept following her around, though, sooner or later she'd see his face.

On Saturday, she was sitting in the waiting room alone. Thad had walked her to the door of the clinic. He'd said to call him if she needed him. Totally dispirited, she felt trapped, unable to safely go anywhere alone. She didn't know what to do about Nita crawling into her bed at night. If Karen did come back, she'd be gone as soon as she found out, but she was pretty sure Karen wasn't going to give her another chance.

She and Nita had silent sex.

"Did you never talk to Carmen when you were doing it?" she had asked one time.

Nita said, "I told you, Carmen was just a friend."

"You think if we don't talk about it, it doesn't happen or what?"

Nita's mouth had been inches from hers, yet she made no move to kiss her. She let Nita take the lead.

"Don't talk." Nita's hand slipped under the T-shirt Sam had worn to bed.

Sam had rolled on top of her. There was only so much foreplay she could resist.

When Julie came to get her, she still didn't know how she was going to tell her about the sex. She was already blushing, just thinking about it.

"So, what's happening?" Julie had given her a number to call if she needed to talk to her, but she hadn't used it.

Sam slid down in the chair and looked at her shoes. "Karen broke up with me."

"I'm sorry to hear that."

"It was my fault." She was mumbling.

"Was it?" Julie asked.

Sam straightened up and looked at Julie and then away. The thing was she wanted Julie to like her. "I did something awful."

"Did you?" Julie said mildly.

"It was stupid." She told her how Karen had caught her and Nita in the act. "I knew she was coming back. I just couldn't say no."

"You know the old saying. "'The flesh is weak.'"

Surprised, Sam said, "That's me. I want Karen back and she won't even talk to me."

"Have you thought about sending her a letter?"

"I sent her a dozen e-mails. She won't answer." She slumped in the chair again. "And DeWitt, the guy who grabbed me and beat Jamie up, doesn't want me talking to you."

"How do you know that?"

"He called me. He's probably out there waiting. I can't go anywhere alone." She fought back tears. "I don't even know what he looks like, so I can't identify him."

Julie was frowning. "Did you tell the police he called?"

Sam nodded. She was crying now and snatched a tissue from the box Julie pushed toward her. She wiped her eyes and nose angrily. "They can't protect me. No one can."

"Have you told your parents any of this?"

"No. Mom would make me come home." Everything that had bothered her when she first started looking for Julie seemed silly now. What mattered was losing Karen and her fear of DeWitt. "I may end up having to go home anyway. My grades suck. My life sucks. I'm sharing Jamie's bodyguard with him."

"Well, since you're pretty much stuck inside and you want to stay in school, maybe you should use this time constructively."

She looked at Julie. "I read the same stuff over and over but it doesn't sink in. I bet you never screwed up."

After a moment of obvious surprise, Julie burst into laughter. "Oh yes, I did. It's what you do after the screwup that counts."

When they went out to Julie's car, there were no vehicles parked on the street, only the two in the parking lot belonging to the phone workers. The angst that seemed to follow Sam around like a black cloud eased.

On the way to the apartment Julie said, "Do you mind if I talk to Dana Talmadge?"

"No," Sam replied. The police officer hadn't been able to protect her. Maybe Julie could do something no one had done, but she doubted it.

Julie called the number Sam had given her and introduced herself and her concern for Sam. "What Sam told me in counseling I can't pass on as you know, but I'm worried about her and her friend Jamie's safety."

"I am too. I've done some digging on Charles DeWitt. He's a loose cannon. He lives on unemployment. The police were called to his residence many times regarding spousal abuse before his wife took the kids and left. I told Sam to call me if he contacted her. My worry is that he'll scare her into silence."

"What can be done to protect them?"

"She wouldn't ask for a restraining order against him."

"Is there no way to revoke bail?"

"An attorney might be able to get bail revoked. Jamie is probably in a better position to ask for revocation."

"I'll see what I can do."

She'd made the call from her cell phone, sitting outside Joe's apartment building, waiting for him to return with Peggy.

When she got home, she carried a sleeping Peggy from her car seat to the house. Peg followed her to Peggy's bedroom, and helped her remove the girl's shoes and jacket. As they covered her, Peggy turned on her side, her thumb in her mouth.

Julie sighed as she and Peg tiptoed out of the room and shut the door. She took her coat off and hung it by the door.

"Hungry?" Peg asked.

Julie looked at Peg and smiled. "Are you for dinner?"

"Aren't you just a little bit tired?"

Julie nodded. "And discouraged."

"C'mon and eat and tell me what you can about your day." Peg put her arm around her and led her to the kitchen.

Julie said, "Why don't I smell spaghetti?"

"Very funny. What you smell is pork roast and garlic mashed potatoes. I made the salad. Mom made the rest."

"Wonderful," she said with a little too much enthusiasm. She appreciated Peg taking the time to cook, but she was a little tired of spaghetti and macaroni and cheese—the kids' favorites.

Between bites, she talked about Jamie and Sam. How Sam, at least, lived in fear of being assaulted. Peg looked appalled. "How come this guy is running around loose?"

"A screw-up, I guess. Sam can't identify him, but the police arrested him for hammering Jamie's car with a tire iron and turning it on Jamie when he tried to stop him. I'm going to call Jamie's aunt. Maybe a lawyer can convince a judge to revoke bail." She put her fork down and leaned back. "I'll call your mom tomorrow and thank her for the good meal."

"I have to go out to the barn and do a few things," Peg said.

"Go ahead. I'll clean up here."

There were no dirty pans. She shoved the plates and utensils in the dishwasher.

She walked slowly toward the stairs as she called Edie. When the call went to voice mail, she told Edie she wanted to talk to her about Jamie and Sam. Exhausted, she climbed the stairs, got undressed and into bed. She was reading over one of her lectures on her laptop, inserting thoughts into the content when she dozed off. She awoke when Peg lifted the computer off her belly.

"Why don't you ask Joe to get the bail revoked? He's a lawyer. Hey, he could probably get something done right away."

"Damn, why didn't I think of that? Worse yet, why didn't I do something last time I saw Sam?"

"You're doing something now, sweetie. Don't go back and beat yourself up. I'll be in bed in a minute."

"Can't wait," she said, pushing in Joe's number on her cell.

He sounded alarmed. "Did something happen?"

"Not to us. Will you do me a favor?"

"If I can. What?" She'd known Joe as long as she'd known Peg. They'd been friends at UW-Madison. Along with Charlie Schmidt, Joe's best friend, they'd made a foursome. She and Joe had eventually married and then divorced. Charlie was the father of Peg's daughter. He had died while embedded in Iraq. It all seemed a lot longer ago than it was.

She told him the story as she knew it, leaving out the part about DeWitt snatching Sam from the porch, and he listened without comment. After, there was so long a pause that she asked, "Well, can you get bail revoked?"

"I could go out and break his slimy neck," Joe said. "Why hasn't anyone else done this?"

"They're kids and we're not lawyers."

"I'll take care of it on Monday."

"Thanks." She was smiling. "It pays to know people in high places. Let me know the outcome. Okay?"

"Well?" Peg demanded when she slipped into bed.

"That was a brilliant idea. He says he'll take care of it on Monday."

"If anyone can do it, Joe can. Do you miss him much?"

"Sometimes. Don't you ever miss the four of us?" She meant Joe and Charlie and Peg and her.

"I miss Charlie more than Joe. I still can't believe I ended up with the prize, though. You." She picked up her book and gave Julie a smacking kiss. "Go back to sleep, Doctor. I'm going to read now."

Julie threw an arm over Peg and snuggled into her. Even the light in her eyes couldn't keep her awake.

Edie called Julie on Sunday when she got home and looked at her messages. She had turned off her phone when she left for Wausau. She hadn't wanted or needed the distractions that Jamie or Claire would present. There were messages on her voice mail from Jamie too, asking her to call.

After talking to Julie, she felt a terrible guilt. Why hadn't she thought of getting an attorney for Jamie? Why hadn't his father thought of it, instead of paying for a bodyguard? Why had it taken Sam's therapist to think of revoking bail?

Jamie answered his phone on the first ring. "Where were you? Thad broke up with me. Now I have no bodyguard. Do you know what that means?"

"Stick tight through Monday and your troubles may be over."

"What do you mean? I'm trapped in my room. Do you know how depressing that is? And Sam is stuck in that apartment." His voice dropped. "Karen broke up with Sam too. She caught her in bed with Nita. Do you have any ideas for her on how to get Karen back?"

"Too much information, Jamie. I'm sure Sam wouldn't want you telling her secrets."

"Yeah. Well, don't tell her I told you. I thought maybe you could help her or me."

"I can't help with Thad or Karen, but I can tell you good news about DeWitt. I think his bail will be revoked tomorrow."

"Huh? What? Who's going to do that?"

"An attorney is going ask that it be revoked, and this attorney has a lot of clout."

"No shit?"

"No, none. My only regret is that I didn't think of it myself. The news came from Sam's therapist."

"Dr. Julie Decker? The one we were looking for?"

"The same." She was smiling. "I skied the Birkie on Saturday."

"Did you win?"

"Come on, Jamie. There were thousands of participants. I was in the third wave and I finished in three hours, twenty-four minutes." She was thrilled with her time, with ending in a virtual tie with Jennifer.

"Kudos upon kudos."

"Are you going to be okay now?"

"I was pretty bummed when Thad walked out. It was too much for him. His grades tanked, like mine. We may get kicked out, Auntie." He sounded more cheerful for some reason.

"Well, now maybe you can concentrate on your studies and raise your grades."

"That's number one on my list of things to do. Are you coming to Madison soon?"

"No." She meant it. Of course, she always meant it.

Lynn came over when dark fell, bringing a pan of lasagna with her. "I've been missing you," she said.

"Me too." She poured them each a glass of merlot.

"How was the Birkie?" Lynn's dark eyes settled on her.

She had once been in love with Lynn, and she briefly wondered where that feeling had gone. Was it a temporary thing that ended when people grew apart or met others who filled their needs better?

"Exciting." She told her about the race and the events leading up to it and after.

Lynn ate while she talked. When Edie fell silent, Lynn said, "Did you ever think that Jennifer might be a better match for you than Claire?"

She paused with a forkful of food halfway to her mouth. It was hot from the microwave and she blew lightly on it. "Aren't you making an assumption? How do you know she's gay?"

"I don't know, but she sounds interested in you."

"I think reading my books confused her. She's not sure about me, but I'm pretty sure she's gay. Pam is reading my books too. Were you in Madison with Frankie?" Funny how that thought no longer bothered her.

"What does Jennifer look like?"

"She's as tall as I am. She's got freckles, reddish hair, brown eyes. She's a terrific skier."

"You could ski together." Lynn took another bite. "I was at Madison. Claire came to the meeting with Janine. They left before it was over."

She felt a little stab of jealousy and frowned.

"Does that bother you?" Lynn asked, her delicate brows lifting. "She's never going to give Janine up."

"I know. I don't care." But she did. She told Lynn that Julie had found someone who ought to be able to get DeWitt's bail revoked. She knew that Lynn believed in fate, but she herself didn't. She believed in connections.

On Tuesday when Claire called, she was working toward the end of *Midnight Magic* and didn't answer. In the story, Tony recovered from his wounds with only a slight limp. He and Elizabeth married. Mary Ann stood beside her. Mary Ann was still standing beside her (figuratively) when the book ended. They made a five some—Tony, Elizabeth, Mary Ann and her daughter and dog, Janie and Riley.

She would have to make some changes before she sent the manuscript to Horizon via e-mail. Sleet spattered against the windows, which made her feel more dismal. The high of the Birkie was always followed by a low. When the phone rang and she saw Claire's name in the display, she sighed.

"Hi, Claire. How are you?"

"Are you coming tomorrow?"

"I skied the Birkie on Saturday." She should call Pam and ask how the Kortelopet went.

"Good. You're not coming, are you?"

"No. I have to work on my book."

"I'd like to see you," Claire said quietly.

"I don't think we're a good match, Claire. You and Janine make a lovely couple." Heart pounding, she waited for Claire's affirmation.

"Will you come one more time?"

How could she refuse? It was a plea, not a demand. "All right, but I can't stay overnight."

Claire opened the door and gave Edie a heart-stopping smile. "Would you like a cup of coffee?" she asked as Edie walked into the living room.

"I'd love one." She followed Claire into the kitchen, where she took off her jacket and hung it on the chair. She studied Claire as she made fresh coffee.

"So, how have you been?"

Claire turned and leaned against the counter. She crossed her arms. "Look. I know I've behaved badly." She met Edie's surprise with a slight smile. "I've been seeing a therapist and I'm on antidepressants. I like you very much." She held Edie's eyes with her own and lifted her chin. "You're a wonderful lover. It made me angry that I couldn't let go of that."

Edie could hardly believe they were having this conversation. "I couldn't either."

"I know." Claire took a deep breath. "You know Somerset Maugham wrote a story about a man who was besotted with a woman who treated him very badly. He was educated. She was not. We're both educated, so there's no excuse for me."

Edie smiled wryly. "Lynn thinks you're my midlife crisis."

"Am I?"

Edie sidestepped the question. "You're a beautiful woman. Who wouldn't want you?"

"You're not answering."

She took a deep breath. "I'm at that age." She had fallen hard, but she thought it was more for Claire's body than Claire herself.

"Come on, one more time, before the antidepressants take away my libido. I'll be glad to see it go." She gave a harsh laugh.

It was different yet the same. She undressed Claire and laid her on the bed. For a moment she just took her in, memorizing her—the ivory skin, the pale nipples and light brown pubic hair, the lovely body. She rolled the two of them into an embrace on the bed, and when she kissed Claire's mouth, her response was hungry and demanding. She kissed her everywhere—her eyebrows, her chin, her neck, her breasts and belly, the insides of her thighs, Claire tugged on her, and she raised her head.

"Come here."

Claire tried to do what Edie had just done to her, but her kisses were too light, her tongue tickled. Edie rolled her over and finished what she had started. Claire arched under her, keening softly as she climaxed.

"Let me," Claire said, when her body stopped shuddering. She turned on her side, facing Edie, her head resting on one hand. With the other she caressed Edie. "You have a nice body. You're like an Amazon."

"Compared to you," Edie said. She closed her eyes and let Claire do what she would, but she was so conscious of the differences between their bodies that she couldn't relax. She found herself thinking of Jennifer, who was her size. She managed to come by closing her eyes and reliving what she'd just done to Claire.

"That was nice," Claire murmured, as they lay side-by-side on the bed. "Will you stay the night?"

She smiled and pulled Claire against her. She had tears in her eyes when she shook her head. "No."

"Let's drink that cup of coffee now."

When they were dressed and had washed in separate bathrooms, Edie sat once again at the small kitchen table.

"You aren't coming back, are you?"

Edie said, "I think it's best I don't."

"I won't ask you."

The change in Claire was so huge that Edie didn't trust it. "Were you very unhappy before counseling?"

"I had a stepfather who really screwed me up. I was so angry all the time, and I was angriest with you because with us it was all about sex. It's not so great being attractive. Maybe he would have left me alone if I'd been ugly, or maybe it wouldn't have mattered." Her arms were crossed tightly and she was biting her lips.

Edie stood up and held her close. "I'm so sorry." Claire's hair smelled wonderful, a reminder that she was still not out from under her spell.

Claire gave a little shrug. "It was a long time ago." She swiped at her eyes.

"If you want me to come back, I will," she said in a moment of weakness. "We don't have to go to bed. We can talk or do something else."

"Give me a few weeks, and then call. I'd like you for a friend. Maybe I'll be capable of that by then."

Deep in thought, she drove home hardly noticing the speeding traffic, even forgetting to call Jamie and Pam as she'd planned. Now that she had new understanding of Claire, she felt as if she'd used her and was deeply ashamed. She'd always known that her passion for Claire was just that, not something more enduring.

The house was dark and cold. She walked through the rooms, turning on lights, turning up the heat. She warmed up leftovers and read the newspaper while eating. She had no heart to work on her manuscript. Instead, she went to bed with a good book.

Thursday she began rereading *Midnight Magic*, making changes as she went. Outside, the sky was a flawless blue. Patches of grass showed through the snow, but she knew there would be more snowfalls before spring arrived.

Friday she was restless. She always received scores of e-mails from political and environmental groups. She looked at all three hundred and forty-two of them and either took action or deleted. Then she put on a light Windbreaker and running pants and went for a three-mile run. At home again, she took a shower. It was late afternoon. She had just finished eating when someone knocked on the door.

Lynn was on her way to Madison. Besides, Lynn would let herself in. She wasn't expecting anyone else, so she peered out the front door's side window to see who was there. Whoever it was had his or her back turned.

She opened the door slightly. The person spun around, and she unlocked the storm and held it open. "What brings you here on a Friday night?" she said with surprise.

"I hoped I'd catch you at home."

"Come on in. It's cold out there."

Jennifer was grinning, her hands stuffed in her jacket pockets. "Is dropping in like this okay?"

"Sure. I'm all by my lonesome. Have you eaten?"

"I'm not that rude. I ate before I left Wausau."

"Well, how about a glass of wine or a cup of decaf."

"Either is great. Listen, I just finished *Seaside Interlude*, so I was thinking of you."

Jennifer must be working her way through Edie's books. "You came to talk about that?" she asked with new surprise.

"I just wanted to see you," Jennifer said. Her cheeks were bright red.

"Let me take your jacket." Jennifer was the only woman she knew who could look her in the eye. They were a matched pair as far as size went. She hung the jacket in the closet. "Coffee or wine?"

"Whatever you're having." Jennifer was still grinning, making Edie smile.

"Wine. I don't often drink alone, so now I can have a glass of wine. White or red?"

"Whatever. I like both."

She opened a bottle of cabernet, rather than finishing the merlot she and Lynn had drunk. "Let's go in the living room. I'll light a fire."

After setting her glass on the hearth, she lit the paper under the kindling. She rested on her haunches, waiting for the fire to take hold.

"Do you live alone?" Jennifer asked.

She closed the screen and picked up her wine, rising to her feet. "Yes."

"Sorry. You must think I'm nosy."

"It's okay to ask. I've always lived alone. It's not always been my choice." She sat in one of the chairs facing the fire. Jennifer was in the other. The couch separated them.

"So, how's work?"

Jennifer laughed. "Busy. How is your latest book coming? I can't wait to read it."

"It may be my last," she said. Did she mean that? Probably not. "I'm kind of tired of writing for Horizon."

"Why?"

"Well, because it seems sort of like I'm deceiving my readers."

"How?"

She glanced at Jennifer, who looked genuinely stumped. Jennifer said, "I love to read, so I think it's pretty impressive to be a popular author."

Edie laughed and said, "My books are read by straight women, and they're pretty light reading and I'm a lesbian." She was surprised at how easily that came out of her mouth. If Jennifer was a lesbian, she had a right to know. If she wasn't, it was time Edie found out.

After a few moments of silence, Edie looked over at her. Her face was an interesting mix of emotions. "What? Are you surprised?"

"No. I wasn't sure. How did you start writing these books?"

"I wrote something I thought might get published and it did." She got up to refill her glass. "Want some more?"

"No. I have to drive."

"You could stay. I have an extra room with a comfy bed."

"I didn't bring any clothes."

Edie shrugged. "You'll fit in mine, I think. I've got an unopened toothbrush."

"Okay. Sure."

She filled both their glasses and returned to the living room. Jennifer was staring at the fire. She looked up and said "Thanks" when Edie handed her the full wineglass.

"You know, it's nice to have a woman friend who is my size. I don't know about you, but I always feel so big around other women."

"I know. I do too," Jennifer said. "What will you do if you stop writing?"

"Oh, I don't think I'll stop writing. I'd like to write at least one lesbian book. I can use my real name then."

"I can't wait to read that."

"Tell me the truth. Would you have picked up one of my books, if you hadn't known me?"

"They're very readable books. I like your writing, but you're right. I wanted to get to know you better." She laughed self-consciously. "I wanted to impress you."

"Can I ask how old you are, Jennifer?"

"Almost thirty-nine. Honest." She held up her right hand.

"I'm fifty," Edie said.

"Well, congratulations! I never would have guessed."

"Hey, I'm turning gray."

"So am I."

Edie hadn't laughed so much in a long time. "I don't see any gray hair."

"I see very little on you. I'd like to spend more time with you. I don't care if you're seventy." Jennifer gave her an ironic smile.

"You like older women?"

"I like you. And besides, once you grow up there are no older women. It's not like I'm sixteen and you're twenty-seven."

"Okay. You've been forewarned." She could see the pulse beating in Jennifer's throat. Her own heartbeat had picked up, but she knew she needed space between Claire and Jennifer. "Look, I just ended an entanglement. I don't want you caught in the dregs."

Jennifer frowned a little. "I didn't know you were involved with anyone. Do you want me to go?"

"Absolutely not. I just want more time to get to know you." Instead of jumping into bed right away, she thought. She had spent time with Jennifer, though. She had even slept with her.

"Okay. Maybe we could go to the Leigh Yawkey Woodson Museum tomorrow."

"There's a nice little art center on the Wisconsin River here in Point. We could go there."

"Sure. I have my skis just in case we're inundated by snow overnight."

Edie laughed. "It always pays to be prepared."

Later, when she showed Jennifer to the extra bedroom, Jennifer gave Edie a kiss that sent chills down to her toes. When it ended, Jennifer looked in her eyes and said, "I've been wanting to do that for a long time."

Edie cleared her throat. "You're a sweet woman. If you need anything, I'll be right across the hall."

"I want you," Jennifer said.

"Let me think about it. Okay?"

"It's your call." She went into the bedroom.

Edie stood outside the closed door. "I'll put the toothbrush on the bathroom counter, just down the hall."

She went to the bathroom, put the toothbrush in its package on the counter, then brushed her teeth and washed her face. In her bedroom, she changed her clothes and got into bed. Lying awake, listening for some sound from Jennifer, she regretted her decision. Finally, though, she fell asleep.

She awoke in the night from a dream, awash with desire. The house was quiet. She padded down the hall to the bathroom to pee. On the way back, she paused outside Jennifer's bedroom door. The dream and desire were still with her.

The door opened quietly under her hand. Her eyes had adjusted to the darkness, but on the way to the bed, she caught her toe on its leg. She hopped around on the other foot, trying not to cry out.

"Hey, is that some new kind of dance?" Jennifer was up on her elbows, her hair askew.

Jennifer's voice startled the pain away. She put her foot down and tried to think of how to explain her intrusion.

"Come over here, why don't you? I could use some body heat."

She felt like a fool, but she sat on the edge of the bed. "I didn't mean to wake you."

"That's okay. I'm glad you changed your mind. Come on, get in with me." Jennifer pulled the covers back and moved over.

She got into the bed, turned toward Jennifer and pushed the heavy hair away from her face. They were eye-to-eye and toe-to-toe. That had never happened before to Edie. She gave Jennifer a serious kiss.

When Jennifer sat up and pulled off her T-shirt, the sudden movement startled Edie out of the moment. Jennifer's breasts were firm, taut, like the rest of her. Edie wriggled out of her own sleep shirt and watched as Jennifer lowered her head to gently take one of Edie's nipples between her lips. She buried her fingers in Jennifer's hair.

Jennifer kissed her way up to Edie's lips. When she got there, Edie took control. She'd always been in charge when making love. Whereas Claire had seemed to love that control, Jennifer resisted it.

"Come on back up here," she whispered when Edie was bunched under the covers They held each other with one arm, breasts and bellies touching, fingers moving in unison. Edie could not distinguish the sounds they made as they climaxed. Even after, they clung to one another until their breathing normalized. Then they fell apart to lie on their backs, separate with only hands and toes touching.

Jennifer turned her head. "What made you change your mind?"

"I awoke from a dream." It could only have been a wet dream. "I don't know if you were in it."

"I was having the same dream," Jennifer said, and they smiled at each other. "Don't go away."

"We can go to my room. The bed is bigger."

"Let's stay here tonight. The best is yet to come."

"Promises, promises," Edie said. She had expected a little shyness afterward, not this easy banter.

It was true, though. Before the sun rose they explored intimacy without any hesitation, as if they'd been making love for years.

CHAPTER FIFTEEN

Sam was on a scary high. For a couple of days, she and Jamie celebrated in his room. Mike, the nerdy hall advisor, was always popping his head in the door, telling Sam she'd have to leave after hours. He'd only recently realized that she sometimes stayed there overnight. She and Jamie would hide their beers behind their backs and tuck the computer chair back under the doorknob. She always hoped when she was there that she'd run into Karen, but so far she'd only seen her roommate Lisa.

She and Jamie talked about whether they would testify at the trial. They were due to be deposed the third Wednesday in March. "What are you going to say?" she asked Jamie.

"I'm going to tell them the truth." His arm was still in a sling and hurt when he tried to use his fingers.

"What if he gets parole?" she asked.

"He's not going to get off. When he gets out of prison, we'll be long gone from here."

"The defense is going to ask me if he's the guy who grabbed me." Her heart catapulted when she said that. "I'll have to lie."

"Yeah, so?"

She admired his bravery, and she tried to put DeWitt out of her mind when she studied, but either he or Karen or Nita always crept in and ruined her concentration.

When she went from the dorm, feeling a sense of freedom, she found Nita in the apartment with a guy from work. He was new to the waiting staff—a senior, named Judd Jelinsky. He was tall and well built and good-looking. All the other girls at Chili Verde had the hots for him. His eyebrows, like Carmen's, merged into one.

He was sitting on the lumpy couch, his large hands hanging between his legs. "Hey, Sam. You live here too, huh?"

"Yeah, I do," she said, her gaze flitting from him to Nita.

Nita sat down next to him. "We're going to study together."

"Great." She went to her room with an uneasy feeling in her guts. Nita had never brought a guy home.

Later, as she sat on her bed with her learning disabilities text propped on her legs, she heard them through the thin walls. He was coming on to Nita, and Nita wasn't putting up much resistance. When the door shut to Nita's room, Sam's chest hurt so much she wondered if she was having a heart attack.

She confronted Nita when he left. "What's going on with you and Jelinsky?"

Nita looked bored. "We're going out."

"What does that mean? You're the one who's been climbing into my bed at night."

"I'm not the way you are."

"Yeah? You could have fooled me."

"I guess I did." Nita turned on her heel and shut her bedroom door behind her.

Sam shouted. "You just wanted to get rid of Karen, didn't you? You can't tell me you didn't like it—all that moaning and stuff."

Nita opened the door a foot. "I put on a good act, didn't I?"

Sam went to back to her bedroom and put her head in her hands. She hurt so much she considered walking out in front of a car. Then Nita would feel bad, but so would her mom and dad and Jamie and her brother and sister and Edie and Julie. Julie. She had her number. Julie had said to call if she needed her.

She pushed in the unfamiliar digits and waited through five rings. When Julie answered, she hung up. After a moment or two, her cell rang. She opened it up without looking at the display.

"'Lo," she said.

"Sam? You called me?" Julie asked.

Her mind froze for a moment before she stumbled over her words. "I didn't mean to bother you. I just, I always think of you when things go really bad."

"I'm flattered. What has gone bad?"

She told her about Nita and then apologized again for calling and whispered, "I thought I wanted to die, but I don't—not really. I think I'll go home this weekend if I can get a ride."

"Good idea. Sam, it will get better. I know sometimes that doesn't seem possible, but then you meet someone, and you will, and things start looking up."

Sam snorted. "Nita's got a boyfriend and Karen acts like I've got leprosy." She had read about leper colonies in a history text three years ago and hadn't forgot the horror.

"Listen. It's a myth that these are the best years of your life. I lost my lover. For a while I lost my way. I think we all do at one time or another. I'm coming to the trial. So is Edie."

"Thanks for talking to me." She was crying.

"Stay on the phone. Let's talk this through. Okay?"

She threw herself on the bed and told Julie how she was afraid they'd find DeWitt not guilty or put him on parole. She said she missed Karen and hated Nita. She said she had trouble concentrating and was afraid she'd flunk out.

Julie told her that she had been put on probation by the university and returned the next year and completed her education. That it hadn't been the end of the world like she'd thought it was.

Sam was silenced by surprise. Julie had been on probation and lost her lover and had not only survived, but got her doctorate in psychology? She wanted to hear the whole story.

"I want to be just like you."

"And I wanted to be just like my psychologist. But whatever you choose to be, Sam, you'll give it that intensity of yours."

Her tears had dried up. "I'm okay." It dawned on her that Julie probably thought she was going to kill herself. "I won't do anything. My mom and dad would be too sad."

"I think it would be a good thing if you told them about DeWitt. They would want to come to the trial."

"Yeah, I will."

"I'd like to talk to Nita if she's there. Would that be okay?"

Surprised, she said, "Yeah, she's here, but why do you want to talk to her?"

"Just for a moment."

She knocked on Nita's door and opened it. Nita was lying on the bed, studying. She looked up and said, "What?" in an annoyed tone.

"Here. Dr. Julie Decker wants to talk to you." She thrust the phone at Nita, who looked puzzled.

Sam stood by the bed and listened.

"Hi," Nita said. "Yes, this is she." She was quiet then, her eyes flitting to Sam and away. "Okay, I'll do that right away. Yes, I'll tell him." She scribbled on the margin of the text.

Sam saw it was a number but couldn't read the digits. It had something to do with her, though. She took the phone back and walked out of the room and into her own. "I'm going to study now, try to catch up on things."

She was still on the phone with Julie when Jamie opened the bedroom door. She looked up in amazement and things fell into place. Jamie was here to make sure she didn't off herself. "Jamie's here. Do you want to talk to him?" She handed him the phone.

"Hey," he said breathlessly. "I ran most of the way."

Julie said something that made him laugh and he handed Sam the phone.

"I'll see you soon," Julie said. "Take care."

She was in awe. Julie cared enough to keep her on the phone till her best friend came to make sure she was all right.

"You wouldn't do anything to yourself, would you? I mean, how would you do it anyway? You don't even own a gun."

"Shut up, Jamie. Don't even talk about it." Nita was standing in the doorway.

She did go home on Friday and tell her parents about DeWitt. Her mom about popped a blood vessel. She was hurt because Sam hadn't told her what was going on. "You would have made me come home for good," Sam said.

Her mom had no answer to that, and her dad said, "We want to be at the trial."

She gave them the date in April. She was messing around with Buddy. The dog was mouthing her hand and mock growling.

Her fifteen-year-old brother and seventeen-year-old sister came into the kitchen after school and were surprised to see her there. Her brother ate a peanut butter sandwich and some cookies and said he was going to meet friends and go to the basketball game.

He punched her on the arm. "Don't they have basketball games there?"

She grabbed him by the head and tousled his hair. "On Saturdays, you beast."

Her sister stuck around and asked her about the university. She had applied and been accepted. "I have to stay in a dorm," she said, making a bored face.

"Yeah, well then you don't have to cook or shop for food. You're better off."

"Maybe you'll still be around and I can room with you my sophomore year."

Unlike Sam in high school, her younger sister had tons of friends. Sam was a little teary eyed because she wanted to room with her. "Maybe," she said.

The day of the trial, she and Jamie were sequestered in the

same room with two other people, who, Jamie thought, were there to keep an eye on them. After what seemed an interminable time, someone opened the door and asked for Jamie. The man who had been in the room with them went with him. Sam was so nervous she had to pee every five minutes. The woman in the room went with her and waited outside the bathroom.

Jamie didn't come back, and the woman explained that he would be allowed to stay in the courtroom after his testimony. When it was her turn, she tried to turn off her mind. Nervously, she glanced around the courtroom. Jamie was sitting with his parents and Edie. She saw her parents and Julie Decker. Not far from Jamie she noticed Nita. In the top row Karen sat alone. As promised, Dana Talmadge was there with Jim Delacourt.

The ringing in her ears got louder as she was sworn in and took the witness chair. From there she could see DeWitt. He looked small in the orange jumper he wore. His hair was kind of long and greasy. She had already decided she would identify him. There was no doubt that he was the guy. He'd been caught with the tire iron. Jamie's arm was taking forever to heal.

It would help if she could hear DeWitt's voice, though. She had told the prosecuting attorney that she would know his voice anywhere. That prosecutor was now asking her to tell her story. She cleared her throat and leaned toward the microphone and repeated the tale of how DeWitt had terrified her. Hearing her voice maximized by the mike made it shake a little.

"Can you identify this person?" she was asked.

She pointed at DeWitt and said, "That's him over there in the orange outfit."

DeWitt jumped to his feet and yelled, "You lie, you bitch!"

The judge banged his gavel and reprimanded the defense attorney for not controlling his client.

The attorney apologized.

Sam barely heard what they said. She knew now that he was the man who had terrified them. "It's him," she said again with more confidence. "He said he'd come back and finish what he started when he dragged me off the porch. If you let him go, he'll probably kill us."

The defense attorney was on his feet. "Objection."

"Objection sustained," the judge said.

Sam glanced at the jury. She couldn't read their minds. She was told to step down, and she joined her parents, sitting between Julie and her mother. Her mother squeezed her hand and she squeezed back.

The judge dismissed the jury to discuss the verdict shortly after she left the stand. Sam and Jamie stood with their families in the hall, debating whether they had time to go to lunch. Edie was talking to Julie. Nita left but not before giving Sam a thumbs-up. Karen was standing by the water fountain.

Sam slipped away and walked up to her. "Hey, thanks for coming."

Karen nodded. "You did a good job. I'm glad you ID'd that scum."

"His voice. I knew his voice." She briefly relived him whispering in her ear, while he held her face down on the seat of that smelly car.

"Those your parents?" Karen asked, nodding at the small crowd in the hallway.

"Yes. Want to meet them?" Her heart began to soar. "Come on. I'll introduce you to my shrink too."

It took less than forty-five minutes for the jury to find DeWitt guilty. He was taken back to jail to await sentencing. They were milling around the hall again, talking about where to go for an early dinner, having skipped lunch—Jamie's family, Sam and her parents and Karen. Julie begged off, saying she had to head back north.

She had a few words for Sam before she left. "I'm proud of you. It couldn't have easy to confront him."

"I recognized his voice."

"I know. Call the office if you want an appointment." She squeezed Sam's shoulder.

"Julie," she said as Julie started to walk away. "Thanks for everything."

Julie waved a hand. "You bet."

Edie went to eat with the others before driving home. First, though, she called Pam. "I'm on my way out of town."

"You can't stay?"

"No, but I wanted to touch base."

They talked for a while before Edie asked her how Claire was.

"Good. She's different, not so snooty. That was an act, you know, a protection device, she said."

"I'm glad to hear it. And things are going well for you?"

"Yes. Donna and I moved in together."

"I'm so glad."

"And you and Jennifer?"

"Well, nothing so exciting as moving in together."

"But you're a couple?" Leave it to Pam to speak her mind.

"Sort of, yes." She was smiling. Did going to bed together make them a couple? It certainly hadn't made her and Claire a couple. It was different with Jennifer, though. Their friendship had been transformed.

At home, she called Lynn to tell her about the trial, before returning Jennifer's call.

"How did it go today?" Jennifer asked.

"All twelve jurors found DeWitt guilty. He's in jail, awaiting sentencing. It was a good day."

"It was, it is. You must be relieved."

"Yes." More than she could put into words.

"Want some company?"

"Don't you have to work tomorrow?"

"Not until nine. That gives me plenty of time. I have something to tell you." Jennifer had been pushing for them to move in together.

One of the problems was where they would live. Jennifer worked in Wausau. Edie could work anywhere. But Jennifer shared her house with Chip, and Edie lived alone.

Edie took a quick shower while waiting. It was still light out when Jennifer arrived. Doves cooed and two robins pecked at the partially frozen ground.

Jennifer let herself in. "It sounds like spring out there."

"I think it arrived while I was looking the other way," Edie said. They were smiling at each other. "Would you like something to eat or drink?"

"No, thanks."

Edie sat on the couch and patted the cushion next to her.

Jennifer plopped down about a foot away. "I've been interviewing in Point. I can work at either Shopko or Walgreens, that is if you'll let me live with you."

"Wow! Why didn't you tell me?"

"I am telling you. You said we needed time to get to know each other. Well, we've had all of March to do that. Besides, I've known you for years."

Edie smiled at Jennifer and said teasingly, "As another skier."

Jennifer met her gaze and said without blinking or smiling, "I'm crazy about you. I've watched you ski for years and been too shy to ask you out. Then those damn books of yours threw me off. I thought maybe you were straight. I want to come home to you."

Edie tried not to laugh. "I'm set in my ways. I've never lived with a lover."

"Well, now is the time to start."

"Okay," she said with a smile. "You've been forewarned. My house is kind of small, though."

"I'll only bring myself and my clothes." Jennifer grinned and moved closer.

Edie laughed then. "By the way, I'm crazy about you too."

**Publications from
Bella Books, Inc.**
Women. Books. Even Better Together.
**P.O. Box 10543
Tallahassee, FL 32302
Phone: 800-729-4992
www.bellabooks.com**

CALM BEFORE THE STORM by Peggy J. Herring. Colonel Marcel Robicheaux doesn't tell and so far no one official has asked, but the amorous pursuit by Jordan McGowen has her worried for both her career and her honor.
978-0-9677753-1-9

THE WILD ONE by Lyn Denison. Rachel Weston is busy keeping home and head together after the death of her husband. Her kids need her and what she doesn't need is the confusion that Quinn Farrelly creates in her body and heart.
978-0-9677753-4-0

LESSONS IN MURDER by Claire McNab. There's a corpse in the school with a neat hole in the head and a Black & Decker drill alongside. Which teacher should Inspector Carol Ashton suspect? Unfortunately, the alluring Sybil Quade is at the top of the list. First in this highly lauded series.
978-1-931513-65-4

WHEN AN ECHO RETURNS by Linda Kay Silva. The bayou where Echo Branson found her sanity has been swept clean by a hurricane—or at least they thought. Then an evil washed up by the storm comes looking for them all, one-by-one. Second in series.
978-1-59493-225-0

DEADLY INTERSECTIONS by Ann Roberts. Everyone is lying, including her own father and her girlfriend. Leaving matters to the professionals is supposed to be easier! Third in series with *PAID IN FULL* and *WHITE OFFERINGS*.
978-1-59493-224-3

SUBSTITUTE FOR LOVE by Karin Kallmaker. No substitutes, ever again! But then Holly's heart, body and soul are captured by Reyna... Reyna with no last name and a secret life that hides a terrible bargain, one written in family blood.
978-1-931513-62-3

MAKING UP FOR LOST TIME by Karin Kallmaker. Take one Next Home Network Star and add one Little White Lie to equal mayhem in little Mendocino and a recipe for sizzling romance. This lighthearted, steamy story is a feast for the senses in a kitchen that is way too hot.
978-1-931513-61-6

2ND FIDDLE by Kate Calloway. Cassidy James's first case left her with a broken heart. At least this new case is fighting the good fight, and she can throw all her passion and energy into it.
978-1-59493-200-7

HUNTING THE WITCH by Ellen Hart. The woman she loves — used to love — offers her help, and Jane Lawless finds it hard to say no. She needs TLC for recent injuries and who better than a doctor? But Julia's jittery demeanor awakens Jane's curiosity. And Jane has never been able to resist a mystery. #9 in series and Lammy-winner.
978-1-59493-206-9

FAÇADES by Alex Marcoux. Everything Anastasia ever wanted — she has it. Sidney is the woman who helped her get it. But keeping it will require a price — the unnamed passion that simmers between them.
978-1-59493-239-7

ELENA UNDONE by Nicole Conn. The risks. The passion. The devastating choices. The ultimate rewards. Nicole Conn rocked the lesbian cinema world with *Claire of the Moon* and has rocked it again with *Elena Undone*. This is the book that tells it all...
978-1-59493-254-0

WHISPERS IN THE WIND by Frankie J. Jones. It began as a camping trip, then a simple hike. Dixon Hayes and Elizabeth Colter uncover an intriguing cave on their hike, changing their world, perhaps irrevocably.
978-1-59493-037-9

WEDDING BELL BLUES by Julia Watts. She'll do anything to save what's left of her family. Anything. It didn't seem like a bad plan...at first. Hailed by readers as Lammy-winner Julia Watts' funniest novel.
978-1-59493-199-4

WILDFIRE by Lynn James. From the moment botanist Devon McKinney meets ranger Elaine Thomas the chemistry is undeniable. Sharing—and protecting—a mountain for the length of their short assignments leads to unexpected passion in this sizzling romance by newcomer Lynn James.
978-1-59493-191-8

LEAVING L.A. by Kate Christie. Eleanor Chapin is on the way to the rest of her life when Tessa Flanagan offers her a lucrative summer job caring for Tessa's daughter Laya. It's only temporary and everyone expects Eleanor to be leaving L.A...
978-1-59493-221-2

SOMETHING TO BELIEVE by Robbi McCoy. When Lauren and Cassie meet on a once-in-a-lifetime river journey through China their feelings are innocent...at first. Ten years later, nothing—and everything—has changed. From Golden Crown winner Robbi McCoy.
978-1-59493-214-4

DEVIL'S ROCK by Gerri Hill. Deputy Andrea Sullivan and Agent Cameron Ross vow to bring a killer to justice. The killer has other plans. Gerri Hill pens another intriguing blend of mystery and romance in this page-turning thriller.
978-1-59493-218-2

SHADOW POINT by Amy Briant. Madison McPeake has just been not-quite fired, told her brother is dead and discovered she has to pick up a five-year old niece she's never met. After she makes it to Shadow Point it seems like someone—or something—doesn't want her to leave. Romance sizzles in this ghost story from Amy Briant.
978-1-59493-216-8

JUKEBOX by Gina Daggett. Debutantes in love. With each other. Two young women chafe at the constraints of parents and society with a friendship that could be more, if they can break free. Gina Daggett is best known as "Lipstick" of the columnist duo Lipstick & Dipstick.
978-1-59493-212-0

BLIND BET by Tracey Richardson. The stakes are high when Ellen Turcotte and Courtney Langford meet at the blackjack tables. Lady Luck has been smiling on Courtney but Ellen is a wild card she may not be able to handle.
978-1-59493-211-3